THE SECRET
OF HARBOR HOUSE

THE SECRET OF HARBOR HOUSE

CLAUDETTE NICOLE

CUTTING EDGE

ISBN-13: 978-1-970848-21-2

Published by
Cutting Edge Books
PO Box 8212
Calabasas, CA 91372
www.cuttingedgebooks.com

CHAPTER ONE

Hush you, now, and listen.

I must tell you this before it is too late. I must tell you this as I wait here to be killed.

Or to kill someone.

To kill someone. Horrible, unthinkable, unbelievable words. Yet I hear them inside me, a terrible whisper, and I know they are real. I shrivel at all that they mean. Once I would have rejected the very idea that I could give even silent voice to such words. Once I would have angrily shouted *no, impossible, never!* And that once was but a short time ago.

But now, here in the silent, waiting dark, I know better. I have learned that words are but clothes, artifices, designs of the tongue to make our naked needs seem less naked. *Survival* is such a word. It makes the unthinkable thinkable, the unreal real and it makes a mockery out of reason, heritage, morality and conscience. It gives the lie to all those things we think make us superior to other creatures. Perhaps, for saints and zealots it is different, but not for the rest of us. I know that now. Here in the dark, as the silent seconds tick away, I know that. So I must tell this and hope somehow you will hear and understand.

When did it all begin? If we must assign beginnings, then it began that day when I first met Derek—a brief meeting yet more than enough. But I don't believe there is ever a single, solitary beginning to anything. There are always many beginnings; some immediate, some hidden away in the past, some made of actions, some of memories, some of joy, some of sorrow. For me, there was a beginning that day so many years ago when I first realized that in everything we say and everything we hear, there are private meanings.

Aunt Catherine made me aware of that, as she did about so many other things. Being raised by her meant more than having all the material comforts, the right schools, and the good summer camps. Those things were important then, of course, as they are to any growing girl, but Aunt Catherine was a well-traveled and well-schooled woman, one of those rare people who cross that bridge from knowledge to wisdom. It is a bridge not that often crossed.

"Stacy Wayland," she would say in a voice that could wither with scorn or warm with sympathy, "the surface words are never enough. If you want to know what they really mean, look for the private meanings behind them. They're always there, and often very different."

That stayed with me, grew with me, as over the years I came to realize the reality of private meanings. In college I took all the psychology courses I could carry although I was an English major. So that was a beginning. And my world was another beginning. I'd grown sick and tired of it. It had been so exciting once, after I graduated from college. I'd found a glamorous job with a large public relations firm and I plunged into the swinging singles set and a life filled with the latest clothes, the theater, parties, men and everybody's affairs on everyone's tongue. It was a wonderful, exciting merry-go-round, the constant carousel where nobody even bothered to grab the brass ring anymore. But a carousel doesn't go anyplace except in a circle, and one day I woke up tired with the inner tiredness that a week at the Hamptons or Nassau would not chase away.

I was tired of a world where pleasure was a thing of small isolations, unconnected moments of temporary meaning. I was tired of fun that was no longer fun because it was lined with purpose and pursued with desperation. I was tired of protesters and pickets, of dirty streets and dirty politicians, of senseless strikes where shouting replaced reason, of a society that seemed to forever walk a tightrope at the edge of chaos. And I was tired of Philip—charming, witty, wonderful Philip—who loved me and needed me so much in bed but so little outside of it. So that was one more beginning among beginnings, for it served to bring me here, too.

There was no terror here for me then—not at first. That came later, with small surgings, tiny lappings of doubt and wonder. At first there was only this place of overpowering beauty, this land of solitary grandeur that still held the seeds of its heritage in a fierce, proud grasp. At first there was only this land of wonderfully strange names, Chickaloon, Natanuska, Moose Creek, Shark Tooth Hill and Turnagain Arm, Kuskokwim Mountains and Nikabuna Lakes, Susitna and Itullik, Lime Village Hungry and Rainy Pass Lodge—names flavored and tasting of massive mountains and roaring rivers, of vast ice-fields and glaciers, of sudden beauty amid monumental cold, names that bespoke a special kind of strength and a special kind of peace, all of them pulled together under the single word; *Alaska*. It was a place, indeed, as Derek phrased it, for "standing on thresholds, for noble experiments."

I came here, first, as a counselor on a teen-age travel camp tour. I'd decided to get off the carousel, finally, the job, the parties, Philip, all of it. I'd gotten off, with no plans except to get away for a while. When I saw the advertisement in the Sunday paper for the tour and for counselors, I seized on it at once. It offered an ideal compromise—I'd be away and alone, yet not entirely alone. I wasn't certain how much solitude I could handle yet. I was never one for quick adjustments. But it had been a good choice. The trip was pleasant, the youngsters without problems. We flew the last part from Vancouver to Anchorage, over the ice fields and the Chugach Mountains. Anchorage, no longer frontier country, still accorded a view of the vast lands northward. I found myself captured by the beckoning power of the land.

It was the last day of the tour that I met Derek. I'd a few hours to myself. I was atop a rise near the north end of the city, looking out at the giant mountains lifting themselves skyward with primordial majesty and wondering how I could return sometime for a longer visit.

Suddenly I was aware that I was being watched—that tiny, vestigial bit of animal sense we still possess, stirring in me. I turned to see the tall, slim figure in a tan car coat with a fur collar, deep brown eyes that glowed like dark embers staring at me out of a straight-nosed face with finely molded lips. It was a lean-cheeked face, intense, with dark hair falling loosely around it.

"I'm sorry—I didn't mean to disturb you," he said. "I have an excuse, though—two, in fact."

He stepped closer and smiled and I felt the vibrant intensity of the man, a steel-wire inner excitement that reached out on its own wavelength, inescapable.

"First, we don't have many visitors here as lovely as you," he said. "And second, I had the distinct feeling you would like to stay here."

His smile widened instantly as he caught the surprise that was admission in my eyes. "It was quite easy to see," he said. I didn't pretend. Pretending was part of my old world that I wanted to shed.

"You're direct," I answered. "I don't really want to go back, but I didn't think it showed all that much." He shrugged and the glowing brown eyes held me with their deep-bright intensity.

"I've an occupational advantage, perhaps. I'm Dr. Derek Closter," he said.

"*Dr.* Closter," I echoed. "I see. I feel a little less transparent now." I saw the deep-fire eyes look past me to the land beyond, narrowing ever so slightly.

"It is a magnificent land," he remarked. "Still unspoiled, still tolerant."

Still tolerant? I repeated the phrase silently and saw him smile as he immediately caught my questioning of it. Derek Closter's sensitivity was too acute, too instant, to be simply occupationally acquired.

"That's right, tolerant," he repeated, "still abiding by the rules of nature. Nature is tolerant. She permits every form of life to live as it sees fit. She renders no judgments. Only man has the intolerance and temerity to do that."

"Aren't judgments necessary for society's existence?" I asked. His smile was almost rueful.

"Are they? Or have we just made them so?" he answered. He paused, then, abruptly, spoke again. "Why go back if you don't want to?" he questioned

"To live, to find a new job, new roots. I'm just here with a travel camp, a summer interlude," I answered. I felt his eyes looking through me, riveting, penetrating.

"Maybe you can find those roots and that job right here," he said. "Not in Anchorage. I'm just here ordering some supplies and looking for someone, but up in that land you were looking at so longingly. Can you give me ten minutes, time for a cup of coffee? I'll tell you about an experiment in tomorrow. How about it, Miss—?"

"Stacy Wayland," I finished. He turned, his touch light at my elbow, steering me to a small coffee shop across the street as though there was no question that I would go. And he was right. I went along as he found a small table inside the shop, sat down opposite me and ordered coffee. He took off the tan coat to reveal a jacket, slightly tight-fitting, and a dark maroon turtleneck shirt. I found it hard to see this attractive man as a doctor, not because he was attractive but because of his intensity. He exuded an excitement, a compelling vibrancy that was more fitting to a missionary than to a doctor. I found out, soon enough, that he was a combination of both.

"Are you a general practitioner here?" I asked. "The typical country doctor visiting far-flung patients?"

"Hardly," he said softly. "I'm a psychiatrist." His quick smile, warm, was a response to the surprise I felt flooding my face.

"I don't blame you for being surprised. My patients are not from up here. They are part of that experiment in tomorrow I mentioned a few minutes ago. They are a very carefully selected group, and they are not really patients, either. They are my guests at Harbor House."

"Harbor House," I echoed. "What a perfectly lovely name."

"Thank you, Stacy Wayland," Derek Closter said, leaning back in his chair. His dark eyes grew darker and more intense as he spoke to me—the missionary now, very much caught up in his gospel. "Harbor House is a most unusual place," he said. "It's a little over a hundred miles north of here, in the Talkeetna Mountains. The first thing you learn about Alaska is that cities or large towns are not centers which reach out to each other with fingers of less populated centers. They end at their borders here and one need only go five miles to find the most untamed, rugged land. The Talkeetna Mountains are wild, fierce country, land where one constructs one's own enclave or one perishes."

"And it was picked purposely?" I asked. His smile was again quick, light, laced with tolerant amusement which he managed to make not at all offensive.

"Of course. Wild, fierce country is conducive to interior exploration. It is always so. That's why the ancient monks and lamas always built their monasteries in isolated places. The more rugged and inhospitable his surroundings, the more man turns into himself, the more he must find his own inner sustenance. But that was not the sole reason why Harbor House was placed here in the Alaskan wilderness. Not that Harbor House itself is rugged or inhospitable. On the contrary. It is a free and easy place. There are no restrictions, no restraints of any kind, no bars or rules."

"But your guests—they would be called patients in other places, I take it," I suggested. Derek's smile was amiable.

"Oh, yes, they would indeed be called patients, inmates, and God knows how many other things," he said. "But at Harbor House there are no inhibiting names."

"Names are judgments," I smiled.

"Aren't they?" he answered, almost laughing back at me and suddenly I was down the long corridor of childhood with all those names that made one cry or grow angry or hide away in embarrassment. Small judgments they were, yet so terribly powerful and I looked at Derek Closter and knew how right he was. I watched him take a deep sip of his coffee and lean forward, his hands executing small birdlike motions in the air as he spoke, as if to help stir that excitement that flowed from him in invisible waves.

"Harbor House is an attempt to see beyond the ordinary seeing, a standing on thresholds, an experiment to open new channels of understanding," he said. "We theorize about what we call mental illness. We experiment on mice in laboratories.

We create little surrogate situations for them and analyze their reactions and then we make conclusions about man. We have a ridiculous obsession with the idea that we can learn about man by studying mice, rats, and chimpanzees. We can't. As the French say, *la vraie étude de l'homme, c'est l'homme*—the proper study of mankind is man. But those we call disturbed we put in sanitariums and asylums. We set them apart. We judge, confine, term them sick or insane, and then expect them to communicate with us. We take those we call less disturbed and ask them to tell us about themselves from couches. It's all nonsense, essentially. No one confined, judged, set apart, made into an object, will take part in a free and open dialogue, which is the heart of communication."

"Will not or cannot?"

"Both. They are closed off, and we are, too. But you cannot see through closed doors, whether they are made of steel, wood or emotions. Harbor House is an experiment in keeping doors open, outer doors and inner doors. They affect each other. It is an attempt to learn about how others really think and about how we see things. You might say it is an experiment in private meanings."

He paused at my smile, his sparkling eyes inquisitive.

"My aunt used that expression," I told him. "It has its own private meaning for me."

He nodded and went on quickly. "Harbor House is a completely unique approach to the entire subject. Naturally, because society has rigid attitudes and conceptions, certain things had to be taken into consideration. Harbor House was put into its remote setting to avoid the pressures and problems that come with organized communities. I received a grant to start with— enough to buy the house and furnish it."

He paused and sat back but the excitement had reached out to swirl around me like so many tingling fingertips. I'd never met anyone with the vibrant fire of this slender, attractive man. It was no surface charm. I'd seen too much of that to be fooled by it any longer. Derek Closter throbbed and radiated with the intensity of his work, his beliefs. As he went on, I found myself listening with mounting excitement.

"I had a young woman assistant, but she left a month ago," he said. "I'm afraid she didn't like the land, the nature of her work, or anything very much. One does have to have a sensitivity for lonely splendor, for the work I'm doing here. I thought she had, and she did try, but it just wasn't for her. I was going to advertise in some of the West Coast papers because I do need someone. Would you be interested, Stacy?"

"I'd have to go back with the tour first," I heard myself saying. "I could return, of course, in two weeks or so."

The words just tumbled from me, as if they had a will of their own, and I grew annoyed at my own surging excitement. But the whole idea seemed a marvelous opportunity—one of those rare occurrences that embrace everything at once. I would be getting away, finding the time to regather my own certainties, and working at something that had always interested me. I knew then and there that I would have returned even if Derek had not been such a captivating, exciting person.

"You would have your own quarters, of course, room and board, and a modest salary. Your work would be primarily to act as another pair of eyes and ears for me, listening, observing, recording. I've a man and woman who do the housework," I heard him going on and I nodded almost absently, my mind already ticking off personal things, clothes I could take, things I needed to buy, subletting my apartment and a host of other details.

"Tell me, do you have a family back home?" Derek asked and went on without waiting for an answer. "You said you didn't want to go back, so I assume there are no close ties with anyone."

"No, no close ties," I replied. "I'm quite on my own. My parents both died when I was very young and a wealthy aunt raised me. She's a wonderful woman, but she spends most of her time traveling abroad these days, so I hardly see her except at holidays."

"Then there's really no reason why you can't join our family at Harbor House," he said.

"I'm leaving here today in a few hours," I answered. "But I can write you my answer as soon as I get home."

Derek's smile was laced with secret wisdom, as though he knew I was replying out of a sense of propriety, not honesty. He stood up and his hand held mine for the briefest moment, a warm, electrical touch. "I hope you'll come. I think you'd do perfectly," he said. His face held a moment of almost arrogant confidence that would have been irritating on anyone else. On Derek it seemed quite appropriate, and I wondered what it would be like to work closely with a man of such acute perception. Fascinating, I concluded quickly.

We said small, polite things, then, and he gave me the address where I was to write him. I stuffed it into my bag without looking at it and left, walking slowly, even casually, while I wanted to race off with schoolgirl excitement. It had been a coincidental meeting—a happenstance—but how many things in this world grow out of just such coincidences. More than we like to admit, I told myself, and I left Alaska that day feeling renewed. I'd forgotten what a wonderful feeling it was.

So all the beginnings had come together and I could envision only good things, sparks for the mind and hope for the heart. I could not know then that one day there would be only terror and a glimpse into the dark places of the soul.

CHAPTER TWO

The trouble with omens is that they so often go unrecognized until it is too late. We're forever looking back at them with the delayed wisdom of hindsight. I had one on that first day I returned to enter this new world, to become a part of Dr. Derek Closter's noble experiment. I saw it for what it was for a moment. For one sudden, shuddering moment, I knew the meaning of being alone—totally and completely alone. For that one moment, I knew that instant of sinking hopelessness, of stark realization that there was no place to go and no one to turn to. It was just a flash—a subliminal moment—but it was there, to disappear unrecognized and unheeded.

I had returned home and had gone through the process of considering Derek's offer in a cold, evaluative light. But it was neither cold nor evaluative, only empty motions I put myself through to satisfy the tiny voice of practicality and logic. I gave myself all the reasons for turning it down, for caution. After all, I didn't really know anything about it beyond what Derek had said. I'd no idea what I might be getting into. But the reasons were all hollow. I'd already been made captive by Derek's vibrancy, by the air of excitement he'd given Harbor House, by the taste of taking part in the tomorrow he'd left with me. And I was a captive of my own determination to find a new niche for myself. I'd been home only two days when my letter of acceptance went to Derek. His letter came at the end of the week, made up mostly of travel instructions which of themselves curled about me with the flavor of pioneering excitement.

I hadn't wasted the week, though. By the time his letter came, I'd succeeded in subletting my apartment. I spent the next week doing all the other things that needed doing—mostly a mad rush of shopping for clothes and hoping I was getting the right ones. The actual good-byes were the easiest part. They'd really all been said, anyway, when I first got off the carousel. I merely sealed them. Philip had the good taste not to try to appear heartbroken, and I was grateful for that in a backhanded way. Finally, the day arrived, bright, clear, a wonderful day for starting new things. I boarded the big jet for Seattle and from there, a second, smaller airliner to Juneau. It was still clear when I landed in Juneau, the air even brighter, etching everything more sharply. In Juneau, following the instructions in Derek's letter, I asked the airport officials for a plane that might take me into the Talkeetna Mountains. They directed me to a small hangar at the far end of the airport. I found a huge, bearded man, his beard the color of old rust, his clothes wrinkled khaki, seated behind a small desk in a tiny cubicle at one side of the hangar. His plane, I saw at a quick glance, was a small monoplane, holding four at the most, I guessed. He was the heart and soul and body of a one-man, independent charter line—one of a number of such lines, I learned. His bearlike appearance hid a garrulous, affable friendliness.

"Sure I'll take you. I fly anyone or anything that needs flying," he said. "Freight, fishermen, goats, hunters, geologists—you name it and I've flown it. I don't usually get pretty girls traveling alone up into this country, though."

"I'm going to work up in the Talkeetna Mountains," I said, almost pridefully as he loaded my bags into the little plane. I wondered if I should try to characterize Harbor House or ask if he knew of it, but I decided against it. It didn't matter because he was garrulous, but not inquisitive, and he flew the little plane with the casual ease of those men who have a daily, almost fond relationship with death and danger. I sat in the seat beside him as we took off and he spiraled the little plane upwards and I felt the soaring, inner lift of going into space, free and birdlike, so totally different from the controlled unemotionality of airline flight. It mirrored, in its own way, my coming here, a few, brief moments of apprehension and then settling back confidently for what lay ahead.

"You've still enough summer left to see the land in its best clothes," he said as we flew over seemingly endless mountain ranges, sometimes flying through passageways between peaks that rose up on both sides. Seeing them this way, almost as though I could reach out and touch them, made me see them for what they truly were, not mere masses of dirt and stone dusted by snow but actual monuments to the living creativity of earth itself. My bearded, talkative pilot pointed out particular mountains and passes and kept up a steady, pleasant, time-filling chatter.

"You'll be about an hour early. We've had a good tailwind," he announced. "I expect you're being met there."

"Oh, yes," I answered. "I wrote and told them when my flight was due to arrive in Juneau."

He grunted. "Most folks up here know schedules are pretty damn uncertain. They'll probably figure out a general idea of flying time. They might even have somebody there waiting," he said. I gripped the edge of the seat as he suddenly banked the little plane and then started to lose altitude. The ground below began to take on more definition, and I saw the dark green of thick forests climbing up along mountainsides and the sparkling blue of crystalclear lakes. We continued losing altitude. The forests became trees, and the trees took on recognizable characteristics—mostly conifers, pines and spruces, giant firs, and tall tamaracks. We were dropping down through the heart of the Talkeetna Mountains, the pilot slipping and sliding his way past sharp peaks, finding openings by what seemed magic and finally almost skimming treetops. I glanced at my watch. It was late afternoon, and I searched ahead for the town I'd been given as my destination, Bear Landing. I saw a narrow, flat stretch ahead, alongside one edge of a large, curving lake of pure cerulean blue. The plane nosed down for the narrow strip of flat soil.

"Bear Landing," the pilot called out.

"Where?" I asked. I saw only three wooden shacks take shape at the far end of the strip, two longer than the third.

"There, that's it," he said. "Bear Landing's only a supply drop. Andy Jackson runs the trading post and sells liquor while his brother takes care of the storage sheds."

The plane's wheels touched the ground. A slight bump, then another, and then we were rolling, braking, coming to a halt at the end of the narrow strip. The three shacks stared at me, solider and heavier than they'd seemed from the air. A big arm reached in front of me and unlatched the door on my side, the plane's engines still idling. Apparently the pilot wasn't going to even turn them off. I stretched my legs out the door, sorry now that I hadn't worn slacks instead of the green skirt climbing high up over my thighs as I swung out of the plane and dropped the short distance to the ground. I glanced about automatically to see how many eyes had been watching. It had been an unnecessary concern. There wasn't a soul in sight. My bags were being reached out of the plane and dropped neatly to the ground. The door was pulled shut by a seemingly unattached arm and then, from inside the plane, the arm waved at me. I returned the wave, squinted as the little craft turned in a tight circle and flung air back at me. It started back along the narrow strip and I watched it gather speed with a sudden rush and then leap skyward. It banked, became a small noisy bird in the cloudless sky, and winged away.

I glanced around me. The three wood huts stood silently, implacable, to my left. To the right, the lake rippled with a cool breeze, bordered with tall spruce that were even more austere than the shacks. Behind me the forest rose in a thick, green wall and, beyond it, the endless mountains. I glanced back at the little plane winging off, and I had the terrible compulsion to call and wave it back and ask it to stay with me till someone came. But it was almost out of sight already and I picked up my bags and moved them to one side of a pathway that ran to the center shack. A hand-carved wood sign hung over the double doors: *Trading Post.* I walked to it, pushed on one of the doors. It swung open. I was inside a huge room filled from top to bottom and end to end with crates, barrels, and piles of skins. The musky odor of fur, hide, and wood hung heavy in the air. Grains, coffee, oats, seed, and meal spilled over the tops of the big barrels. Boxes marked *tea*, sacks stamped *flour*, crates upon crates of canned goods. Piled high atop each other were stacks of furs and skins, some made into coats and jackets, others simply strewn carelessly about. A long counter ran along one side of the hut, piled high with jars of spices and herbs and oils.

A figure materialized at the far end where there was a cleared space at the wooden counter. I saw a small man with long, braided black hair and the high-cheekboned face of an Indian or an Eskimo or a mixture of both, a face that seemed as though it were forever pressed flat against a windowpane with every feature broadened and blunted. He wore a shawl or cape—I couldn't be sure which—of dark brown tones. His small black eyes regarded me intensely, but I could find neither curiosity nor surprise in them.

"Do you know Dr. Closter?" I asked, hearing the tentative-ness in my voice. "He's supposed to have someone meet me here. I don't suppose there's any way of getting in touch with him, is there? My flight arrived early."

"Mr. Jackson away," the figure grunted. "Come back maybe two days."

"I see, thank you," I nodded and retreated outside, certain that we had exhausted our level of communication. I glanced at my watch. If Derek had estimated the usual flight time I had at least a half hour to wait. I walked to the edge of the lake and scanned the clear blue of it. The sky was the sky I would come to know well—clean and brilliant, unsullied. I knelt down and felt the water. It was warmer than I'd expected, clean and light in my fingers. The blue of the sky had begun to darken, carrying a trace of pinkness that was becoming blue gray at the horizon line. I turned slowly, scanning the deep green of the conifers that surrounded Bear Landing like a thick collar. I began to walk along the edge of the lake, following its slow curve.

The ground was firm. The trees grew almost to the water's edge. A hare hopped into view, then away, and I paused to watch it go. I walked on, watching the water push against the shore as a wind gathered strength. The shoreline curved and Bear Landing vanished from sight and the sky grew purple with oncoming night. A bird, gray-feathered, darted from the trees, circled, and disappeared back into their greenness. I halted, feeling very alone again, but there was something else now. This wild, raw land seemed to threaten and protect at once. *I will make you small and insignificant and alone with my strength*, it seemed to say, *but I will let you borrow strength from me, too. I am here to take and to give.* Unexplainably, I felt I would need to borrow strength from this wild land, and I turned and hurried back along the lake until finally the three wood huts of Bear Landing were before me again. My bags, looking as lost as I felt, sat to one side. Using the largest one as a perch, I sat down. It was then that I noticed the road, leading down from the side of one of the huts, winding out from the trees. I was watching it when I heard the sound of a car engine. It sounded like the clarion call of triumphant trumpets to me, and I stood up just as an old and very battered jeep emerged from the trees and bounced down to where I waited.

A young man got out, medium height, wearing jeans and an open-necked shirt. I saw light brown hair and cool, blue eyes in an attractive face that seemed to hang somewhere between sternness and sadness. I started toward him, saw his blue eyes focus on me, caught the moment of appreciation in them.

"Hello. I arrived early," I said. I've been waiting for you."

His smile was slow, rueful, and held apology in it, curiously. "I wish that were so," he said, and I felt the tiny crease lines on my brow.

"I'm Stacy Wayland. Didn't Dr. Closter tell you to pick me up?" I said. The slow smile vanished and I saw something flicker in his blue eyes.

"I'm not from Harbor House," he said. "I just drove down to pick up some supplies I ordered."

"Oh, I just assumed," I stammered, feeling as foolish as disappointed. "I'm sorry."

"I'm not," he said, holding out a big, warm hand. "I'm Cary Brooks. I've a cabin up in the hills." He paused letting me have the next line.

"I don't suppose you'd know how I could get in touch with Dr. Closter, would you?" I inquired.

"I'm afraid there's not even a phone up here," he answered. "You did say they were expecting you, didn't you?"

"Yes, I'm going to work at Harbor House as Dr. Closter's assistant," I said. The cool blue eyes seemed to harden and search my face but he said nothing. "I'm replacing the girl who left last month," I said.

"Elise Donner?" he commented.

"Was that her name?"

"Yes, and it was closer to two months ago," Cary Brooks said quietly.

"You knew her?"

"I knew she worked there. I keep to myself, though my cabin isn't all that far from Harbor House. I came up here to paint, and I'm sticking to that.

"You're an artist?" I commented and he nodded. Expressions shifted in the blue eyes like someone changing clothes behind a screen—movement, but nothing clear enough to recognize.

"Look, if you wait till I load my supplies, I'll drop you off there," he offered. "As I said, it's not that far from me."

"That'd be wonderful, if you're sure it isn't inconveniencing you," I replied.

"No, I'm just a bit higher on the mountain," he said. He turned and started into the trading post and I went with him. The figure inside looked up and, with a flick of his eyes, gestured to a small mound of supplies placed in a neat pile. Cary loaded sacks and boxes in his arms and I took up two of the sacks and followed. "No need for that," he protested. "I'll get them all."

"Let me help, please," I insisted. I walked to the jeep beside him as he deposited the supplies in the back of the vehicle. I turned, caught his long, sideways appraisal.

"How did Dr. Closter ever find you?" he asked.

"Really sort of a chance meeting," I answered, and told him briefly how I'd met Derek. Cary's eyes were veiled again as he listened—extremely attentively, it seemed.

"I understand the girl who left was very beautiful, too," he remarked, but his face was unsmiling, almost stem.

"Thank you," I murmured.

"Dr. Closter has been lucky once again," he said, and I suddenly had the distinct feeling that he was choosing words carefully, a controlled evenness in his speech. But he started around to the other side of the jeep and I shrugged away the thought. The purple haze had turned to a dark gray-blue and the air took on a sharp bite. Along the far edge of the lake, where it slowly curved away, the line of tall pines there still snared a last few glints of the setting sun. I was just about to climb into the jeep when the blue pickup truck nosed out of the trees and down the road. It rolled up almost alongside, halted and a man stepped from the cab, a gray figure in a gray shirt and gray trousers with high shoulders that made his head seem to set deep in between them like one of those ill-made dolls with no neck. He had a square face with opaque eyes, large irises with tiny pupils, almost like those of a cat. It was not just his clothes that gave the grayness to him. His large, expressionless face seemed made of gray clay, a strange, bloodless feel to it.

"Miss Wayland?" he said, his voice as flat and expressionless as his face. "I'm Matland, from Harbor House. I got started late—engine trouble."

It was not an apology, simply a statement. He picked up my bags and put them in the back of the truck. Cary Brooks returned to my side of the jeep.

"I'm sorry he wasn't delayed a little longer. I'd have been on my way with you," he said.

"Thanks anyway for the offer," I said. "You helped by just showing up. I was beginning to get really worried."

"If you're out wandering about sometime, come visit me. Just go back from where you'll be. I'm the only cabin," he smiled.

"Thank you. I might just do that," I told him. He nodded, serious instantly, and as he turned away I caught the tiny twitch of a tightened jaw muscle. I went to the pickup truck where the gray-faced man, Matland, waited. As I climbed into the cab I glanced back at Cary Brooks. He was watching me, something in his eyes I couldn't read, more than curiosity, more than idle interest, a depth to it that almost seemed to edge concern. It stayed with me as Matland sent the truck climbing up the roadway, faintly disturbing, like something slightly out of place.

The darkness lowered itself quickly now, the trees forming patterns, deckled edges against the last remnants of light still clinging to the sky. The road seemed in constant danger of being swallowed up by the huge white pines that bordered both sides. Matland switched on headlights as the dark enveloped the little truck, driving with a grim implacability that seemed to be part of the man; his hands, large and square, fingered the wheel with a tight grip. He made no attempt to talk, his silence not simply silence but a wall. I've always hated walls. Like Robert Frost, I always asked to know what was being walled in or walled out.

"Is it far?" I began.

"Ten, maybe twelve miles," the reply growled back.

"Have you been at Harbor House long?" I tried. The gray face turned for a moment, the tiny pupils of his eyes hardly more than slits.

"Longer than some places," he said and drew silence in on himself again.

"Do you like it there?" I persisted.

"It'll do," Matland said. Answers that were really no answers, replies that said nothing. The man held a surly truculence deep in him.

"I'm sure I'll like it and I hope everyone will like me," I pressed. The gray-clay face turned, longer this time, the cat's eyes boring through me.

"It's not a place for outsiders," the man said, returning his eyes to the road ahead. I held the words for a moment. Just a remark, a passing comment? Hardly, I told myself. I was an outsider, at least as yet, and there had been the touch of disapproval in the comment. Perhaps, I wondered, the hint of a warning in it. Matland's wall was not to be pierced, I decided, and I settled myself outside it, not unhappy to be there. The man radiated hostility, and it was perhaps best walled in. I concentrated on watching the headlights pry into the trees as the road curved and then, widening, grew flatter. Suddenly we were in a cleared area. Harbor House rose up in front of me, two lights flicking on outside to illuminate the premises. I saw a house that might have been ludicrous were it not so monstrously ugly. A center section rose up and came forward from two short sections on each side so that it sat squatting like a giant toad with its two hind legs out from its belly.

I saw the open-timber of Tudor, the gables of Jacobean, the cupolas of Pennsylvania Gothic, the gambrel roof of New England, and the dormers of Dutch Colonial, all painted an unrelieved charcoal gray—a monstrosity that was at once everything and nothing. I found myself hoping the ugliness was all on the outside. Harbor House indeed, I reflected. It harbored architectural aberrations as well as human ones. The cutting reaction sent a moment of guilt through me, but it was real, and I was not one for denying the reality of my own feelings, even if only silently voiced.

Matland swung the truck to the front door of the house and I saw Derek come out. He wore dark trousers and a deep red lounging jacket over an open-necked shirt. His eyes, deeper and more alive than I'd remembered them, found mine at once, and the electric vitality of the man reached out like an unseen lasso. His arms reached upwards, half-lifted me down from the cab of the truck and his smile was wide with that steel-spring aliveness of those few souls who are attuned to and aware of every little thing around them.

"You're tired," he said at once, "but more lovely than I remembered."

I was feeling tired and didn't deny it. "And you're hungry, I imagine," Derek said, and again was completely right. "There's no formal dinner hour tonight—we usually skip two days a week—but I'll have something sent to your room as soon as you're settled. Most everyone eats in their rooms on these evenings."

I nodded, glad not to have to meet everyone now. I went with Derek, his hand on my arm, into the house and a square foyer with rooms branching out from it. I saw a wood-paneled living room, furnished with two couches and good, solid pine furniture and from it, with two entrances, one off the hallway, a dining room with a solid, polished oval table and a Sheraton-styled sideboard. As I walked further into the foyer I saw a smaller room, a library of sorts with one book-lined wall and again, good, solid furniture. The interior of the house was, thankfully, more or less all of one piece. Aware that Derek had been watching my quick appraisal, I turned to his glowing, vibrant eyes.

"You told me you'd furnished the house. You didn't get these pieces from around here, I take it," I commented, noting a lovely corner cupboard in the living room.

"No, I went about picking them up all over. I don't even remember where, for most of them," he answered. I followed him into the living room as he made a sweeping gesture with one arm. "Most of the guests spend their evenings here and in the library. Everyone can do exactly as he or she wishes," Derek said. "Living quarters are in both wings, which really go from one section to the other, and are practically one."

He led me back into the hallway and I noted the wall lamps, a half-shell of translucent glass around each one, giving the hallway a dim, nineteen-hundreds look about it. At the end of the corridor, a stairway led to the second floor of the center section of the house. "The kitchen is just before the stairway, and my rooms are at the top of the stairs. I use them as living quarters and office," Derek said.

A door opened just before us and I glimpsed pots and pans as a woman stepped into the hallway. Tall, wearing a dark skirt and a wool blouse, she had blonde hair braided and wrapped around her head. She was a big woman and her eyes—cold blue—speared me from out of a totally unsympathetic face that was without any softness at all in it. She was perhaps forty, I guessed, and not unattractive in a commanding, rather amazon way.

"This is our housekeeper and cook, Una Stenner," Derek introduced. "She's been looking forward to your coming, as has everyone else here."

Una Stenner nodded with a flick of her eyes. She didn't impress me as looking forward to my coming at all, I thought to myself.

"Aaron is not eating again," the woman said to Derek, her voice as unsympathetic as her face.

"He's punishing himself again. If it doesn't pass by tomorrow, I'll look into it," Derek told her. Una Stenner turned on her heel and marched back into the kitchen, her bottom too broad, too heavy, yet not without a crude sensuality. Derek's hand touched mine and his smile flashed warmly, sweeping everything else aside. "Come, I'll show you to your room," he said, and I hurried with him into the east wing, just before the stairway. I saw a short corridor with rooms opening from it and as we passed the first door it opened and Derek halted. A woman poked her head out, then her body, round and short, and I saw frizzy brown hair spilling around a round face with makeup applied too heavily, giving her a toy-soldier face.

"Marlyn," Derek said. "This is Stacy." The woman stepped out of the doorway in a frayed robe and slippers to come toward me. She was nearing fifty, I guessed, but her round face held a certain youthfulness.

"Hello, love, how are you?" the woman said, her voice a deep contralto, one of those voices that seem to always hold a chuckle ready to burst out. Her eyes, small and sharp in the roundness of her face, darted over me quickly, as though she were searching, judging. Suddenly her eyes snapped shut and then opened again.

"Where's Rudi?" Derek asked her.

"He went downstairs to the library to get a book," the woman said, never taking the bright, sharp eyes from me.

"Rudi and Marlyn are very close friends," Derek explained, a kind of mock gravity in his eyes. Marlyn moved closer to me, her eyes traveling slowly, now, over my face, moving across my every feature.

"You'll be loved here, dearie; you'll be loved," she said after a moment. "Yes, indeed you will." She smiled cheerfully.

"That's very nice. I hope so," I replied.

"Yes, you'll be loved," the woman smiled at me. "And you'll be killed, too," she added.

I felt my jaw go slack for a brief moment. The words had been delivered with the same bright cheerfulness as the others. "Marlyn sees all. Marlyn tells all," the woman finished and, with another cheerful smile, almost wrinkling her nose at me, she hurried back into her room and closed the door. I shook off my initial astonishment.

"What did all that mean?" I asked Derek.

"Nothing at all but Marlyn's delusions. Marlyn was a fortune teller, a soothsayer—one of the ones with real gifts of prophecy, if you listen to Marlyn's account. But she was a typical charlatan, I'm afraid. She claims she still has the vision of prophecy, of course, but she has only what she always had, an overwhelming desire to really have the things she claims to have," Derek said. His smile came again, lighting up the corridor. "You can't let everything you'll hear around here bother you," he said.

"No, of course not. I guess she just took me by surprise. It was so unexpected. And she sounded so cheerful."

"Marlyn always sounds cheerful, no matter what she says. It's part of her training as a fortune teller, she claims. But no case histories tonight. There'll be time tomorrow for that," Derek said. He was right again. I felt fatigue creeping over me. We halted and he pushed a door open and led me into a room, the walls a soft lime, two windows facing the grounds outside and draped in deep red. I saw a bed with an echoing deep red bedspread on it and a knotty pine dresser. A bathroom opened up from one side of the room. "One of the few rooms with its own bath," Derek said. "The hot water runs slowly, but it runs. We have our own somewhat ancient hot water heater."

My bags, I saw, had been placed beside the bed. Matland had obviously carried them here through the rear door. I glanced at the door and saw the chain bolt fixed to the inside and just then Una Stenner appeared, a tray of food held out from her heavy breasts. She placed it on a folding table alongside the small end table next to the bed. "Thank you very much," I said. The woman turned and left the room without glancing at me. Derek seemed not to notice her brusqueness. Perhaps he was too used to it to notice anymore. I felt that she certainly made a fine companion to Matland.

"I'll leave you now," Derek said. I turned to him. "Have something to eat, unpack, and relax. I'll stop by later, before I go to bed. His hand pressed mine. His smile was enveloping. "I'm very glad you decided to come," he said. He turned and left, not waiting for me to say anything, obviously aware it was better that way. I peeked beneath the covered trays and found lamb chops and potatoes and a side dish of peas. It was all very hot and steaming, so I decided to change first. There was a long mirror in the bathroom and I kept the blouse on and changed to a pair of light blue slacks that fit extremely well. Finally I sat down to eat. When I'd finished, I felt better for the infusion of new energy. I knew it wouldn't last too long, so I quickly finished unpacking. I put the small portable radio I'd brought on the end table beside the bed, hung my clothes in the large closet, and went to the windows to look outside. It was almost pitch black; the moon, if there was one, still not high enough to reach over the towering mountains that formed the frame for the small, cleared area. I examined the rest of the room then, found a small shelf of books, some novels, a few short story collections, nothing I'd read and so they were welcome enough. The small, polite knock interrupted my casual ferreting, and I opened the door to Derek. He walked in quickly, a bottle of brandy and two glasses in his hands.

"The brandy is for you," he announced. "I'll just have one glass with you, a nightcap." I watched the deep glow in his eyes as he poured the brandy and he handed me one of the glasses, the bright, brimming mood he brought with him filling the room. "To the new and beautiful addition to Harbor House," he toasted. I drank with him, the warm, tingling sensation welcome, another small recharging of energies.

"Tomorrow, after you meet everyone, I'll go over each case history, and we'll outline a program for you," he said. "But, like everything else, a program here is only a flexible guide. I want you to feel free to spend as much time with anyone you wish, to establish whatever relationship you think important. Reaching others is really a matter of rapport, isn't it? One must sense one's way intuitively."

"I suppose so," I said. "The girl I'm replacing—Elise Donner—did she do the same kind of thing I'm going to do?"

"Yes, but you'll be much better at it. You can't do something well if you don't like it, or the people you're doing it with, can you?"

The question was rhetorical, and I didn't offer a reply. "I don't remember that I told you her name," Derek said. "Did Matland tell you?"

"No, I met a man—an artist—while I was waiting at Bear Landing. He was about to drive me here when Matland arrived. He seemed to know of her."

"Ah, yes, the fellow with the cabin up in the mountains. He arrived about three months ago," Derek said. "Elise wandered about. They might have met." He fell silent, lost for a moment in his own thoughts, and I detected a tiny frown on his broad forehead. For that moment, it was as though a current in a wire had been turned off and then, equally abruptly, his smile flashed and the current was on again.

"You are practically spilling over with questions about the operation of Harbor House and its objectives," he said, and I had to laugh with him again. He was able to pick up my feelings with such effortlessness. "Everything in time," he continued, a small, whimsical smile in his deep eyes. "But I would say this now. I make no pretenses of rank here. I am Dr. Closter and that is understood by everyone, but I do not use the title or insist that others do. They call me whatever they wish and in whatever way they wish. Titles are almost as inhibiting as judgments, don't you think?"

The little lights of laughter were still dancing in his eyes as I answered. "Possibly, but I was raised to respect titles. My family was quite formal. It might be inhibiting to me not to use them in a formal situation."

His laughter was bright, quick and he extended his palms upwards at me. "You do whatever you wish, Stacy, whatever feels right for you," he said. "You'll find many different things here at Harbor House, but one must expect that when dealing with those who have stepped beyond what society defines as the norm. None of us, even the most withdrawn, can entirely escape the stamp of society. We're marked too early and too thoroughly to simply erase it. The totally withdrawn try to escape. So you will find many of the more common symptoms from time to time, depression, anxiety, blocking, compromise formation, and sometimes maladaptive behavior. But I daresay you'll find more surprises than you expect here at Harbor House."

He stood up, reaching out and pulling me up with him, letting his eyes take time to linger on the upward curve of my breasts, wander down to my waist and hips. I always enjoyed frank admiration. It's a compliment without words and I enjoyed his appreciative eyes now.

"In a way, bringing you up here is very wrong," he said, and chuckled at the question that formed in my eyes immediately. "This is a wild and lonely place, and it's a bit like putting something beautiful into a closet."

"Not at all. I wanted to come," I said. And, silently, I added a thought of my own. His electric vibrancy and frank appreciation would more than suffice. Derek turned quickly, pausing at the door.

"Breakfast is casual, in the dining room from nine to ten. I'll introduce you to everyone then," he said. His smile reached out warmly again and then he was gone, closing the door after him.

I put the chain bolt on, more the habit of years of big-city living than anything else. I undressed, enjoyed the freedom of being without clothes even though the room was chilly. In the bathroom, I turned on the hot water in the tub. It was warm enough, but even more exasperatingly slow than Derek had indicated. I finally decided to make do with half a tub and to develop more patience in the future. I bathed quickly and slipped into flannel pajamas as the night chill seeped through the room. I slid beneath the cover and switched off the small lamp on the night table to lay in the darkness and generate warmth.

I was too tired to fall asleep quickly. It had been one of those days when too much happens too quickly. It had started with eagerness and excitement, grown into nervous apprehension, and now ended on a mote of quiet anticipation. But I was here, far from everything I'd known and perhaps feeling a little more alone than I wanted to admit. The letter I'd sent Aunt Catherine would catch up to her someplace in her travels. It had been a final cutting-off of my other world and I'd been surprised at how difficult it had been to write. But I was here and Matland's words rose up to sway before me. I was the outsider in a place not for outsiders. I hoped that would change quickly.

In the silent darkness my mind made its own paths, idle wanderings, slow pursuits of stray emotions and stray thoughts. It was terribly still in the house, and I almost leaped from the bed when the sound from outside split the stillness—the hoot of an owl, a wild, untamed sound, not at all like the barn owls I used to hear at camp when I was younger. I rose and went to the window. My eyes, already adjusted to the darkness, found him quickly enough, on the branch of a tree directly across from the window. It was a large, full-feathered bird—a great gray owl—and I watched him for a few minutes as his haunting cry reverberated in the air. Finally, feeling the chill again, I went back to bed and he stopped, as though he'd had enough of disrupting the night.

The silence took back the room, then, and I lay still once again. I was beginning to drift off to sleep when another sound came to me, drifting through the closed door of the room, faint but clear—a soft sound, not quite a gasp, not quite a cry. I listened, awake instantly again, the woman's voice making the small sounds in a regular, rhythmic pattern, each a little stronger than the other, each a fraction longer. I knew the sound and felt my abdomen tighten in the response of recognition. I listened and did not believe my ears, yet I could not disbelieve as the small gasps gathered urgency as their rhythm increased. I swung from the bed and unlatched the door, opening it slightly on the dark hallway. The sound came from down the corridor someplace— no mistaking it now—but I hadn't mistaken it anyway, different for each woman, yet the same for all. Again I felt the response of my own body as I thought of Philip beside me in the darkness of my apartment, the intertwining of needing and wanting that had been mine. Yes, I knew the sound, and my skin was wet with tiny drops of perspiration.

The softly gasping, urging voice was the only thing I did not know, except that it was not Una Stenner's voice. It was too light, too young and soft. Nor was it Marlyn's contralto. The sound rose now, each gasp quicker, desire racing beyond itself until, with a rushing, bursting cry, it hung shuddering in the night and was still.

I closed the door and turned away, furious at the trembling that was in me, the terrible surgings of all those needs I thought I could so easily put aside. In bed, disbelief came flooding over me again, not at myself now, but at the ecstasy I had unwillingly eavesdropped upon. Derek had stressed the freedom and lack of restrictions here at Harbor House. The *guests*—and I used his euphemism—were partakers in *an experiment in tomorrow, in new ways of understanding.* I had of course interpreted those words in my own way, structuring them automatically to my own concepts. Private meanings again, I grimaced, and I'd been wrong, very wrong. No restrictions meant just that, apparently. Derek's noble experiment had taken on new dimensions indeed, and my list of questions to ask him had grown suddenly longer.

I held back my first critical reaction, that skepticism we always bring to that which takes us by surprise. Harbor House didn't deserve such judgments. I didn't want to bring the corrosiveness of skepticism to it. Derek would detect it at once and be disappointed, perhaps even hurt, I reflected. He was a fervent believer in Harbor House, whatever it was and whatever it meant, I saw that the very first time we met. I would not compromise that now, not till I was no longer the newcomer, not till I could embrace its promise or see its futility. In accepting his offer to come here, I had made more than simply an agreement to be his assistant. I had made an agreement to come in openness, to bring a willingness to believe with him. I would keep the agreement, I told myself, closing my eyes. Fatigue, refusing denial any longer, pressed down upon me, but I went to sleep restlessly, the echoes of ecstacy still clinging, even Marlyn's contradictory prophecy returning for a brief moment, then fading away before sleep. If the house held any further sounds in the night, I didn't hear them.

CHAPTER THREE

woke early and, as when I was a little girl and someplace new for the first time, I rushed to the window to look outside. I saw sun striking off the mountaintops and below, the deep green, thick pines and firs shimmering with dew, looking as though they'd just been washed down with a giant hose. The window opened easily and, shaking off the morning chill, I inhaled the smell of the forests, wet wood and pine needles and damp earth and musk, all mingled together in a timeless, primal fragrance. Later, when the sun came down into the forest, the damp, new-morning smell would give way, and the scent of pine and fir and spruce would be dominant. But now there was the special magic of morning, and, with surprise, I found myself thinking about Cary Brooks in his little cabin someplace in the hills, and I wondered if he were up with palette and brush to try and make the moment stand still.

Turning from the window, I dressed hurriedly, deciding on blue corduroy slacks and a soft pink sweater that was both warm and clinging. I opened the door and tiptoed into the hallway. I saw the door at the end of the corridor and, pushing it open, I was outside. Looking around me, I knew that this is how the world must have been for untold eons, supremely indifferent to man, possessing all that tried to possess it. I saw brush move to the right, and a red fox ambled into sight along the edge of the trees, his coat burnished gold and thick, a white underside showing at the chest He cast a glance at me with sharp, unafraid eyes, and he walked with ownership, making me feel an outsider again as I turned and went back into the house.

Matland was in the hallway, his gray-clay face turning as I entered. Una Stenner stepped from the kitchen and handed him a large silver coffee service. She glanced at me, her face expressionless, only the cold blue eyes acknowledging my presence. I heard the sounds of the house waking, water running, doors opening, footsteps and the murmur of voices. As I reached the center section at the stairs, Derek came down, a beige sweater casually thrown over brown slacks, his smile instant and enveloping as he saw me.

"Lovely in the morning, the true test of an attractive woman," he said. "And an early bird."

"Not always," I laughed. "Call it anticipation for the moment." His hand took my arm, that firm yet gentle touch that was his.

"Come on, we'll have breakfast and meet some of the others," he said.

"Some?" I asked, surprised.

"I never know who'll show for breakfast but I think today it will be most everyone, to meet you, of course," he said.

My questions about the night tugged at me. I pushed them back. There'd be plenty time for that, I told my impatient self. As he steered me to the open double doors of the dining room, I suddenly realized how apprehensive I was. We are all conditioned, in a thousand subtle and unsubtle ways, and to change that conditioning is like reaching inside yourself and tearing out a part of you. It is a painful and often slow process. To Derek, these people were really his guests. His euphemisms were not euphemisms to him. To me they would be patients, and I had to make sure not to show that. I was glad for his strength, his presence beside me, and I wondered if I'd ever be able to see quite as Derek did. The ability to step outside yourself, to see and think and feel as others do, is a charismatic gift. I hoped Derek could share it with me.

We entered the dining room and I saw that the coffee service had been set up along one wall, on the sideboard, with plates of buns, rolls and fruit—a buffet breakfast. I focused on the round, squat body of Marlyn, first, still in the frayed robe. "Hello, love," she called out, coming toward me with a waddling little walk. I felt Derek's arm pull from me.

"I'll get coffee. Milk and sugar?" he said and I nodded. Marlyn was beside me now and my eyes took in a portly, medium-height man, gray-haired with a somewhat jowled face, a network of tiny red veins just under the skin. Near him, a thin, hollow-eyed figure leaned against the wall, his face sensitive, ascetic with dark curly hair and an aquiline nose, a Semitic face that could have come from the wall paintings of ancient Judea. That would be Aaron, of course, I murmured silently, the Aaron who wasn't eating.

"Come on, love, say hello to Rudi," Marlyn exclaimed and propelled me toward the ruddy-faced man. He put out a hand to pump mine, his voice smooth and well modulated.

"Glad you got here, Stacy. Derek told us you were coming," he said. "Derek needs help. You can't be efficient without good help. I always told them that at the company. A good road-man needs good people behind him, right?"

I was nodding when Derek appeared at my elbow to hand me a cup of coffee. "Rudi was a top salesman," he said to me as I sipped. I saw Rudi seem to swell, a small turn of his head, shoulders squaring a fraction.

"That's right, the very top," he said, pride—almost arrogance—in his voice. Aaron, I saw, watched with round, haunted eyes, and I moved toward him, leaving Marlyn's deep cheerful voice in the background.

"Hello, Aaron. I'm Stacy," I started, flashing my most charming smile. The round orbs stirred, hinted at an acknowledgment, but he said nothing and remained pressed against the wall. "I hope we'll have a chance to talk soon," I said. Aaron's eyes watched me, deep brown spots of nothing, taking in my words, my presence, as a sponge soaks up a spill.

Derek's touch at my arm made me turn as I sipped deeply again of the coffee. The girl came toward me from the doorway, moving as though she were blown by a gentle, unfelt wind in a floor-length, loose-fitting gown which nonetheless pressed against round, high breasts. I saw auburn hair against an alabaster skin, a face of delicate, breathtaking beauty that held a mournful sweetness in it.

"Stacy, this is Nora," I heard Derek's voice saying as the girl halted before me, her smile wistfully soft, her eyes quiet, like a still blue lake.

"Stacy. What a lovely name. I wish it were mine," she said, and I knew the voice at once, none of the fervent urgency in it now, but the timbre the same, the basic tonality unmistakable. I fought down my instinctive surprise by concentrating on her beauty, seeming unflawed, yet somewhere, hovering in it, a quality of woundedness.

"Nora does all our summer gardening," Derek said. "And when the winter sets in, she keeps all kinds of plants alive in her room."

I watched Nora's eyes grow soft with a kind of private reminiscence. "You must love them, you know," she said to me. "Plants respond to love."

"Doesn't everything?" I asked gently and Nora tilted her head to one side for a moment and pursed finely formed lips.

"Everything should," she said finally. "But hardly anything does."

"I'll get you some coffee, Nora," Derek said, moving away for a moment. I watched the girl's soft eyes follow him, stay with him and I saw something that bordered on worship come into them.

"Dr. Closter is quite marvelous, isn't he?" I probed. She turned to me with the worship still hanging in her eyes.

"Derek? Oh, yes, Derek is something special. He's part of us," Nora said, the small smile wistfully guileless.

"Isn't that a nice thing to say!" Derek's voice cut in and he was standing beside me, handing Nora a cup of coffee as his eyes met mine in a small, silent exchange. It had been more than nice, of course. It had been the highest form of compliment. It meant that his was no longer a doctor-patient relationship here. He had been accepted fully, as a friend, as something special, in Nora's words. It was a remarkable achievement and as the full meaning of it continued to pull at me I felt a sweep of excitement at being here to take part in it. Nora was studying me over the rim of her cup, I saw, and her soft blue eyes grew warm with suddenness.

"We're going to be friends, Stacy," she said. "I can feel things like that."

"Of course we are, Nora," I answered. "You were friends with Elise Donner, weren't you?"

"Yes, but we'll be better friends," the girl said and, abruptly, she turned away and moved to Marlyn and Rudi. I caught Derek's eyes on me, slightly narrowed, studying me and tinged with amusement I was certain he had a remark held back and Matland, approaching, halted my question. The man's square head seemed as neckless as it had to me yesterday. I watched his cat's eyes flick over me as he halted before Derek.

"The insulation is gone around the hot-water pipes. I'll have to order it. I'll need a check," Matland announced. Derek turned to me.

"My office, upstairs, fifteen minutes?" he said. "We've a number of things to go over."

"Including whatever you were thinking a moment ago?" I asked and drew a quick laugh from him.

"Including that," he said, turning and walking from the room. Matland had gone to the coffee and was pouring himself a cup and I scanned the others, my thoughts on Nora again and I found myself trying to fit a partner to this delicately beautiful girl. Rudi? No. I rejected the thought, perhaps out of hand, and moved on to Aaron. He was certainly more suitable, an ascetic sensitivity to complement her wistful loveliness. But he was still hard against the wall, in a state of at least semiwithdrawal. He would not have been actively positive enough for sex last night, I was reasonably certain. My eyes moved to Matland and saw him watching Nora, holding her with a glance of slitted intensity. Matland? The thought repelled, asked to be cast aside. Yet I could not ignore the possibility. This was a world where my own reactions, my own reasoned logic, were at best poor guidelines. I accepted the outside possibility, but no more than that.

The others were intent on breakfasting and I didn't want to press myself on them, not until I'd talked further with Derek. I took half a buttered muffin and wandered from the room. I was in the hallway, examining the old, deep-red drapes framing the windows when the door opened and a tall man, straight in the black suit and roman collar of a priest entered. He had an attractive, well-modeled face that carried both warmth and discipline in it. He came toward me at once, arms outstretched in welcome, gray blue eyes twinkling.

"You must be Stacy. I'm Father Hodges," he said warmly.

"Good morning, Father," I said and saw the gray blue eyes twinkle at once.

"It comes easy to you," he said. "One can tell, instantly. There's a certain ring to it."

I laughed. "Saint Theresa's Academy, outside Garrison," I said. "Four years."

"Ah, the Ursulines, a fine group of teachers," Father Hodges said, and was so very right. I wasn't Catholic by birth, but Aunt Catherine had been a devoted believer in quality education. The Ursulines ran the best educational plant in the area, so I was sent there. I left, four years later, not made over, but with far more than mere empirical knowledge.

"You're a brave young woman, coming all the way out here to help Derek. I pray you won't regret it," Father Hodges said.

"No chance of that," I answered confidently.

"You must tell me what it's like back in the big cities these days. It's been so long for me and I was always a big-city boy— New York, in fact, Cathedral, the seminary, the whole route to a parish there," he said.

"I'd love to, Father, but right now Dr. Closter expects me. Later today?"

"At your convenience, my dear Stacy," he said. "It'll give me something to look forward to till then."

His warm, generous smile followed me up the stairs to the second floor. I saw a short corridor and just outside an open door, Derek talking to Matland there. He gestured to the door. "Go on in, be right with you," he said. I went inside the room, saw a heavy old desk, and behind it a wall filled with books. I could recognize only those my school psych courses had touched upon, Bleuler's writings on schizophrenia, Janet on psychic energy, Wundt on experimental psychology and, of course, Jung, Freud, Kraepelin and Krafft-Ebing. A fireplace and a stone mantel took up most of another wall and assorted chairs were scattered about. A large, framed montage of posters from the Vienna State Opera decorated the opposite wall and little porcelain figures stood at various spots. Many of them were Hummel pieces. It all gave the room a distinctly European flavor. I saw the open door to an adjoining room, a large bed inside it, and a dresser which looked surprisingly disordered. Derek, like most intense, completely work-oriented individuals, had little patience with neatness, obviously.

"I picked it all up at an auction—the entire room," the voice behind me said. I turned to see Derek closing the door to the hall. "I bought it intact, everything in it. It was a bargain. I was told it belonged to a wealthy Viennese."

"It's very nice, really. I expected rows of file cabinets stuffed full of case histories," I said.

"I have them," he replied, pushing a chair at me. "But I've memorized them all." He pulled another chair to the side of the desk and sat down across from me.

"I met Father Hodges," I said. "You didn't mention that you included the clergy in your work here."

"Ah, you met Tom," Derek smiled. "Good. He's the only one of my guests who usually skips breakfast."

"Guests?" I heard the word tumble out of me, automatic, before I could catch it and saw Derek's amused smile. I felt the color flooding into my face and uttered a silent *damn*.

"Don't look so dismayed," Derek said, smiling.

"I'm sorry," I answered, furious at my own transparency, embarrassment now stepping on the heels of surprise. "I just keep being taken aback, that's all, like last night."

"Last night?"

"I heard things," I began, trying to choose words, wanting to be neither crude nor prim. "Sounds—rather unmistakable sounds," I said.

"Oh?" Derek's amusement stayed in his eyes. "A door must have been left open."

"Yes. I'm quite sure whose door, now," I said and I watched as Derek sat back in the chair, letting his fingertips lean on each other to form an inverted V.

"Tell me, Stacy, if you had been in a motel last night and heard what you heard, would you have been taken aback?" he asked.

"No. No, of course not," I said, feeling quite small suddenly. "You're absolutely right. I'm just not conditioned enough yet. You've told me something of Harbor House, but I'm only beginning to understand the scope of what you're doing here. Nora, this morning, the things she said, they were really quite remarkable. You're a friend, here, a confidant."

"That was a first step, an absolute necessity," Derek said. "Just as all the other things are necessary to create the climate needed, an atmosphere of complete normality and equal acceptance. That means individual freedom, individual dignity. And it means what you heard last night; all that is a part of normal human experience. After all, sex is a form of communication, not only with someone else but with oneself. Only in such a climate is there any chance for learning about those who have stepped past society's concepts of normality. Only in such a climate can we understand the mind and the emotions. After all, we all harbor reasons, justifications for the things we do. The so-called disturbed are no different, and until we truly understand their justifications we will not understand our own. That, Stacy, is the clinical aspect of Harbor House, that experiment in understanding I spoke of to you."

"And the therapeutic aspects?"

Derek's smile grew almost abstract, a dreaminess coming into his eyes, as though the question raised fond memories.

"The therapeutic aspects, of course. There must always be therapeutic aspects—the goal at the end of the trail," he said. "The goal of Harbor House, therapeutically, is not merely to return those here to society but to create a revised concept of the entire area of the mind and its workings. You could say that the therapeutic goal is a new level of accommodation."

He halted, and I realized how once again he'd swept me up in the missionary zeal of his intensity. He laughed abruptly, breaking the mood, moving in his chair. "Enough of theory. We must get down to more practical aspects," he said. "First, a word about the maintenance of Harbor House, which I'm sure has entered your mind. The original grant covered the purchase of the house and furnishings. A second grant covered the first two years of operation. We are just starting our third. In addition, either the families or concerned organizations paid a two-year advance for each guest."

"How did you choose each person?" I asked.

"Through professional contacts. From case histories I chose those who would give me the clinical, social and personality mixture I felt important to the project. Co-operation from official agencies, families, and guardians were easy to obtain, for varying reasons, mostly self-serving. The agencies welcomed one less occupant for their facilities, and families were more than willing to push something traumatic even further away."

Derek paused again and a note of satisfaction came into his handsome features. "It has been a good two years, very productive," he said. "I anticipate even more satisfying results with you here to help me."

"And I promise not to be surprised anymore," I said, sounding more confident than I felt. "Mr. Hodges was my last."

"Father Hodges," Derek corrected.

"You call him that because he prefers it?"

"No, because he is a priest—an ordained priest of the Roman Catholic Church," Derek answered, paused, and then smiled slyly. "I thought you weren't going to be surprised anymore."

"I wasn't. That promise didn't last long, did it?" I said, shamefully.

"Father Hodges's presence here as one of the guests is a human condition. I don't know what this means theologically. I'm sure there are complications, but I'm no theologian. However, he is a priest."

" 'Thou art a priest of God forever,' " I murmured silently, remembering the words from the ordination ceremonies I'd attended when I was at Saint Theresa's.

"But let's get back to you," Derek said. "I was going to go over each of my guests with you, but I've decided against that. It might be a bit much all at once, so let's take one or two at a time. Your pick this morning."

Nora's wistful beauty came to me at once. My reply was unhesitating. "Nora," I said. "Let's start with Nora. I see nothing wrong in her at all, of course, only a terrible sadness."

"A terrible sadness," Derek echoed. "Maybe that's all there is—a sadness too terrible for the world to understand."

"And so they call it by other names," I followed.

"Exactly. We tend to reject that which we cannot under-stand; we resent that which makes us uncomfortable. People such as Nora make the world ask questions of itself it's afraid to ask. Her proper name is Nora Conlan, her family was middle-class, typical in every respect of millions like them, churchgoing people, believers in all the ethics and virtues that are part of the American culture. Nora had a younger brother, Eddie, three years younger than she. Apparently as very young children they were very close. Even as a small child, Nora instinctively recognized the need for protectiveness on her part. Eddie was retarded and almost spastic. At first, of course, she saw only that he was younger and dependent on her. Later, as she grew older, she recognized Eddie's differences from other children. The real problem began with school, the cruelty of children."

"It can be so terribly cruel. There's something of the wolf pack in it when they get going on someone," I said.

"Human nature unvarnished, without the restraints of social amenities," Derek said. "Nora's little brother, though retarded, could feel, could be hurt, and in school he was tormented, ridiculed, both emotionally and physically. The parents, as so often happens, were unwilling to admit that their child could not make it in an ordinary school. And, of course, there was after-school play. Eddie didn't fare any better there, and Nora's protectiveness grew consuming and compulsive. She began to be the target for the other children because of her protecting Eddie. Between fights, she went into periods of severe depression. Night after night she stayed with Eddie as he went to sleep, holding him, talking to him.

"When she was eleven and Eddie was eight, her parents finally decided to act. They realized that Eddie had to be put into a special school, for his sake and for Nora's. It's interesting that her case history notes that when they told her that he would go to a school where he wouldn't be hurt and tormented, she refused to accept that. 'Eddie will always be hurt, all his life,' she told them. "That's not right; it's not fair. He doesn't deserve that, and I'm not going to let that happen.'

"They passed over her remarks and a few days later, when her parents came home after having been shopping, they found Nora holding little Eddie in her arms in the kitchen. 'He won't be hurt anymore, by anyone,' she told them. 'It's better this way. He'll be all right now.'

"Nora had killed her younger brother. She'd made soup for him with a tasteless insecticide in it that had been around the house."

Derek halted, dark, deep eyes intent on me. I couldn't hide the shock and emptiness that flooded over me.

"Her case notes show that she was at first confused, then angered, then shocked by her parents' reaction to what she had done. She thoroughly expected at the very least, understanding, at the most, approval. Instead she was judged unbalanced, even dangerous. She was committed and sent away. Her actions had been beyond the norm, her solutions inverted and twisted beyond rationality."

"You sound as though you don't agree with that decision," I suggested.

Derek's smile was brief, a momentary expression. "Of course her actions were beyond the norm," he said. "The question is whether that, by itself, makes her unbalanced, insane, fit only to be put away. Nora was brought up, as we all are, to believe in love as the supreme thing in human relationships. To do good, to love unselfishly, is taught us as a goal which is to be sought at all times. It is taught us at home, at school, in the churches. Love thy fellowman, love thy enemies, love and honor thy father and mother, love and you will receive love. The Good Samaritan. To help even a total stranger, is an act of love. We are weaned on loving, nurtured on the principles of love as the ideal of human behavior. Some of us believe it more than others, but it is part of the fabric of our conscious and subconscious collective thinking. Can you say that Nora's act was not an act of love?"

"No, I can't. To her it was that, surely."

"To her it was a deed completely justified from inside and outside, justified by society's own teachings and principles. To society, it was an act of madness. There is too large a gap there. We must close it."

"By that new level of accommodation?" I smiled.

"Exactly. You are dubious, of course," he said, and I felt transparent again, a twinge of resentment at his ability to see into me accompanying a moment's uncomfortableness. "That's to be expected, at first," he went on. "I've made an irrational act appear to have been both rational and justifiable, and you automatically rebel at that. It reverses all the rules. It threatens that which you've grown up to believe. But I expect that in time you will find a completely new set of guidelines for yourself; not by anything I will tell you, but by what you'll see and hear yourself here at Harbor House."

He halted and, with a small smile, closed off that part of our talk. He went on brightly, a clinical matter-of-fact tone coloring his voice now.

"Your work here will be to talk to the guests, to listen, to absorb, and then to return to your room and make notes. You will make notes of what was said, the things that stayed with you, your impressions, everything and anything you wish to put down. They will become part of the notes I make. All will be analyzed monthly. They all go to form a picture, notes and more notes. It's important that you put down your own reactions. Don't try for objectivity. I'm a believer in Heisenberg, his Principle of Uncertainty—observing disturbs the observer. The act of observing affects both observed and observer. It puts to rest the pretense of detached observation, and we are better for it. Now the observer's role can be evaluated within the entire context."

Derek paused. "As I said before, you are free to talk to everyone or to concentrate on one. I imagine you'll want to talk to everyone—at first, anyway. We have a siesta period after lunch, an hour or so."

"Good enough," I said, sensing he was finished with his briefing for the moment. "But I'd like to know one thing more. Aaron—is he schizophrenic?" I dug into memory, psych courses coming to life again.

"A classic example," Derek said. "He had a very aggressive mother and a shy, retiring father. The mother was a pusher. She wanted her son to excel at sports, all contact play, be outward and thoroughly extroverted. The father, a teacher at a small private school, a lover of obscure poets and obscure playwrights, wanted Aaron to be like him. They fought constantly over the boy, in all the vicious and subtle ways such battles are waged, and the boy tried to please both, naturally. He tried to be one thing for the mother and another for the father. Tom between them, he assumed two roles and in time became two people, no longer in fantasy but in fact, the roles not roles anymore but actualities. The result, classic schizophrenia with all the rotating symptoms of delusion, dissociation, withdrawal, and the completely split, schizoid personality."

"Then you take a strictly psychological view of schizophrenia," I commented. "You don't accept those studies which indicate that it has an organic pathology."

"Acquired tissue characteristics, a histogenic and genogenic root?" Derek smiled. "Which came first, the chicken or the egg? Are biochemical and organic changes a genogenic blueprint or a reflection?"

"Of psychogenic disturbances," I finished.

"Exactly," Derek said. He rose suddenly, impatiently, obviously disliking the questions that had come up. He paused for a moment, plunged into private thoughts, and then his smile reappeared. He reached down and pulled me up with him, his fiery eyes amused again, soft lights dancing in them. I felt stimulated, made part of Harbor House now and caught up in the vibrancy of Derek's own feelings. I felt wonderfully alive.

"There are note pads in the library. Take one and keep it in your room for your notes. I'll see you later," Derek said, letting go of my hands. I turned away and, at the door, paused to look back.

"When I was talking to Nora at breakfast, what was it you were thinking as you listened?" I questioned. "You promised you'd tell me."

His answer was given unsmilingly; not a reprimand, yet something that edged close to it. "Don't talk down to anyone here. They are all your equal in most respects, your superior in many," he said. His bright smile flashed a moment later, as if to assure me that his reply was not to be taken any way but objectively, yet I couldn't help feeling that he was not at all objective in it.

"I'll remember that, Derek," I said and, with a rush of surprise, realized that it was the first time I'd called him by his first name. I left quickly, liking the sound of it on my tongue.

Downstairs, I heard the murmur of voices from the dining room, Marlyn's hearty chuckle coming through loudest. I was about to move toward the room when, through the hall window, I saw a small panel truck drive up outside, slow down, and a man lean out to toss a bundle of mail, tied together. I watched it land on the ground. The truck drove off at once. I went to the door and opened it to watch the truck disappear down the narrow roadway, the driver not looking back. I picked up the bundle and was bringing it into the house when Marlyn stepped into the foyer.

"Mail," she cried out. "The mail's come." Excitement seemed to shudder through her as she came toward me, her round body fairly shaking. "It comes every month or so in the summer and sometimes not for months at all in the winter," she said to me as I placed the small package on a chair. I saw Rudi emerge from the dining room, then Nora sweep out behind him. "Stacy will give it out," Marlyn called to no one and everyone. I tugged at the string on the bundle, snapping it finally, and saw Aaron come out into the foyer, still pressing close to the walls like an animal fearful of leaving the safety of its den. Another figure appeared, and I glanced up to see the tall, straight shape in the black suit and Roman collar, blue gray eyes watching me with calmness, encouragement. With a sudden stab, a mental non sequitur, I wondered if he could have been Nora's companion in the night, if that were the human condition that had brought him here to Harbor House. I shook away the thought and straightened up, the mail held in the crook of my arm. Two catalogs for Marlyn were on top. She snatched them gleefully from me.

"Marlyn sends for everything," Rudi announced. "She's a chronic coupon clipper. Is my issue of *New Products* there?"

I thumbed through the envelopes quickly and found it. Rudi took it with a pleasant nod. "I like keeping up with the times," he said.

"A letter for Father Tom Hodges," I said, holding out the envelope. I caught the return address as I did so—Mary Immaculate Church in New York.

"My monthly sermon from Father Martin," Father Hodges said. "He never fails to write. A good man, Father Martin."

Two magazines were next, both for Marlyn. She chortled happily as I handed them to her. The next envelope was light blue, a neat, feminine handwriting on it. "And here's a letter for Elise Donner," I announced in some surprise.

"It's probably been a month getting here," Rudi said. I was trying to make out the postmark when I heard the door open and then the voice, fury in it. I looked up to see Una Stenner storming toward me. Her face darkened, frowning. She whipped words out at me.

"What are you doing?" she cried. "Here—give me that."

The woman's frame seemed even larger as she loomed over me, her hand pulling the letter out of my fingers. She glanced down at it and her cold, hard eyes blazed back at me. But not before I'd seen something beside fury in them, almost a sudden alarm. "I give out the mail around here. Nobody else," she barked at me and took the rest of the bundle.

"I'm sorry. No one told me," I answered stiffly.

"I'm sure Stacy meant no affront," I heard Father Hodges say, his voice more than calm, a quiet admonition in it. Una Stenner turned on him. Her jaw muscles made little ripples along the side of her cheek as she worked to control herself.

"Now she knows!" the woman said, finally, gaining hold of her fury. She shot a quick, hard glance at me and I held back my own irritation. I watched her push the letter to Elise Donner into the pocket of her apron and proceed to hand out the rest of the mail.

I turned away, unwilling to think about unwarranted angers. I told myself that Una Stenner was one of those individuals who feel constantly threatened and jealously guard their own small tasks to reinforce their own small importances. But that instant moment of alarm had been in her anger, and the fact buried itself away inside me where it would lie dormant until something else happened to bring it to life. Damn being astute, I swore silently. It was a burden more than a help sometimes. I was almost to the library when the voice, close behind me, spoke. I felt myself jump as I whirled. Aaron was there, at my heels. "Do you like poetry?" he asked.

I hadn't heard a sound and automatically I glanced down to his feet. He wore ordinary white sneakers.

"I'm sorry—you startled me. My, you do walk softly, Aaron," I smiled. He stood waiting, watching me, the ascetic, mobile face, the long, delicate nose holding the echos of Galilee. "Why, yes, Aaron, I like poetry. Very much, in fact," I said.

His eyes, fixed on me, were deep, haunted, yet in them something stirred, an awakening, a coming alive. I paused at the library door. "Let's sit in here and talk about poetry, Aaron," I said. "I'd like that."

He followed me in and waited as I sat down on the couch. Aaron was the only one in whom I'd seen any obvious signs of disturbance, but that was to be expected. The states of schizophrenia were much more obvious than many other types of emotional disturbance. But I was glad to see the curtain still lifting in his deep eyes as he slowly emerged from his state of withdrawal. I motioned to him and he came to sit down beside me, perching tentatively at the very edge of the couch as though, at the slightest wrong move on my part, he would dash away to safety.

"I suppose you have favorite poets, don't you, Aaron?" I began. "Everybody has favorites. I love Yeats and Rupert Brooke, Dryden and Keats. When I'm feeling very sober-minded there's William Blake and Pope and even Browning. Different poets for different moods. Poetry is a thing of mood and feeling. Don't you think so, Aaron?"

Aaron's eyes continued to gather life, in a way not unlike the manner in which a baby chick breaks out of its shell, little movements of gathering intensity.

"Different poets for different moods?" he echoed questioningly. "Different people for different moods. We're all so many different people, you know."

"Are we really?" I probed.

"Of course we are," he answered. "Most of us are afraid to admit it. We make believe we're different people when no on is around, or we keep it all inside us. That's cowardly." He halted, clasped his hands around his left knee and looked dream-ily upwards. "Do I have a favorite poet?" he mused aloud. "Sometimes my favorite poet is me."

"Oh?"

He waited a moment and then, in a voice at once soft yet holding quickness in it, a half-smile edging his lips, he began to recite.

> Spin around,
>> who do you see?
> Spin around,
>> it isn't me.
> Spin once more,
>> it's someone new,
> Guess again
>> and tell me who?

He glanced at me and a smile of slow satisfaction traveled across his face.

> Some like sunlit days
>> full of laughter and life,
> I like darkness ways,
>> full of sorrow and strife.
> There's nothing in the open places,
>> where everyone sees and everyone knows,
> But in the deep and secret spaces,
>> I follow where the darkness goes.

He stopped and his eyes turned fully on me. "Poetry and dark places—they go together, you know," he said. I waited for him to go on, but he stopped there.

"I shouldn't think that," I said finally. "Poetry is something beautiful, something moving. Didn't someone once call it spoken music?"

He regarded me with a long, unmoving stare before answering. I felt suddenly uncomfortable.

His tone was, if not contemptuous, certainly patronizing as he answered. "Simonides of Ceos called painting silent poetry, and poetry, speaking painting," he said.

"I stand corrected. And you don't agree with that, Aaron?" I probed. He twisted his shoulders in a pained parody of a shrug.

"Pretty words," he said. "T.S. Eliot had hold of it. He said that poetry was not a turning loose of emotion, but an escape from emotion. It's not the expression of personality, but an escape from personality. He knew about the dark places and poetry. He knew about escaping."

"And you know, too, Aaron," I suggested. I saw him settle back on the couch.

"I know. We all know. Some of us just know more," he said. He began to talk, then, telling me incidents about his childhood, pausing to recite a few lines here and there, each couplet filled with the same brooding preoccupation with inner darkness and silent secrets. I pulled things from him, and then had to wonder if I'd pulled anything more than he wanted me to have. I thought I'd developed a rapport with Aaron as we talked. I wished I were certain when finally, abruptly, he tired of the game, if it indeed had been a game to him. He rose, gave me a shy smile and walked from the room. I watched him leave, moving quickly, and I felt slightly victorious. If I hadn't established a true rapport, all signs of withdrawal were gone from him and that was enough of an accomplishment. I looked at my watch and was astonished to find that the morning was over. I hurried to my room, hearing Derek's voice coming from the living room, followed by Marlyn's deep chuckle.

In my room, I hurried to set down all I'd heard and thought during the long talk with Aaron. I wrote furiously, transcribing and commenting while it was all so fresh in my mind. Partway through, I had the thought that it was all so needless. Derek must have long since covered with Aaron those things I had this morning. But I continued writing, remembering how Derek had said it was important I put down my own reactions and thoughts. It all goes to form a picture, he had said, and I continued to scribble furiously.

It was after one o'clock when I halted, realizing that I was tired with that drained, depleted kind of tiredness that follows intense concentration. I put all that I'd written into the bottom drawer of the bureau and stretched out on the bed, preferring rest to lunch. As I lay there, half-awake, half-asleep, I found myself thinking of Derek, his recitation of Nora's case history. He had indeed made the irrational sound completely rational, and he had been so right about my subconscious, automatic rejection of that. There was in Derek a kind of wisdom that went far beyond simply acquired knowledge, I decided again. I had caught a tiny part of his thrusting enthusiasm, but I had so much more to go. How long would it take me to see the others as Derek saw them, I wondered. Perhaps, with his help, not too long.

Una Stenner's cold, angry face drifted in front of my closed eyes. The conscious mind dismisses; the unconscious mocks such presumptuousness. The alarm in the woman's anger pushed at me, a puzzling, disturbing thing and suddenly I was seeing Cary Brooks's eyes watching me as I drove away with Matland. I didn't like things that were out of place—words or glances. They clung like wet leaves to a log. I sat up, restlessness seizing hold of me, equally out of place and unexplainable, yet equally undeniable.

I swung from the bed and went outside, moving through the very still house. I chose the rear door, and with only a few strides, I was into the deep green wall that rose up just back of the house. The ground rose gently, trees offering small footpaths between them, and I filled my lungs with the strong scent of pine and spruce. I crested a small rise and looked back down at Harbor House below. It was mostly hidden from view and, as an ugly, wart-ridden old toad looks less unattractive hidden in the bulrushes, so did the house appear less monstrous through the trees. I turned away and continued walking, pausing to examine little bits of brilliance that dotted the forest floor, some of them familiar, recognizable yet slightly different. Bunchberry that was not nearly so large as those back home. Fireweed that was more delicately brilliant. Woodfem that was tougher, stringier.

A sound, sudden scurrying of tiny feet, made me halt quickly and I glimpsed a brown, furry creature—not a rabbit—disappear into the brush. It didn't reappear. I walked on. The mountainside flattened slightly, and I found myself on a ridge, halting before a hooded flower that rose up in solitary splendor, deep violet with veins of purple running through it. I knelt down to examine it and saw another just a little ways on.

"That's called a purple monkshood," the voice said. Only the softness of it prevented my whirling in fright. I half-turned and looked up to see the tall figure standing between trees, the cool blue eyes serious, the same slightly sad gravity in his face.

"Cary Brooks," I said. "Hello again."

His smile was sudden and full of warmth. "Hello," he said simply.

"You do have a way of turning up unexpectedly," I said.

"I was out poking about and saw you coming. If you keep on his trail, you reach my cabin." He moved from between the trees and I glanced at the small, clear plastic sack he carried in one hand. I saw bits of bark, some mushrooms, and three or four rocks in it along with some grasses. "Collecting items for detailed blow-ups and cutaways, things the camera can't do. I'm working on material for a book on Alaskan wildlife and supportive terrain," he said, hoisting the little bag up for me. "Unfortunately, I spend too much time painting what I want to paint for my own pleasure." A puff of wind blew his light brown hair across his forehead and suddenly he looked very young, a tall, lanky, serious-faced boy.

"That purple monkshood, believe it or not, is a member of the buttercup family," he told me.

"There's certainly no family resemblance," I commented, and he laughed softly.

"None at all," he agreed. "Up higher you'll find mountain cranberry, brilliant red berries more often than not covered with iced dew. In some of the mountain glades you can find dogwood and sometimes what they call Lapland rosebay, rhododendron that grows only six inches high. But that's mostly found along the tundra."

"It's more than beautiful here, isn't it?" I said. "There's something more here—call it what you will—a spirit, a presence."

"I call it a foreverness, and I feel a warning force in it," he said.

"A warning force? That's not quite what I meant by a presence," I said.

"I know what you meant. I mean the same thing. You sense a presence, the existence of a force greater than man, call it whatever you will, nature, an omnipotent being or simply the presence of God. But whatever, there's a warning force in that presence, telling man not to despoil and desecrate this beauty or someday, in some way, he will suffer for it. The Lord thy God is a consuming fire, even a jealous God. That's Deuteronomy, I believe."

"My, do you always quote scripture to reinforce your points?"

"Hardly ever," Cary Brooks grinned. "That just happened to surface from somewhere back in my Sunday-school days." His eyes returned to the giant peaks that rose from deep green, misty bases. "But man won't listen," he went on. "He'll try to change this to suit himself and his own needs."

"I refuse to be such a pessimist," I answered. His smile, boyish, a gentleness in it, answered me; his question seemed merely polite. Only his eyes became wary again, veiled and refusing to echo the smile.

"How do you like your work at Harbor House?" he asked.

"I like it very much. It's different from anything I've ever done, certainly in depth, and I'm learning new and wonderful things," I answered.

"New horizons opening up," he commented, and. I thought I caught just the hint of wry amusement in the words.

"Yes, and Derek—Dr. Closter—is a very exciting person to work with. He fills everything with his own vitality and aliveness." I saw his eyes studying me again as I spoke, not with the frank admiration I'd seen in Derek's glance, but with something questioning. A thought hovered in the forefront of my own mind, trying to escape into words. I decided to let it do so.

"How much do you know about Harbor House?" I asked, making the question casual, offhanded.

"Not a great deal, but maybe more than anyone else around here. That's not saying much. There's hardly anyone else around here," he answered. "The house itself is something of a monstrosity aesthetically, and I became interested in a place like that sitting out here with a handful of people in it. I've a contact in the district office in Anchorage, and I had him look up whatever deeds they had on file there. The house was originally built by a rich old recluse who died soon after it was finished. It sat there for years until Dr. Closter bought it."

"I see. And what do you know about it now?" I probed. I saw Cary Brooks's smile broaden, telling me he knew I was fishing.

"I know it's being used as a sanitarium for a selected group of the mentally and emotionally disturbed," he answered.

"It's not just a sanitarium," I cut in hastily. "Harbor House is an experiment to open new channels of understanding all around."

"That sounds suspiciously like a quotation," I heard him say with deliberate mildness.

"All right, maybe it is, but it's the truth. Derek Closter has a concept, an approach to the problems of emotional disturbances that could revolutionize our thinking in this entire area."

"Do you agree with his theories?" Cary asked, a sudden brusqueness in his tone.

"I think so. As I said, it's all so new to me that I'm still learning, listening, absorbing," I replied.

"Meanwhile, Harbor House is full of surprises," he said, and he laughed at my quick, almost startled glance. "That's called insight," he grinned down at me. "That extra measure of sensitivity common to artists, wild animals, and the mad."

His eyes had taken on silent laughter as he watched the small parade of thoughts that flashed across my face. It was a gentle laughter, though, not malicious. I finally shrugged in admission.

"Yes, there have been surprises," I said. "Maybe because I wasn't expecting what I should have expected. But I'm learning."

"You're very beautiful against this backdrop of the trees and the mountains," Cary said, his eyes narrowing. "A very

cosmopolitan, polished beauty against a primitive, rugged setting. I'd like to paint you here."

"I believe you mean that," I said, watching his eyes rove
across my face and body with that special appraisal of the artist
that was both subjective and objective, personal and detached
at once.

"I do. Would you sit for me sometime, for some sketches, at
least?" he asked. "It'd be a change of scene from Harbor House."

"Perhaps, sometime. It's flattering to be asked."

"I'm sure you don't need ego building," he said drily.

"We all need it. It comes under the heading of reassurance.
And I'd better start back," I finished. "I really walked further
than I'd intended."

"Yes, of course," he said, and I felt an invisible curtain drop
between us. He seemed to be choosing words carefully again.
"You're welcome whenever you want to visit, any time of the day
or night," he said, nothing more than polite pleasantness. Yet
there was something more. I felt it, knew it, with the knowing
that can't be measured out. Perceptions, insights, sensitivities,
they seemed to be endemic here, I thought wryly. Even I was
being caught up in their climate. Or was I just being overimagi-
native? Cary Brooks watched as I went back down the pathways,
his waiting form finally disappearing behind trees and foliage.
I picked my way back, filling my lungs with all the sweetness of
pine as though I could store it somewhere for later use. Reaching
the end of the trees, the house only a few yards from me, I hurried toward it when I saw the figure to my right, dressed in white
slacks and a white sweater, doing deep knee-bends on the grass.
The dark eyes acknowledged my presence, the ascetic, fine-
featured face intent on the exercises.

"Hello, Aaron," I said. He ended the deep knee-bends with
a lithe spring on the balls of his feet, his face breaking into an

assured, confident smile. The sensitive, dreamy shyness was completely gone. I was standing before the sportsman, full of physical energy and extroverted enthusiasm.

"Lots of exercise and fresh air, nothing like it," he said, his voice deeper, louder. "Did you know that the highest score ever in the decathlon was made by Yang Chuan-Kwang of Taiwan, over eight thousand points?"

"No, I didn't," I muttered.

"In nineteen sixty-one, a forty-two-year-old Argentine man swam from England to France and, after only four minutes rest, swam all the way back again. That's what exercise and sports can do for one," Aaron said. "An Englishman chinned himself seventy-eight times a few years ago."

"Remarkable," I said, retreating toward the house, an unwarranted feeling of disappointment sweeping through me—unwarranted because I should have known better. I'd expected Aaron to go from his other state into something more normal, and, I realized now, there was no clinical justification for expecting that. I went into the house deciding that of the two, I liked Aaron's other self much better. Inside, Matland was at the foot of the steps, showing Derek a section of corroded drainpipe. I saw Derek shrug, his eyes finding me at once, and Matland trudged off with an annoyed glance at me.

"How is it going?" Derek said, his smile encompassing me with a quick, flashing brilliance.

"I spent the morning with Aaron," I said. "One of the Aarons, anyway. I just saw the other one outside."

"More surprises," he said and my lips tightened in wry admission.

"I guess so," I said.

"You expected too much," he answered. I nodded, grateful once more for his instant sensitivity and I made a mental note to tell Cary Brooks to include doctors in his little comment about the supersensitive. I wondered about telling Derek of the incident with Una Stenner and decided it was neither the time nor the place and perhaps not even worth the mentioning. But he had caught the split-second of hesitation.

"What is it?" he asked, his deep eyes intent.

"Nothing," I lied. "I was just going to tell you how happy I am that I'm here." Surprises and incongruous prophecies notwithstanding, I added to myself.

"Good. I'll see you at dinner. I've some budget work to do," Derek said. He pressed my hand, a spontaneous, warm gesture and then he was bounding up the steps and leaving behind the vibrant glow of his compelling intensity. I was glad I hadn't brought up Una Stenner's rage. Derek was too involved, too absorbed in the meaningful aspect of Harbor House to bother with such insignificant things. I turned, glimpsed Nora at the end of the east corridor, and then Rudi stepped into view, a large tin pail in his hand.

"Stacy, come with me to the barn," he boomed out. "I'm going to get some goat's milk for Una."

"Goat's milk? Barn? I haven't seen any barn," I said.

"It's just a little place behind the trees. Come on, I'll show you."

I followed as, his eyes crackling brightly, he led me outside and around to the left side of the house. A line of spruce extended, fencelike, in a straight path and I rounded the end one to see the small neat barn tucked away just behind them.

"We keep a half dozen goats and kids, just for the milk," Rudi said. "Nothing like goat's milk for nutrition, you know."

"It's an acquired taste, I'm afraid," I answered. Rudi smiled back. "We get the regular, commercial cow's milk in, too," he said. "Whenever supplies come in. Powdered milk, too."

He pulled the barn door open and the pungent odor of goat swept over me. I saw two grown goats, one billy goat and a dam and three kids. I knelt down as the clatter of small hooves rushed at me to push strong little bodies hard against my legs. Rudi had already seized the dam and was positioning the pail under her swollen teats.

"By midwinter those youngsters will be giving milk," he said. "I learned how to milk cows and goats when I worked my territory."

"What did you do, Rudi?" I questioned as I pushed back against small, hard heads of wiry fur that demanded attention.

"Agricultural sales—everything for the farmer and cattleman from tractors to fertilizers, including medical and feed supplies," Rudi said as he sat down on a small milking stool and I heard the sharp, rhythmic sound of milk hitting the pail. "For nearly ten years I had the top sales record in the company," Rudi went on, "and all my customers were the little farmers and small cattlemen. I didn't have any of the big combines. That's why when a farmer needed help foaling a mare or when one of his boys took sick and left him short-handed, I'd pitch in and help if I was there. Hell, you want to keep a top sales record, you help out your customers."

"It sounds as though you were a very welcome person on your route," I said. Rudi's voice grew softer, reminiscence in it over the steady sound of the milk squirting into the pail.

"Yes, they liked me real well. Everybody did," he said. I moved, brushing off the kids who continued to push against me, glancing into the small stalls of the little barn as Rudi stayed at his task. They were lined with hay and water pails hung on each stall front. I saw a feeding trough in the rear and a handful of rakes and shovels against the wall. The sound of the milking stopped and I turned as Rudi swung the pail out from the goat.

"Enough for now," he said. "We'll get this right back to Una. She uses it in making bread and biscuits."

I hurried with him, helped shut the barn door and returned to the house beside him. Once more, only Aaron had exhibited anything other than completely normal behavior. Certainly Rudi had been absolutely ordinary in every respect. Yet he was here and, like Nora, something had brought him here. As we came around the end of the line of spruces I saw Nora standing at the door of the house and I could think only of beauty and the beast as the gray hideousness of the house loomed over her fragile delicacy.

"You were out visiting our little family," she exclaimed. "Aren't they nice?"

"They get loose sometimes and Nora always is the one to find them," Rudi said. "She has something really special with animals."

"You offer them love, that's all. When they accept it, they don't surround it with conditions. They don't qualify love," Nora said. The words, by themselves, were full with the taste of bitterness but as Nora said them, a small, rueful smile turning her lips, they sounded not at all bitter. Only regretful, I thought. Rudi held the door open and I went inside, Nora coming in behind me. Derek was just coming down the stairs, a manila file folder in one hand. His glance swept over Rudi and the pail at once.

"You're getting thoroughly acquainted with Harbor House," he smiled. "Good. That's what I want."

"I'm changing for dinner. See you then," Nora said as she swept past me.

"Is dinner that formal?" I asked Derek. His hand curled around my arm and I responded to the warm comfort of his touch at once.

"As with everything else, here, Stacy, you do whatever you wish. Nora likes to dress for dinner, so she does. Marlyn does sometimes, Aaron never. It's completely up to you," he said. My eyes looked past him as Rudi went into the kitchen. Una Stenner poked her head out from the door and cast a glance at me. Again there was something in her eyes—not alarm, not anger this time, but an uncertainty, almost a worried expression. I was rapidly concluding that Una Stenner was herself a very disturbed person.

"Did Rudi tell you about himself?" Derek asked and brought my attention back to him.

"Yes, he told me about his being a top salesman. He certainly didn't touch on anything to explain his being here."

"Rudi was a top salesman on the rural territory routes, just as he told you, I'm sure. He was very close to his customers, knew them all and their families and he did have a top sales record for a long time. He had a huge territory and he covered it well. But a time came when farm and cattle conditions went sour all over, too much rain and not enough grain, bad crops, bad cattle and hog prices at the market. His customers were all hurting, some close to collapsing. Rudi gave them whatever they needed to stay in operation, whether it was feed, equipment, or medical supplies. It maintained his tremendous sales record, but in actuality he was subsidizing half the state at one point at his company's expense."

"And then?"

"An audit caught up to him. He had gotten by as long as he did by pyramiding payments, balancing some payments against others, filling out false vouchers and falsifying records in general. Of course, his company had him arrested on charges of theft, misrepresenting his sales for commissions, giving away the company's property and assets, plus a host of other allied charges. Then they demanded payment from all those whom he'd given things, accusing them of being party to a scheme to defraud. All those Rudi had helped turned against him then."

"Didn't they think they'd eventually have to pay for all the things he'd let them have?"

"Nobody wanted to look too hard at anything. Nobody wanted to look a gift horse in the mouth. Besides, Rudi had told them he'd worked out long-term, deferred-payment accounts, and they had no worries over obligations."

"All to maintain a sales record?" I questioned.

"I doubt that. He was really involved with the troubles of his customers. He had become something of a benevolent figure. I'd say the role took charge of him and he thought he could help everyone and work it out later. But not only did the company prosecute, but those he helped turned on him, accused him of having made them party to fraud. Instead of thanks and approval in the name of humanity, he was pilloried. Rudi came apart. He went into a severe psychosis with extreme depression, rage, irrationality, paranoia. Even his family turned against him. He must have been insane to even think he could have gotten away with his schemes—that was the consensus—and so he was judged and committed. He was severely disturbed at the time of commitment but, as you see, he came back out of it. The first question is, of course, whether his actions were ever irrational, ever a mark of insanity."

"You mean, what if he had somehow gotten the time to put everything in order," I followed.

"Yes, what then? In time he would have collected on the deferred accounts, when the farmers were able to pay. He's still certain of that. He would have been almost a saintly figure then. He would have been someone of faith, belief, trust, a shrewd judge of human nature. If he had succeeded, he would not have been called irrational, insane, a twisted egomaniac."

"But success or failure doesn't govern rationality, of course," I put in. Derek's smile was fleeting.

"Doesn't it? Think how often men have been called visionaries when they succeeded. Another man, equally visionary, who fails, is called a fool or crazy," he said.

"That gap again," I remarked. "Society is wrong someplace."

"I never used the word *wrong*, Stacy," Derek said, little lines of amusement crinkling the corners of his eyes.

"All right—let's say the inconsistencies of society," I answered. He shrugged, almost offhandedly.

"Inconsistencies, a good word, that. But wrongs result from inconsistencies, don't they?"

"Yes, I suppose they do. But perhaps Rudi's actions were inconsistent with normality. Anything—even the most well-intentioned act—carried to extremes becomes something else, a travesty of itself."

"Perhaps," Derek said, his smile broadening. "Don't try to make too many conclusions too fast. I'll see you at dinner."

He hurried away and I turned to go to my room, his gentle, wise admonition staying with me. I found myself smiling inwardly. He was not telling me what to think but only to think, to see in different ways, to look with different eyes. And he was succeeding. He didn't come at me pedantically, not even with his own version of the Socratic approach. He simply told me facts and pointed out elements surrounding those facts and left me to see the rest myself. One couldn't hear about Nora, Aaron, and Rudi, as Derek brilliantly capsuled their case histories, and not think about inconsistencies, and from inconsistencies to a new accommodation in human relationships, one thought fathering the other.

I went down the hall and passed Marlyn's room, the door open. She was seated at a dressing table, her back to me, carefully applying the small, toy-soldier circles of rouge to her cheeks. The room was a clutter of hanging things—slips, robes, dresses, stockings, coats, everything hanging from, over or around something. It looked like the backstage of a theater with pieces of scenic backdrops hanging at various heights and levels. I went on to my room, closed the door after me, and thought about changing for dinner. I decided on a compromise. I'd change from slacks into a skirt.

I'd stepped out of the slacks, the rush of cool air on my legs a pleasant sensation, when I noticed the folded square of light blue note paper atop the dresser. One of my bottles of lotion had been placed on it to hold it down. I laid the slacks on the bed and slid the stationery from under the bottle. Unfolding the paper, I recognized the script at once. It was the letter that had come to Elise Donner, the same neat, feminine handwriting now marching across the page in even, tidy lines. I read, and felt the frown deepening along my brow.

Dear Elise

It was wonderful to hear how happy you are up there in the middle of nowhere. You sound like you really like your work and your boss. He must be a fascinating man.

But you said you'd write soon, again—a real letter and not just a note. I haven't heard a word. No one has. I asked Judy and she hasn't heard since your note to her. What happened? Let's hear more about how happy you are. Let's hear something, at least.

Love,
Barbara

I finished the letter, staring down at it, reading the words again as I sank down on the edge of the bed. It became a thing of two parts. There were the words themselves, simple, answering Elise Donner's note, their meaning so clear, so unmistakable. And there was the letter itself, put in my room for me to read, meanings within, meanings, connected, entwined, circles inside circles. Elise Donner had written that she was very happy here, yet I was told she had left because she was unhappy. Why? A grab-bag of emotions offered themselves, puzzlement, surprise, a touch of resentment. Had Derek simply lied to me about the reason for Elise Donner's leaving Harbor House for his own selfish purposes? I rebelled at the thought. There had to be more than that. Perhaps something had happened to make her leave suddenly—something he felt might discourage me wrongly, perhaps even upset me. But I disliked being duped, even with the best of intentions, and I was sure Derek had only those at heart.

I stared down at the letter again and more questions swirled up from it. Had it been left for me as an act of friendship or malice? Had it been left to warn me, to alert me to something, or simply to irritate and upset? And who had stolen into my room to leave it? Una Stenner? The woman could do it, I was certain, as a small thrust back at me for treading on her prerogatives. The insecure are capable of vicious little answers prodded on by their own fearfulness.

The question circled, their meanings beyond reach and I felt the impatience gathering inside me. I'd always been a prey to the unresolved, essentially *gestalt*, bothered by tasks left in mid-air, comfortable only with things structured, integrated and whole. I decided to go to Derek, wanting explanations, certain he would have completely valid ones, probably ones to make me ashamed of my irritation, yet needing to hear them whatever they were. I slipped on the skirt I was going to wear for dinner and left the room. I had started down the corridor when, near the stairs, I saw Matland, his square back to me, the seemingly neckless figure partly visible by the stair post. I couldn't see Una Stenner but I heard her voice as she spoke to him, strained and harsh.

"No, it didn't fall out of my apron. I tell you I put it in my room as soon as I finished in the kitchen," I heard her say.

"And you think someone took it," Matland said.

"Of course. I didn't even have a chance to read it," the woman hissed back.

"The new one—maybe she took it?" Matland suggested. Una Stenner's voice snapped at him. "No, she's not that type. It was one of the others, damn them."

I had halted and now I moved backward, retreating to my room. I closed the door softly behind me and leaned against it. Una Stenner had not left the letter for me, to irritate or push uncomfortableness at me. And she hadn't read the letter. Then why was a letter to Elise Donner so distressing to her? I'd been right about the alarm that had seized her glance when she saw I had the letter in my hand. Had she been afraid of what might have been inside it? It had said nothing about her—yet she couldn't know that, of course. And Matland obviously was involved. Perhaps they had something to do with Elise Donner leaving? I felt a sudden excitement rising inside. I would say nothing to Derek yet. Perhaps he was not aware of things going on here, I decided. I wouldn't run to him with the first bit of strangeness to appear. I'd go to him when I knew who had left the letter, with more than questions and sudden frights. It wouldn't be all that hard to find out, I was certain. When I found that out, the other answers would most probably make themselves clear, too. Whoever had left the letter knew why Elise Donner had left here.

One of my bags had a small, hidden compartment in it. I put the letter inside it, closed it, and went out into the corridor and to dinner. When I reached the dining room, I saw that the oval table had been set with a gracious and classic silver service, a large candlabra acting as a centerpiece. Matland was beginning to serve from a sideboard. Only Marlyn and Derek were at the table. Marlyn wore a long, print dress, loose and round-necked, something that might have once been an evening gown but now looked more like a tired lounging robe.

"Hello, love," she called out cheerily. Derek rose, bringing me around to sit beside him, his eyes soft, almost prideful as he looked at me.

"Rudi told me how he enjoyed your visit to the barn with him," Derek said. "You're being everything I'd hoped you'd be. You've fitted yourself right into the mainstream of life here. I'm more than pleased, Stacy, more than pleased."

The warm intensity that was Derek curled around compliments as thoroughly as it did concepts and I felt my response, automatic, almost a tropism to his vibrancy. "I'm glad, Derek," I said softly and felt the surge of pride in his pleasure. Whatever I might finally uncover about the letter and Elise Donner, I knew then, once again, that Derek's reasons would be justifiable. I glanced away as Aaron strode into the room in his white sweater and white slacks. Rudi and Father Hodges came next and then Nora swept through the doorway in a filmy, full-length pink dress. Marlyn's voice cut the air.

> Hark, hark, the dogs do bark,
> the beggars are coming to town;
> Some in rags, some in tags,
> and some in velvet gowns."

She had hardly finished the old nursery rhyme when I heard Derek, his voice hard-edged and cold. It was the first time I'd ever heard him be sharp to anyone. "Why do you say that, Marlyn?" he bit out. "No one feels a beggar here; no one is."

Marlyn's quick shrug seemed to show unconcern at Derek's displeasure, but I saw her look away quickly and tiny lines tighten the corners of her mouth.

"You know Marlyn, always the cynic," Rudi said. I caught the protectiveness in his voice, as one child stands up for another to a displeased teacher or parent.

"Words don't mean anything, anyway," Aaron said.

"Ah, but they do," Father Hodges corrected gently. He had seated himself directly across from me, Nora beside him. "We are conditioned by words. They have hidden impact on us. *Beggar* is philosophically and psychologically demeaning to modem man. *Supplicant*, on the other hand, holds nothing abrasive in it—yet what is a supplicant but a beggar?"

"You prove the need for new definitions, not just of words but of concepts, attitudes, conclusions. We need to redefine not only our words but our thinking. The old is no good anymore," Derek said. He had returned to his usual calm but controlled intensity and good humor.

"Of course, I'm not for tossing away the old so casually," Father Hodges smiled. "One tends to toss away the soup with the bones."

"Naturally. Religious thought is anchored in anterior definitions," Derek replied.

"When new knowledge discards old wisdoms, it ultimately fails," Father Hodges countered.

Derek's eyes were dark, twinkling lights as he glanced at me. "Father Hodges has a particular dichotomy. He disagrees while he agrees. He continues to seek a syncretic answer."

"And there is none?" I questioned.

"Love is the answer," Nora said. "Love and loving. It's really quite that simple and quite that easy."

"Hah! Love is never easy, and it's sure as hell never simple," Marlyn burst out.

"Knowledge redefined is the answer," Derek said. "Till now, knowledge has been considered an empirical substance, the province of scientific inquiry. Only that which is determinable on man's own terms is considered knowledge. A few theoretic thinkers have begun to question this. The psychologist, Abraham Maslow, phrased it well. 'We have learned to think of knowledge as verbal, explicit, rational, Aristotelian, realistic,' he said. "But equally important are mystery, ambiguity, illogical contradiction, and transcendent experience.' In short, we've worshipped at mathematical altars and made a religion out of rationality. This is all insufficient. We must recognize the limitation of empiricism. We must recognize that rationality must include the irrational, reality must include unreality."

I glanced at Father Hodges. His eyes were reflective, a small smile touching his mouth. Derek, I saw, also watched him but with a sharp-edged intentness.

"Of course I agree with that," Father Hodges said slowly. "But I don't think one can set up one's own Goddess of Reason, not even Derek."

I felt the frown of perplexity creasing my forehead. "Father refers to the French Revolution when an attempt was made to substitute a new religion for Christianity," Derek chuckled. "So many of Father Hodges's predecessors were involved with the intrigues and sins of the royal court that the revolutionaries condemned Christianity, also. The Goddess of Reason was the central figure in this new religion."

"Replacing the Virgin Mother, of course—a kind of admission right there," Father Hodges injected.

"The role of the Goddess during the Feast of Reason ceremonies was taken by various well-known young women, the actresses Mademoiselle Aubray and Maillard, the opera singer Mademoiselle Condeille. During the ceremony, the Goddess of Reason was surrounded by municipal figures and ballerinas carrying torches of truth."

"The attempt failed, obviously. Christianity survives, the substitute has long since disappeared," Father Hodges said.

"I take it you mean that Derek cannot substitute a new sense of reason for the attitudes of society," I commented.

Father Hodges smiled, a gratuitousness in it. "Something like that," he said, and I knew he hadn't meant that at all. Whatever he had meant, only Derek seemed to be aware of. I decided against pressing. I wouldn't compound errors nor wander further out of my depth. Both Derek and Father Hodges had a special brilliance I couldn't match. I backed off as the topics turned to less profound talk and everyone ate hungrily. I found myself thinking and listening with both admiration and a sense of disbelief. Certainly the conversation was the equal of that at any dinner party of educated and voluble people, except for Aaron's shallow role-playing. Indeed, the comments had been far more stimulating than at many such gatherings I had attended. If these were the disturbed, then I had to wonder if there was no Alice-in-Wonderland aspect to our sociological definitions. Certainly these before me could function and function well in an open society—indeed better than many I'd seen on the other side of that dividing line. I hadn't witnessed any of the tensions, anxieties and general hang-ups I used to see among my friends and office associates.

Derek was undoubtedly aware I'd realize that. Was this one more way of his to bring me to reexamine my own thinking? Probably, I decided. It would be impossible to partake of Harbor House and not look again at one's own conditioned thinking. That was of itself an accomplishment. But conditioning is a tenacious thing, and reservations continued to cling silently though I was becoming confident of their eventual resolution. I had almost forgotten about the letter when, as the main part of the meal ended, it was brought back to me with renewed force.

"I've eaten too much, as usual," Rudi said. "Which means that now I can lie down and look over my magazine."

"Rudi looks forward to the expected," Marlyn said. "He revels in habit."

"That's dull and meaningless. Only unexpected things are important," Nora said. She looked down at her plate.

"I like things peaceful. Unexpected things aren't important, just upsetting," Rudi said, pushing himself away from the table.

"Unexpected things are warnings," Nora said, her eyes still cast downward. I felt myself growing excited.

"Are they always, Nora?" I asked. I kept my glance at her delicate beauty, but she refused to look up. I was suddenly certain one of my questions had been answered; who had left the letter for me. Nora rose abruptly, still not looking at me, fixing her eyes on a point in space and speaking to no one and everyone.

"I'm going to bed. I don't feel there's much love here tonight," she announced with quiet firmness.

"Oh, now, don't say that, Nora. Love comes in many ways, even hidden away in acid cynicism," Father Hodges said. Nora continued to stare into space, her beauty frozen, as if she had been momentarily suspended in time and movement.

"No," she said suddenly. "It doesn't come that way at all." She turned and started from the room.

"I'll walk you to your room, Nora," Father Hodges said, hurrying after her, and I wondered again about that first night of sweet sounds. Mostly, though, I watched her go off with frustration. There'd be no talking to Nora tonight. I pushed down the questions that had already lined up to be given voice.

"I'd like some more fresh coffee," I heard Derek saying to me. "How about having some in the library with me?"

I nodded and he rose. "See you there in five minutes," he said. I was still thinking about Nora, certain that it was she who had left the letter. I began making plans to find the best way of approaching the subject in the morning, when Marlyn's voice cut into my thoughts. She was still at the table, looking matronly and slightly forlorn.

"Things going well, love?" she said to me and I nodded quickly.

"Very well. I hope everyone enjoys having me here as much as I enjoy being here," I answered.

"Of course they do. I told you you'd be loved here," the woman said. "Marlyn knows."

"Yes, so you did. You said something else, too," I reminded her. She smiled cheerfully.

"Of course, dearie. Marlyn tells it the way it is," she said. I wanted to find derision, silent laughter, at the woman's words, but suddenly I couldn't find anything but uneasiness. Marlyn's prophecies were charlatanism, I told myself. Derek had said as much. Yet the letter to Elise Donner hung in my mind, and suddenly I knew it had been left for me as a warning, knew it with the crystal clarity that goes beyond material facts. I'm being ridiculous, I told myself. I'd get to the bottom of it in the morning. It would be revealed as not worth the thinking about, I reassured myself, and refused to listen to that part of me that rejected my refusal. Marlyn rose then and with a quick little wave, hurried from the room. I went into the library just as Derek was filling two cups from a coffee pitcher. I sat down on the sofa and he handed me a cup, an easy, amused tolerance reaching out from him. I thought about bringing up the letter when his words snuffed out the thought at once.

"Dinner was another kind of surprise, wasn't it?" he said softly, his eyes alight with tiny glints of quiet laughter.

"Maybe," I said, unwilling to admit to further surprises and certainly not the surprise of the letter, not yet, anyway. "Tell me about Marlyn. She and Father Hodges are the only two! still have no background on."

"Did you enjoy dinner?" Derek asked, passing over my question, the laughter still in his eyes, an unspoken kind of teasing. I heard myself sound more brusque than I wanted to sound.

"It served its purpose, if that's what you want to know," I tossed back at him. "It was brilliant, absorbing and quite sobering."

Derek's laugh was quick, low and infectious. "*Touché*," he said. "You're quite wonderful, Stacy." He went on quickly, giving me no time for awkward replies. "Now about Marlyn Cruise, which is her proper name though she never uses the last part. As a young woman, she found herself with very strong psychic abilities. She predicted a number of things about family and friends. As she grew older, she began to devote more time to developing her psychic abilities. She got a sponsor and opened up commercially, gaining a rather sizable reputation very quickly. Her case history shows a number of validated instances of her extrasensory powers, prophecies, predictions, telecommunication."

"ESP is beyond dispute as a phenomenon, though unexplainable on present-day terms. But no one has yet been shown to have a sustained, controlled command of it, the fortune-teller kind of thing," I commented.

"Exactly. The entire telepsychic ability seems one of unplanned reception on the part of the receiver. Even Rhine's experiments have only shown that some people have greater sensitivity to receive than others though there has been some evidence of concentrated psychic communication. Anyway, Marlyn attained a real measure of fame as a psychic, and she did have some valid instances. However, she began to believe completely in her ability as a prophet. Her natural psychic abilities gave her a slightly higher ratio of success than the ordinary fortune-teller kind of fake. The behavior of ESP alone virtually dictated that. But that same behavior dictated that, when making prophecies on a commercial basis, she was doomed to many more failures than successes. But Marlyn had begun to see herself as someone able to help people better their lives by predicting things in their future. She saw herself as a real prophetess. What she couldn't cope with were her mistakes, her failures, what psychics call misses."

"Couldn't cope with them commercially, personally, or psychically?" I questioned.

"All three. All were inextricably entwined. She felt that each miss was a failure, a mark against her and a blow to those who had trusted in her abilities. Marlyn may have taken herself into charlatanism, she may have taken her abilities beyond what they were, but it was an error of misguided self-belief. She really felt for those who came to her for help, for the importance of her psychic abilities. Naturally, she could no longer separate the real, valid telepsychic visions from those she imagined as real, except by the proof, whether they were borne out or not. And each failure was an inner blow."

"They caused an emotional breakdown?"

"Not that simply. Marlyn took to fulfilling her prophecies. She made come true those that failed, at least the most important to her thinking. She was determined not to fail those who had come to her. She told a woman she would be happier without her husband and would leave him when she found him with a young girl. When it didn't happen, she arranged for a willing girl to involve the husband for the wife to find out. Once again, she received financial rewards, but it seemed that that wasn't the motivating force. Each miss was letting down those who needed her help. A businessman with severe financial problems came to her. She told him his store would burn down and the insurance would solve his problems."

"It didn't happen so she arranged for it to come true."

"That's right. Of course, most of these things came to light after the fact, when people—even those she arranged to help—became suspicious. She had to involve too many others, hired help, in the task of making her prophecies come true, An investigation uncovered the entire thing. The evidence was overwhelming."

"You say she believed in herself. How did she justify arranging these made-to-order prophecies?"

"She believed totally in herself and still does. She believed, or at least she told herself so, that each one of her prophecies *would* have come true. Her clients just couldn't afford the time to wait. They hadn't the faith to wait."

"So she helped things along."

Derek shrugged his agreement. "Marlyn was first tried on criminal charges, convicted, and later judged mentally disturbed and committed."

I sensed something held back—almost a hint of disapproval—in his flat tone as he concluded. "Don't you feel that was a socially justifiable conclusion?" I asked.

"Of course it was," Derek said, small lights of amusement glinting in his eyes. He drained his cup in a moment of silence and then regarded me with a speculative look.

"Unquestionably, Marlyn had deceived herself," he said. "She had delusions of sainthood in an oblique kind of way. But we tend to forget in our modern, technological age, that the ability to prophesy has been a root part of man's background. We are not living in a prophetic age today; yet even now, anyone who can show any valid psychic ability is quickly sought by millions. The rest of us may stand on the sidelines, but we stand there wanting to believe in the existence of a prophet. All our religions are filled with prophets and prophesying. We even distinguish between major and minor prophets in the Bible and the Koran claims that some two hundred thousand prophets have existed, only six of them being of major significance—Mohammed, Jesus, Moses, Noah, Abraham and Adam. All ancient peoples considered the prophet a figure of veneration. In ancient Greece, to be able to prophesy was to be touched by the gods. This entire business of predicting events and prophesying about them is a very basic part of man's striving, yearning and cultural history. Is it so difficult to understand how someone touched by the magic of psychic ability can delude oneself into being another Delphic oracle? I feel we must build a society of less justification and more understanding."

"Including the irrational?" I smiled.

"If you like," Derek chuckled. "Incidentally, Marlyn told the judge that committed her that he would die in seven days."

"And?"

"A week later he died of a heart attack."

A small, icy wind swept through me. Ninety percent self-delusion and fraud, ten percent psychic ability. Into which part did Marlyn's prophecy to me fall? I wrenched myself away from the question, unwilling to wrestle with it with Derek beside me. I seized on something clinical to ask, something to fill the mind with impersonal thoughts.

"How do you expect to reach your goal—this new level of accommodation with society—without any outpatient work?" I asked, keeping my mind riveted on the topic.

"Ah, that period of final, therapeutic testing," Derek commented with a smile. "Of course, you're speaking of the usual approach to outpatient therapy."

"I guess so," I admitted. "Putting the subject into the mainstream of social situations, into the areas of tension producing situations."

"But what if that, like so much of our approaches to mental disturbance, is also inadequate, if not actually wrong?" Derek said.

"You feel it is, apparently."

"I feel it is because, once again, it is society testing and evaluating on its own standards of normal behavior. Again, there is no tolerance, no accommodation. The subject involved in outpatient care succeeds or fails depending purely on *his* accommodation to society's attitudes, which, you have seen, can be so terribly misdirected and unjustified."

"So how do you manage outpatient work here?"

"Quite perfectly, Stacy," Derek said. "First, my concept of outpatient therapy is a period in which the subject tests his ability to develop solitary self-reliance. If you can adjust to being alone for extended periods, if you can adjust to yourself, to the inner-directed tensions of your own being, then you can adjust to any outside tensions."

I turned Derek's words over as I heard them, in no way willing to challenge their concept, yet not quite willing to accept them as I had accepted other things he had pointed out.

"Certainly these surroundings are perfect for such outpatient work," he added.

"Yes, certainly, for your concept they are. Then you've done that kind of outpatient therapy here? Successfully?" I asked. Derek turned his palms upwards.

"Success is not something I even consider until the race is run, until the game is over," he said. I saw his eyes hold mine, then look away. "I am satisfied so far," he said flatly, closing off the subject, obviously unwilling to go into it any further at this time. His answer, I realized in an almost subconscious way, had not really answered my question. He turned back to me again, his hand reaching out, closing on my arm, a warm, comforting touch. I saw his eyes grow serious.

"Thanks for coming, Stacy. I mean that," he said. "You've really worked a minor transformation here—for me, at least," His lean, intense attractiveness created an enveloping shell around us. His thanks had credited me with a decision that had really been more of a response. Attraction—that powerful, indefinable communication—certainly fitted into the definition of psychic phenomena, I thought silently. It was indeed an experience of receiving, and, sometimes, of returning. Derek was too acute not to detect my own response to his electric presence and I decided not to play games.

"I think my coming was a *fait accompli* five minutes after we met," I replied. "A lot of things had come together then, and you gave them direction, focus."

"Hooray for catalytic agents," he smiled, rising, his hands pressing my shoulders for a brief instant. "Work beckons. More about this soon, though." He grinned down at me and then hurried away. I stayed only a few moments alone in the library. Una Stenner entered to take away the coffee and cups, her angular face set, and letters and prophecies rushed back over me. I left at once, ignoring the woman as she had ignored me. I paused in the hall and wished I could leave behind the growing uneasiness as simply as I'd left the woman in the room. I half-turned toward my room when Father Hodges crossed the hallway, his easy, calm pleasantness reaching out at once.

"On my way to celebrate mass," he called to me. "There's a little room at the far end of the corridor. I usually say mass first thing in the morning but if not, the last thing in the day."

Years rose up to pull at me and I thought back of all the daily masses I had attended at Saint Theresa's and suddenly I longed for the peace, the quiet strength of those interludes.

"May I attend?" I asked Father Hodges. His smile seemed full of understanding.

"Of course, Stacy, my dear. Sometimes I have just about everyone here, and other times I'm quite alone. I'm afraid this will be one of the alone times, except for you, now."

I walked beside him down the corridor to the end, allowing quick glances at this pleasant, quick-minded man. He was the only one left whose story I had yet to learn. I found it increasingly hard to believe there was a story, any aberrant behavior possible for him. Certainly I'd seen nothing to even intimate he belonged here. But then, except for Aaron, I'd seen nothing much from anyone. Whatever his story, I'd hear it from him, I decided, as Father Hodges opened the door of the little room. I saw an altar had been set up along the far end of the room, a table, long, narrow, covered with the three linen cloths, the altar cloth reaching the floor at both sides. The two beeswax candles flanked the modest crucifix and the missal waited at the right on a bookstand. A pair of wooden benches faced the altar and he motioned me to the first one. I sat down.

"Be back in a moment," he said. "Without altar boys and all the rest of the trimmings, we do the best we can. But then, the ancient Christians lacked many of our modern-day touches, too. The results were the same."

He left, disappearing into an adjoining room, not much more than a closet as far as I could glimpse. He returned in his vestments, chasuble, stole and maniple, carrying the chalice, corporal and purifactor in one hand. The veil, paten and host in the other. His back to me, he arranged things on the altar with quick, deft motions and then I heard his voice, strong and clear, a different voice now, holding in it the sound of organs and choirs.

"In Nomine Patris, et Filii, et Spiritus Sancti. Amen. Introibo ad altare Dei," the voice intoned. I closed my eyes and listened, following the Latin which had been so tenaciously drilled into me. It was as music, sonorous sound, letting the mind drift with it. I drifted back in time, closing out the moment with the echoes of yesterday. Even when he switched into English, I heard only the sound and not the words until suddenly, the conscious mind rebelling against being ignored, a word, then a sentence, then a phrase filtered through me. My eyes opened as I began to listen now, Father Hodges before the altar, the chalice in his hand, *"Eternal Rest give to them, O Lord; and let perpetual light shine upon them."* The phrases continued to drift to me and I felt the frown sliding across my forehead. Listening, now, I groped back through memory, phrases I knew yet should have known better, the mass, yet something more…. *"Absolve, O Lord, the souls of all the faithful departed from every bond of sin … those souls of whom we this day make commemoration … may be numbered among those whom thou hast redeemed."* The phrases stretched out, hung together and found meaning finally. It was the mass, but the mass for the dead. I sat quietly until I heard the final *"The Father, the Son and the Holy Spirit … Pater, et Filius, et Spiritus Sanctus. Amen."*

Father Hodges stepped from the altar, disappeared into the small adjoining room and returned in moments, free of his vestments. I had waited.

"Why, Father?" I asked. "Why the mass for the dead?"

"That's the only mass I ever say, Stacy," he answered. "Good night, my dear."

He strode away, straight, purposeful, disappearing down the hall. I continued to stand in the little room for a moment, gathering myself from his reply that had taken me so aback. Finally, I walked from the room, still hearing his words, an answer that was not an answer at all. I went to my room, a terrible sadness going with me.

CHAPTER FOUR

F ear is like a fanged, black bat in the night. It swoops and darts and rushes about before it decides to land. It had not found a place in me yet, and I refused to admit its presence. Yet it was there, hovering and circling just outside the borders of conscious recognition.

I had latched the door, undressed and lay in the dark room, the terrible sadness still lingering, but being pushed aside by more demanding emotions, apprehension, uncertainty, the gnawing uneasiness that continuously returned. The sadness was unjustified, I told myself. I'd no right to it at all. I'd no right to expect that those here were free of individual peculiarities. I'd rushed into an unrealistic, naïve acceptance of the remarkable things I'd seen here, perhaps carried along too completely by Derek's concepts and conclusions. He would not want that himself, I was certain. And yet, in one sudden stroke, all the disarming normality I'd accepted had been, if not shattered, certainly shaken. Harbor House, I decided, was not unlike the house of mirrors in an amusement park. Images were not just images, reflections of reality, but two-way distortions. Things were not as they seemed. There was indeed normality, even brilliance; yet there was more—undercurrents, movements inside a separate, closed world. Derek had begun to open my eyes to see broader horizons of human behavior, to the acceptance of a deeper conceptual understanding. Yet I wondered, now, if he was perhaps too involved with his work to see objectively. Did he dismiss things better not dismissed? I thought of his remark about Heisenberg's Principle of Uncertainty, observing affects the observer. Did he look the other way sometimes? Did he make excuses in pursuit of that new accommodation, that new understanding he so believed in?

The questions paraded themselves through my thoughts, and I felt a bit guilty reviewing them, like a general reviewing troops he knew did not really deserve to be reviewed. I had no reason to question Derek's astuteness, his ability to see clearly and objectively. I was reaching out to assign reasons because of my own uneasiness. Father Hodges's unexpected reply had been its own thing, striking into me in its own way, but it would have been merely surprising were it not for the letter and what it implied. And for Marlyn's glib prophesying. They were the primal cries that demanded answers. There was no way to turn aside from them. Una Stenner feared that letter and shared her fear with Matland. I had been told a lie. Elise Donner had not been unhappy here.

I turned on my side, burying my face in the pillow, restless but determined to sleep till the morning came to provide the opportunity for answers. I'd find a way to Nora, somehow. Pushing away further speculation, I finally managed to sleep, uneasiness settling down to rest alongside me. While outside, the black bat of fear continued to swoop and circle, waiting for a time to land.

I woke early, clothed in grim determination. I wanted not only answers for myself, but the chance to show Derek that I possessed the initiative and sensitivity to deal with the unexpected. As I bathed, I toyed with various approaches to Nora and decided only that firmness at the right moment would-be crucial. Finally, dressed in maroon slacks and a light-blue shirt, I went down the hallway to the dining room and the usual buffet breakfast. I passed Una Stenner, the woman's face set in a frozen, unreveal-ing mask. But in her cold blue eyes I saw worry. I couldn't hold back a tiny glint of satisfaction.

Everyone was at breakfast already and I was greeted warmly. Derek broke off a conversation with Rudi to come to my side. My eyes sought out Nora and I returned her small, shy smile of greeting. I watched her, hoping for some small sign, perhaps only a sharp glance or a moment of guarded questioning in her eyes. But there was nothing, only the sweet-sad loveliness of her. Father Hodges nodded brightly at me over his coffee cup. I reminded myself that he was next on my list of things to do—a very different but hardly less anxious set of questions hoarded inside me for him.

"I'm afraid it's a day of hard labor for me," I heard Derek saying. "There's trouble with the pump. This afternoon I'll have to drive to Palmer to get a new part. There and back will be an all-night trip."

"I'm sorry," I said.

"I'm reserving tomorrow right now. I'll use executive privi-lege. Maybe we could get away for a little picnic," he said.

"I'd like that. I may have a few things to go over with you by then," I added blandly.

"Fine. I know I'll have things to tell you," he said, his smile flashing, showering brightness. I felt his hand press my arm in a quick, private gesture and then he was going off to where I saw Matland waiting in the hall. Father Hodges and Rudi were drift-ing from the room and Nora still sipped her coffee. Aaron, in a dark green shirt and dark trousers, stood to one side, quietness clinging to him like an invisible shroud. His eyes, as they glanced up to mine, edged the withdrawn expression of a few days ago. Aaron was his other self this morning. I knew I ought to engage him again but I backed from the thought, wanting to stay free to get to Nora. Aaron had other plans.

"Let's talk again this morning, Stacy," he said.

"Why, of course, Aaron, if you like," I recovered quickly—at least I thought I had.

"You don't want to talk to me," Aaron said, a childish petulance entering his voice.

"Of course I do," I protested, guilt giving me extra forcefulness. "We'll go into the library and talk about whatever you like." I paused, glancing at Nora. "Perhaps you'd like to come, too, Nora?" I suggested. Actually, I wanted Nora where I could eventually get to her, before she perhaps became involved with someone else.

"No, I'll be gardening all day today. It's a perfect day for it," Nora said, her glance almost too quick to catch. I murmured silent agreement. The garden would be a good place to talk, perhaps the best. But now I followed Aaron to the library. He began to talk freely, sitting beside me, poetry first, mostly Eliot. I let him go on, and he began to talk about his father but in a detached and distant way, as though he were talking about a man he'd once met rather than his own flesh-and-blood father. I listened, wanting to give myself fully to the conversation, but it was impossible. Nora and the letter refused to let me, questions leapfrogging in my mind, unwilling to accept the delay. I found myself giving Aaron only the outer shell of my attention, feigning interest, giving responses that were more glib than concerned. But I felt I played the role perfectly, listening with what seemed absolute attention, taking part with an extruded involvement. It was late morning when he halted, the mood run its course, depleted of its drive and I was ashamed of the relief that swept over me. Aaron had just wanted someone to act as a sounding board, mostly, to release himself of words and pent-up emotions. I'd served that well enough.

He rose and I saw his eyes staring at me with a sudden sharpness, almost an anger, as though he were giving me a final, disapproving appraisal.

"You shouldn't have said yes if you didn't want to talk," he said abruptly, no petulance now but an icy coldness. Astonishment and guilt competed with each other inside me. Aaron turned and strode away, and I had the chilling feeling that he had known all along. Was I that poor an actress? Or were his sensitivities beyond deceiving? I heard Cary Brooks again, his remark about that extra measure of sensitivity given to artists, wild animals and the mad. Perhaps it had been a little of both with Aaron—his extra sensitivity and my own inadequate deception. The incident beyond immediate repair, I hurried outside and around to the side of the house. Nora's slender figure, in a pair of denim coveralls, knelt beside a long row she was spading. What appeared to me as tomato vines covered the ground just beyond her.

I called to her as I approached and she half-turned to me, halting her work, the spade in her hand. The denim coveralls did nothing to hide or diminish her delicate beauty, a porcelainlike quality to it, as though it was so easily shatterable. I sank down on the ground beside her, resting on both knees. She began to spade again. "Do you like gardening, Stacy?" she asked.

"I think I might. I've never done much of it," I replied. I decided suddenly to be bold. We were alone, and other interruptions could come up at any time. Besides, the delay of the morning had eaten away subtlety and patience. "Remember how angry Una became when I was giving out the mail?" I began. "She became very upset when I saw that letter to Elise Donner. She took it from me and shoved it into her apron, remember?"

Nora continued to spade, the sound of it a short, chopping noise. "That letter turned up in my room. Someone left it for me to read, as a warning of something."

I paused and Nora glanced at me, her eyes veiled, saying nothing. She returned to her rhythmic spading at once.

"It was an unexpected thing, and unexpected things are always important, aren't they, Nora?" I pressed. "You believe that, don't you? You said it yourself last night."

Nora's glance was instantaneous again, but this time I saw discomfort in her eyes. "I'm very grateful for having had the chance to read that letter, Nora. Leaving it for me was an act of goodness, of friendship, maybe even of love," I said. "I know who left it for me, Nora."

Nora's eyes met mine again and now they were touched by apprehension, like those of an animal afraid it's going to be trapped. I decided to press harder.

"You left the letter, Nora. You stole it away from Una and left it for me. Why? What did you want me to know?" I said. Her eyes darted at me now and I saw something approaching panic in them and I felt frightened. I was pushing too hard, perhaps. I was hardly experienced at this sort of thing with anyone, certainly not with someone as delicately tuned as Nora. I reached out, put my hand on her shoulder.

"Please don't be afraid. I won't tell anyone. I promise," I placated. "I just want to know all the rest now. Why did Elise Donner leave Harbor House? Why was I told she was unhappy here when she obviously wasn't?"

I kept my hand on her shoulder and she turned to look at me, her eyes round and frightened, but the wild panic gone from them. Now and then, as I watched, I saw it return. She looked past me and I turned to see Matland just outside the corner of the house, tools in his hand. His squat figure paused to look toward us, somehow terribly appropriate beside the ill-fitting, ugly grayness that was the exterior of Harbor House. Nora looked down as she furiously attacked the ground with her spade.

"It's all right. Don't be afraid," I said again. She answered without looking at me.

"No, it's not all right. I can't talk, not here. There are ears everywhere, eyes everywhere," she said tensely.

"Where, then, Nora? I want to know what that letter meant," I half-whispered.

"Tonight, an hour after dark," Nora said, not looking up and continuing to dig furiously at the ground. "Behind the house there's a trail up into the mountains."

"Yes, I know."

"A little way up there's a ridge and a clearing. I'll meet you there."

"An hour after dark," I repeated. "All right, I'll be there."

"Please go now. It's best we're not seen talking," Nora said, fear in her voice.

"Don't be frightened, Nora. I can talk with anyone I wish," I told her. Her eyes met mine for an instant, trapped panic in their roundness again and I rose, not wanting to upset her further and helpless to allay her fright. I turned and started toward the house. Matland was no longer there, and my eyes roved across the gray house where nothing fitted quite together, its excesses not simply ugliness but a perversion of beauty radiating a kind of inverted pride. How faithfully did it reflect many of those inside it, I wondered, as I hurried into the foyer. Nora's fear and the letter to Elise Donner filled me with a steel-spring excitement that was preferable to uneasiness and uncertainty. The day had started into the afternoon already and I saw that Una Stenner had put out a self-service luncheon, vegetable soup in a huge silver tureen and cold chicken and ham. I was too tightly wound to eat very much and settled for a little of the soup. Aaron came in and, except for a hostile stare, ignored me. I made no effort to reach out to him, deciding to wait till his mood changed. I ate alone in a corner of the room, and when I was finished I put my plate on the table. Matland passed me as I started from the room, the gray-clay face set, but the little, opaque cat's eyes were moving with quick, restless motions.

"Has Dr. Closter left yet?" I asked him. He paused only to nod, and then hurried on to clear away plates. I moved into the hall and saw Father Hodges with notepaper and pen in hand. I had to hold myself back from rushing to him. He would help occupy the rest of the day and keep my mind from running off in excited speculation. He halted and smiled at me. I couldn't help feeling the quiet strength of the man, the strength of someone at ease with himself and with the world, the strength of someone with inner discipline and outer peace. And then I heard his words in the little room and everything was out of focus again.

"Do you have time to talk, Father?" I asked.

"Of course, Stacy, my dear," he said. "I was going to begin a letter to Father Martin, but there's plenty of time for that. Besides, I write him in chapters, sending it on when I've almost a small book."

He strode into the living room and I followed, groping for words to begin with when, with a small, wise smile touching his lips, he rescued me.

"It's last night, of course," he said. "You were distressed by the mass and by what I said to you."

"Yes," I admitted.

"And you're rational self demands that the illogical be made logical," he added and I heard the echoes of Derek's remarks to me.

"Is that wrong?" I replied, feeling unaccountably annoyed and defensive. He considered the question, lips pursed and the sad-stern face seemed drawn, strained.

"Not wrong, perhaps. Just impossible," he answered slowly.

"Why?" I threw back sharply. This was no Aaron needing patience in his role-playing, not this sharp mind I'd seen matching wits with Derek.

"Because you cannot see through my eyes, feel with my emotions, and think with my mind," he said.

"Rubbish," I snapped. "Since when does understanding require role exchanging?"

"There are times, my dear Stacy. You will learn that," he said, resignation in his voice. Or was it sadness. "So let us not talk about understanding. It's too fragile a process, at best. Let us talk, as the Walrus said, 'of shoes and ships and sealing wax, of cabbages and kings,' particularly cabbages and kings." He paused, a smile flooding his face suddenly as he sat down in an armchair. "I thought I was a king and found out I was a cabbage," he said. "A gross reduction of issues, of course, but not without its own truth. You see, I believed in, and still believe in, the truth of the Gospel, *let us love not in word or in tongue but in deed.*" That's 1 John three-eighteen. There are more such commands than I've voice to quote. *"Open thine hand to thy needy in thy land. The needy shall not always be forgotten, the expectations of the poor shall not perish forever.*" They are all there, not just to remain there as lovely phrases, good words, but to be translated into the needs of the world as they are today. I became a priest because I believed, of course, and especially in the divine mission of the priesthood. The miracles Jesus performed were not just to show his divinity. They were performed to tell us something. With each one He gave not only comfort but practical help, whether it was feeding the multitude with the loaves and fishes, the curing of the ill or the draught of fishes after the Resurrection. Even the changing of water into wine at Cana was a deed of practical help. Aid, assistance, the spirit at work on the gut-level where it's needed. What a travesty that has become."

"Why do you say that?" I asked. I saw his face grow more set, a darkness creep into his eyes as he spoke to me.

"You are neither a theologian nor are you familiar with the internal aspects of the administration of the Church, from the parish to the Vatican. But you can believe me that the fresh winds, the spirit of Vatican Two, has been blowing only across the surface. Look at the vital social problems of this country alone. Look at the ghettos, the family disintegration, the crisis in living. Look at housing, one of the basic factors in man's ability to live a decent life. Commercial interests, banks, builders, are not coping with the problem. They have their legitimate limitations and interests. Government is not really doing it. Its paternalism is too bureaucratic and diffused. It is perhaps not truly in the province of government, anyway."

"But it is in the province of the church."

"Of course. Spiritually, biblically and practically. The Church is organized on a parish level. It has its roots in the people, or it is supposed to have. Dioceses and archdioceses have hundreds of millions of dollars. They have power and strength. They could step in to fill the vacuum that government and banks and commercial interests fail to fill. They have the ability to really attack our social problems at that gut-level area. If love, imagination and the spirit of Christ were ruling them that's what they would do."

"What is ruling them?"

"Accountants in Roman collars. Businessmen in birettas. The other churches are equally guilty, but I can only speak of the one I know best. Christianity, you know, was never meant to be a cautious thing. It was meant to be a living, imaginative, leading force. It was not meant to amass hundreds of millions of dollars in banks and in real estate. It was not meant to deal in corporate portfolios and stock transfers. It was not meant to play the financier's role of amassing wealth."

"But aren't those things done to provide services to the people?"

Father Hodges laughed, a short, brutal guffaw that startled me and his eyes were cold as quartz.

"Supposedly," he shot out. "Supposedly. Only the amassing of wealth becomes a Frankenstein. It takes over and becomes the end-all of being."

"But aren't the schools and the charities all examples of the spirit of the Church operating on that gut level of yours?" I poked at him. He fastened a hard stare on me.

"I could answer in John Boyle O'Reilly's words, 'the organized charity, scrimped and iced, in the name of a cautious, statistical Christ.' But you are guilty of misplaced recognition, Stacy. The schools were originally begun to protect and preserve the faith. That they educate millions of young people today is a bit of fallout, a dividend, if you like. Their original purpose, their *raison d'être*, still remains the same from the Church's view, to protect the faith. So, essentially, they are self-serving, directed inwards, not outwards, to the needs of the Church, not mankind. Charities are in essence painted with the same brush."

He rose, abruptly, and began to pace as he spoke, his face clouded, anger filling his every movement.

"I was in a parish in what is called one of the borderline ghetto areas. Things could be saved. It wasn't hard to see what needed doing, and it was not merely youth clubs and basketball tournaments. I drew up a plan where the parish would back, with its resources and those of the Church, new and rehabilitated housing. It was a plan for giving the people a piece of today and a foothold on tomorrow, for a new climate, a sense of responsibility and ownership. And it was workable and feasible. I met with caution and more caution, with talk of money and interest and return on investment. My God, return on investment, the words of bankers and good enough words in their houses but not in the house of God and not from the lips of his priests. Talk about blasphemy. *People* should be the Church's return on its investment. That is the Church's stewardship. I went to the chancery and showed them my plan. It was needed, workable, reasonable."

"They didn't agree."

"The higher I went, the more caution and inertia I found. I heard the same advice on investment values, dollar return, capital risks and I met more men who have exchanged the principles of Christ for the principles of Wall Street."

"Nobody listened to you," I said. Father Hodges stopped his pacing and gazed at me.

"When I was a youngster and offered perfectly valid suggestions only to be dismissed or ignored, I would get furious. I'd go and sit by myself and cry out my rage. But, after all, I was only a youngster offering my views, right as they were, I used to tell myself. As a priest, I would offer the words of God, the views of Christ and they would not be rejected. How wrong I was."

"And how angry you got?" I pressed.

"Yes, how very angry. They said I tried to kill the cardinal."

I felt a tremor go through me, unexpected shock. "Did you try?" I asked.

"Of course not," he said. "I did finally get an interview with him on my plan. By then I'm afraid I'd reached the breaking point and on that very morning a fire in an abandoned house killed three children in the adjoining building. When the cardinal gave me the same caution, the same platitudes, only in loftier language, I went a bit berserk. I ran from his office, two of his aides chasing me. I ran into the cathedral and began destroying the altar, stripping it of everything that was on it, linens, altar cloths, even ripping away at the crucifix. The cardinal came and ordered me to stop. He was aghast, but I flung a heavy candelabra at him and continued to destroy everything I could."

"Why?"

"I was destroying their fraudulence, ripping away their facade. They had no right to stand before God's altar when they refused to stand behind God's love. They had no right to invoke His name when they filtered His love through investments, dollar returns and statistical caution."

He paused and I saw his fists clenching and unclenching and then, after a moment, his hands straighten out as he regained control of himself.

"They called the police and took me away," he said. "They called me deranged, mad, and tried their childish treatments on me. They did not work, of course. I was not mad. I am not mad. They are the ones who are mad, the destroyers of things holy. They released me from their sanitarium in a few weeks, and I destroyed the altar of the parish church and I was seized again. I told them, then, that I would destroy every altar where the love of money hid the love of God, where dollars and not people were the primary consideration. So they put me away and killed me."

"Killed you?" I blurted in surprise.

"There are many ways of killing something. You can dispose of the physical presence, and you can dispose of the philosophical presence. You can put something away so that it no longer exists in any meaningful or bothersome way. The results are quite the same. It is dead, its existence done with, for all worldly purposes, killed. And so now I only say the mass for the dead."

"For yourself, for your own death?"

"For everything that has been killed and will be killed. Because all the good things are dead. Love is dead, reason is dead, the spirit is dead. Only the mass for the dead has meaning."

There was still a cold rage inside him, just beneath the surface of his control. I felt more than saw it.

"Perhaps it's not all that bad," I said. "There's always hope. You see, I didn't need to see through your eyes to understand the things you told me. I didn't need to exchange roles."

He smiled and it was the same smile I'd seen at dinner when I'd misinterpreted his remarks to Derek over reason and society. It held the same gratuitousness in it and I knew that I was off the mark again.

"It would appear that way, wouldn't it?" was all he said then, and once again I had an unfinished feeling, as though everything I'd listened to was not enough and that the point of it lay somewhere else, still beyond my grasp. Father Hodges glanced at his watch.

"I feel like starting my letter to Father Martin. You have put me in the mood, my dear Stacy, started the intellectual wheel turning. See you later," he said. He strode off, straight, disciplined, and I rose and walked slowly to my room, the word *discipline* dancing along with me, executing a mocking little rigadoon. He was disciplined, controlled, and yet obviously that discipline had shattered completely. Did that mean everything, the shattering of discipline? Was that the key to it all, discipline? Was that the distinction between madness and sanity? No, I answered, angry at myself, that was a gross oversimplification. I heard Father Hodges's words as he had said them. *I was not mad. I am not mad.* I wanted to accept them, to agree with them, yet I could not. I had embraced Derek's concepts, understood the things he had shown me, yet it was still an intellectual embrace, the emotions were still not part of it. The emotions bound, and imprisoned with a discipline of their own. That word again, springing up instantly, I thought impatiently. Perhaps it was more important than I realized. Derek spoke of including the illogical in the logical, and Father Hodges had said it was impossible to make the illogical logical. He had said I would have to exchange roles, to see through his eyes and to understand. Yet I had understood his story, his logic, his feelings. But he had smiled that gratuitous, patient little smile at me when I'd noted that. The contradictions were not really contradictory, I was certain. There were signs, explanations, a glossary to explain, but I couldn't read it. I would need more help from Derek, help in closing those gaps, in redefining definitions.

I reached my room and closed the door behind me. Undressing to panties only, I stretched out across the bed. It would all be less unnerving after I learned the meaning behind the letter, I told myself. Till then, everything would hold shadowed meanings that were probably more of my own creations than anything else. It was almost dinnertime. I focused my eyes on the clock. I'd skip dinner tonight. I was too tense to eat, anyway, my stomach quivering inside me.

Everything had been so perfect here, the work, the challenge, the rugged splendor of the land and, of course, the excitement that was Derek. I had found new horizons for myself, new ideas and I had been thoroughly happy until the letter was left for me. I would clear that tonight, I vowed. I would restore perfection. I lay still and watched the day dim, grayness creeping into the room, finally slipping into night. The excitement that had seized me earlier returned now and as the dark deepened I counted off minutes, then seconds. Time isn't at all a changeless absolute, I decided, but a capricious, unpredictable thing, sometimes leaden, sometimes dazzlingly fast. This was one of the leaden moments. The dark had come and the clock seemed to move with agonizing slowness. I shook the clock once to make certain it was running even though I could clearly see the second hand move.

Finally, I swung from the bed and dressed. I went to my suitcase and took out the letter, pushing it into my pocket. I wanted to go over it line for line with Nora. I had a flashlight in my bag and I took that, too. Opening the hall door carefully I slipped into the hall, the murmur of voices drifting from the distant library. I moved to the rear door and opened it, quietly, stepping into the night and closing it behind me. I stood for a moment, letting my eyes grow accustomed to the blackness. It was a dubious wait and I began to move toward the mass of trees only a few yards beyond, grateful for the inky deepness of the night. I didn't dare use the flashlight yet and I groped my way forward, finding the trees, using my feet to discover the narrow pathway. With hands stretched out ahead of me, I began to climb, moving from tree to tree. It was a stygian world where only touch was of any value and each step was a slow, tentative one. I found myself shuffling, using my feet to stay on the path, drawing back at each touch of heavy underbrush, then going on again. I still didn't dare use the light but my progress was much slower than I'd expected and I tried to hurry only to pitch headlong over a rock. Swearing softly, I pulled myself up and groped on along the trees. Finally, cupping my hands around the light, I switched it on, keeping it directed down at the ground. Enough light escaped to show me that the trees were forming a solid wall between the pathway and the house below. I moved forward with the light held at my side. The circle of whiteness was round enough to light the way and finally I shone the light ahead, seeing the path widen and the ridge appear.

"Nora," I called out, aware that I was a little late. "It's me, Stacy." There was no answer and I moved forward.

"Nora?" I called again, halted and waited, but there was no answer. The trees to my right rustled and I spun, shining the light, glimpsing a small, furry shape disappear. My breath rushed from me in a soft hiss of relief and I turned the light forward again. "Nora," I called once more and moved forward. The pathway widened a little more and I walked on slowly. The night was cool but I felt my blouse sticking to me, little beads of perspiration trickling down between my breasts. Damn! I uttered the word under my breath. I hadn't allowed enough time to climb the path in the dark, but I wasn't that late. Had she waited only a few minutes and then left? I would have met her on the way up, then, I answered my question. Unless she knew another path down from here. But Cary Brooks had said this was the only path. I halted, let the light move slowly in a semicircle along the trees, a white spear cutting the blackness.

I heard the scream, acid-sharp, yet swallowed up by the thick trees. It reverberated in my head, a searing, cutting sound and, as if in a dream, I realized it was my own scream. The flashlight spear stayed riveted, fixed on Nora. Her delicate beauty now hideously streaked by rivers of blood running down her face, and down the ripped-away front of her coveralls. The white light gave the horrendous scene a make-believe, klieg-light air. Only it was real, the lines of red widening slowly, moving, expanding into small, sickening drops. The scream stopped and I heard my whispered words. "My God. Oh my God." They repeated themselves, as if coming from someone alongside me. A terrible fascination refused to let me look away, pulled me toward her and I felt my steps moving forward. She was slashed, horribly slashed and hung against the trees, draped there like a ghastly figurine from the *Grand Guignol*. My stomach turned over and I thought I was going to be sick. I stood as if in hypnosis, transfixed in horror.

The spell exploded when the trees to one side rustled, the sound loud, abrasive, snapping my shock as a tightly wound rubber band snaps. Another scream ripped from my throat as I turned and ran, fell, cried out and pushed myself to my feet to run again. The flashlight was in my hand, making erratic motions as I ran headlong, disdaining its cautious light. I felt stones slipping from beneath my feet, my legs twisting, feet going out from under me and I was falling, my shoulder hitting the ground. I felt the dirt break away, and I was falling over the edge of the ridge, arms flailing out to find something to hang onto and finding only air. I was falling headfirst now. My body turning in the air. The blackness a void with neither up nor down. Something hard smashed against my head, cutting off my scream. The blackness became bright orange for an instant and then pain and horror and terror were slipping away and there was nothing. The last thing I remembered was wondering whether this was what death was like, this slipping away into nothing, all feeling, all knowing, all being dissolving away and then I knew no more.

The nothingness lasted, how long I didn't know. When it ended it did so with something akin to the first coming to life, a slow awakening, a knowing of the senses. Definitions first, warmth, air, touch. I was not dead, I told myself through closed eyes. Then more definitions, movement, response, the feeling of skin. I let my eyes open by themselves, contracting at first as light struck them, then reopening to see a soft, flickering yellowness. Orientations came next, shapes and forms. I saw a wood-beamed ceiling, wooden walls. My hands felt the mattress and I knew I was on a bed in a room. I moved my hands, felt the warm smoothness of skin, my skin, ran my fingers up along my ribs, over the soft roundness of my breasts. A sheet lay across me and I lifted my head and felt the sharp pain in my temple, fought it down and felt the warm compress fall from my head to land on the sheet. I moved it, brushed it to the floor and raised myself up on one elbow. My blouse and bra lay across a chair nearby. I saw I was in a small alcove of a cabin—the main room visible—a fireplace burning brightly. A figure moved into sight, and came toward me, the light from the fire giving it form and definition. I saw Cary Brooks, his blue eyes dark with concern.

"Hello. How do you feel?" he asked, not expecting an answer, I knew, and I gave him none. He halted at a small table and poured whiskey from a bottle, handing the glass to me. "Drink this," he said, pulling me to a sitting position. The sheet slipped from me and I clutched at it with one hand and then decided it wasn't all that important. It cooperated anyway by staying fairly well in place. He sat on the edge of the bed as I sipped the whiskey and fiery tentacles reached out through my body.

"You went off the edge of the ridge. You were lucky. There's a small ledge a dozen or so feet below. You could have missed it and gone all the way down," he said matter-of-factly. I felt the whiskey's strength inside me, and the terror began to return. He saw it come into my eyes and spoke quickly.

"I saw her," he said. "I was out trying to set up some flash triggers for night photos when I heard your screams. I was near my place, but sound carries up in these mountains. I came down as quickly as I could and found you on the ledge. You'd hit your head on a piece of rock jutting out as you went over the edge."

"I was running. A noise in the trees set me off. I just ran in terror," I explained, ignoring the pain in my temple to press my hands to my face. I was seeing Nora's torn, slashed form again and that moment of sheer, horror-stricken panic flooded back over me. I felt Cary's hand on my shoulder, warm, comforting.

"She'd gone there to meet me. I was a few minutes late," I told him, looking up at his serious face. I paused, leaving the question hanging. I knew the answer yet I had to ask it. "Could it have been a wild animal?" I offered. His lips pressed together in grimness.

"Could it have been? There's always that outside chance, that ten-thousand-to-one chance. An angry grizzly could tear someone that way, but I haven't seen any signs of a grizzly around here," he said.

"She had something to tell me. Someone stopped her before she could talk," I said.

"Someone at Harbor House?" Cary Brooks asked. I shrugged my reply, a gesture of uncertainty.

"You suspect someone?" he pressed. I hesitated, full of suspicions, yet unwilling to accuse. I settled for evasion.

"I don't know. I'm not sure of anything," I returned. I looked up at Cary Brooks, a sense of unreality clinging to me. Nora's torn body was vivid in my mind yet it all seemed impossible, dreamlike. I retreated, into unemotional facts and particulars, details to occupy the mind and surround reality with things to be grasped, hiding places of their own special sort.

"How did you get me up from the ledge?" I questioned.

"Rope. I came down first, found what had happened, and then went back here and got the rope and went back again," he answered.

Gratitude rushed over me with its own warmth. "How do you thank someone for saving your life?" I asked.

"You don't. There's no need for that," Cary said, and then, pausing, glanced at my round, bare shoulders. "I was getting your blouse all wet soaking your temple," he went on. "I took it off, and your bra, and applied very wet hot compresses." He paused again, and this time a faint smile edged his lips. "A friend of mine is an expert restorer of paintings. He's often told me how exciting and rewarding it is when he removes outer layers of a canvas and finds something even more beautiful underneath. Now I understand how he feels."

I wanted to make some bright comment to acknowledge the compliment, but the best I could manage was a small smile. His eyes told me he understood. My head was beginning to throb again, and I thought of Nora and the letter. Automatically, my hand went to the pocket of my slacks. The letter was gone.

"I had a letter in my pocket," I said, alarm seizing my voice. "Did you find it?"

Cary shook his head. "Didn't go through your slacks," he said. "It's connected with what happened, isn't it?"

I nodded, my eyes holding his steady glance. "I lost it, then. It must have fallen out of my pocket," I said.

"Maybe when I dragged you up with the rope. It was efficient, but hardly delicate. It could be lost forever now at the bottom of the mountain," Cary said. He watched as I seemed to shrink together, a sudden chill coursing through me though the little room was warm. "I'll make some tea," he said, getting to his feet. "I think you'd best stay here till morning."

"Yes, please," I answered, words rushing from me. "I don't want to go back tonight. Derek—Dr. Closter is away. He'll be back in the morning. I don't want to go back till then."

"Are you afraid for your own life?" Cary asked.

"No. At least, I don't think so. I don't know," I replied, confusion always an honest thing. "No, it's ridiculous," I added, summoning confidence out of nowhere.

"Is it?" he commented. "As ridiculous as that girl down there?"

"Her name was Nora," I said. It was somehow important that she have a name, an identity, a meaning to her death. "What will happen to her now?" I questioned.

"I wrapped a sheet around her. Morning will be time enough to do what needs to be done," Cary said. He went into the main part of the cabin and I slipped into my blouse. It was torn and dirt-marked, but it would have to do. I followed into the larger section and saw it was comfortably cluttered, full of artist's things—palettes and brushes, sketch pads and untouched, white canvases that seemed to wait to be used. There were other canvases, oils of nature studies, very accomplished. Cary was brewing the tea in one corner of the cabin, using a small Franklin stove. I saw a half dozen canvases, faces to the wall, in another corner and I strolled over to them, turning them around to see them. They were very different than the nature studies, all abstract, impressionist pieces, deep blues and purples with brilliant red flashes whirling about in them. They were striking in a macabre way, and I could think only of Dante's Inferno.

"Mood pieces," he said at my elbow and I turned. He handed me a mug of hot tea. "I was playing at abstract painting—strictly mood things."

I looked again at the canvases. His mood must have been one of dark, turbulent anger, I thought silently. There was none of that now in Cary Brooks, I thought. He hadn't Derek's electric excitement, but he had his own attractiveness, a deep, quiet purposefulness and a sly humor just beneath the surface of his calm exterior.

"Want to tell me more about why you and the girl were meeting up here in the dark of the night?" he asked. He sat down on one of two old, but comfortable, chairs, and I took the other.

"There's not much to tell," I said between sips, the hot tea feeling good, warming. "She had let me know about something that bothered me. She was going to tell me more. It was about Elise Donner."

"Oh?" he said questioningly. I glanced at him, but his eyes were only mildly curious. I wondered how much to say, feeling somewhat traitorous. He caught my thought somehow. "It's no longer a case of telling tales out of school," he said. "There's been a killing, now."

I flinched from the word, the sound of it ugly, shudder-provoking. I didn't want to hear the word, not even think about it. To think about it was to think about who and why and about Harbor House itself. In one sharp, sudden stroke, the curtain of normality had been torn aside—the rationality of concept shattered. But I was really being traitorous now, I told myself. I was making conclusions I'd no right to make, not without first talking to Derek. I returned to Cary Brooks's patiently waiting face.

"It seems I wasn't given the right reason for Elise Donner's leaving," I said. "She wasn't unhappy here. There was something more to it."

"And Nora knew the truth," Cary Brooks said, an edge of sharpness creeping into his voice.

"Apparently," I replied.

"Do you think you've been given wrong impressions about Harbor House in general?" he asked, casualness returning to his voice.

"No," I said, too quickly, and was immediately annoyed with myself. "Derek's work is remarkable and his concepts are valid. We need new guidelines, new standards for judging human behavior, and helping those we call disturbed."

"A new approach to madness," Cary said. The word—naked, brutal—shocked as though cold water had been flung in my face. My distaste apparent, Cary smiled at me.

"You object to the word. I object to euphemisms," he said. "*Disturbed* has become a linguistic wastebasket, a term for all degrees of behavior, but more importantly, an example of how we avoid facing unpleasantness."

"Perhaps because the word reflects what we subconsciously realize is our lack of understanding," I returned. "You're against euphemisms. Well, I'm against wrong definitions." I paused, groping, refusing to simply quote Derek, trying to put his thoughts into words of my own. "Madness needs redefinition," I pronounced.

"I'll agree to that," Cary said.

"The guests at Harbor House are not as irrational or as illogical as we would like to believe," I said, sounding more certain than my own conditioned reservations permitted. "They can evaluate, judge, reason. They are not stupid. In fact, most are quite brilliant."

"Brilliance is no bar to madness," Cary replied. "History proves that. Neither is age or education. I've always heard that the mad have a special kind of brilliance, a cleverness all their own."

"There are a lot of old canards about yet," I answered. "But I do think that perhaps madness, to use your word, may require brilliance, or at the very least a mind developed beyond the ordinary. Conversely, stupidity may be a kind of protection against madness."

"Dr. Closter's positive thinking?" Cary remarked.

"Isn't positive better than negative?"

"Emotionally, yes; intellectually, no," he snapped back. "Positive bias can distort the process of evaluating as well as negative bias can."

"All right, but since coming to Harbor House I've had to look at some of the distortions in our sociological definitions which are, if nothing else, certainly intolerant," I said. I found words tumbling out of me. I wanted to talk, to let words fill space and keep the mind occupied with their sound alone. I began telling Cary about Harbor House, about Nora and Rudi and Father Hodges, Marlyn and Aaron, and about the conversation at dinner the night before. I wanted everything to become case histories, embracing an air of clinical detachment, the safety of unemotional thought. Cary listened intently, making few comments, and I knew I was being overexcited and unable—or more correctly, unwilling—to do anything about it. I finally began to run down when suddenly the thought burst inside me, an explosion of the obvious, as all sudden discoveries are, falling from my lips with a sense of awe.

"They've something in common, all of them," I said. Cary frowned. "Don't you see it?" I asked with the impatience of the newly enlightened. "They all have one thing in common."

Cary's lips pursed. "A unifying thread? There might be a number of them."

"No, only one that means anything," I said. "Love."

I saw his frown deepen.

"That's right, love," I went on, growing excited at my discovery. "Each person at Harbor House tried to help someone else. Each of them loved, wanted to do good. Even poor Aaron tried to please two parents and wound up becoming two people. From Nora's love for her little brother to Father Hodges's love for the needy of his parish, each of them wanted to make the world a little better for someone else. Each of them was hurt by what was happening to others. Their methods of helping, the things they did, may have gone over into twisted and distorted thinking, they may have slipped into obsessive, compulsive behavior, but the original, motivating force was love."

I halted, feeling the impact of what I was saying. I wondered if Derek had chosen them all because of that. Probably, I decided, remembering how he said they were all carefully chosen.

"An extra helping of empathy?" Cary mused aloud.

"That's right, an extra measure of love. Maybe that's the one key factor in what we call madness. I'd call it an extra susceptibility to the needs of others, the pains and hurts of the world. And after all, isn't that what love is in the truest meaning of the word?"

"You make it sound like a plus factor," Cary said.

"Maybe it is," I answered. "Even what happened tonight fits. Nora was killed because she wanted to help me, because she cared about me."

"And did love kill her?" he speared, cold water again.

"I don't know. I don't know that madness killed her," I answered. I searched his face to see if there was mockery there, but found only the calm seriousness that was Cary Brooks and suddenly I was very tired, too tired to think any longer. Behind the tiredness, confusion, uncertainty and fear returning to the foreground of my mind, I felt my head tilt back against the chair and my eyes close. I slept, almost at once, grateful for the erasure of thought, fatigue silencing the subconscious mind as well. I didn't know Cary had carried me back to the bed in the adjoining alcove, not till I woke there in the morning.

Sunlight, brilliant gold shafts spearing into the cabin, signaled the new day and I sat up slowly, pressing fingers to my temple. It hurt to the touch but the throbbing had stopped. An inviting odor drifted to my nostrils, fresh coffee. I swung my feet to the floor as Cary peered around the edge of the alcove.

"The bathroom's to the left.' It's pretty primitive, but at least it's attached to the house," he said. I went past him with sleep still clinging to me. Later, washed and freshened with cold water, I returned to the room and he handed me a mug of fresh coffee. I sipped the coffee eagerly and accepted a slice of toast.

"I didn't expect you'd be really hungry," Cary said, and I nodded agreement. I sank into a chair, realizing how desperately I had wanted the night to have been a bad dream. But it hadn't been a dream. I was here, in Cary's little cabin, and the night rushed back over me. I looked at Cary and felt the dull anguish mirrored on my face.

"I don't want to go back down past her," I said dully, words pulling from me as though they were tied down with leaden weights. "Is there another way?"

"Yes, the road where the jeep is kept. It's around the other way and circles the other side of the mountain," he said.

My eyes told him I'd take it no matter what the climb. I sat drawn into myself, sipping the coffee. With the morning, new thoughts came to torment. If I'd gone to Derek, if I hadn't tried to poke about on my own, Nora would probably be alive. The accusation was too brutal to allow rejection, when I was both accuser and accused.

"It could have been avoided, perhaps. It could all be my fault," I murmured aloud. I looked at Cary wanting someone else's denial yet ready to spurn glibness. I got neither.

"Maybe," he said thoughtfully. "You don't know that yet."

"Will I ever?" I asked, finishing the coffee.

"Possibly," he said. His face was set. I met his eyes and they looked away, concern in them as on that first day when Matland picked me up. Matland. The name shuddered inside me. He and the woman—I saw them as a unit, a pair. To accuse them, even to myself, would be unfair, yet the subconscious mind whispered accusations. Certainly racing suspicions.

"Ready to go back?" Cary said, breaking into dark thoughts. I nodded and rose, following after him with a numb, half-alive feeling. The trail was non-existent until, somehow, he came to the end of a small road and I saw the jeep parked there. As I climbed into the seat beside the wheel and he came in beside me, he paused, his eyes serious, holding mine.

"I'm sorry for what happened. But I'm still going to paint you here," he said.

"All right. Sometime," I answered. It would be a new experience, anyway, and now it was almost an obligation. But I kept that thought to myself. He wouldn't want it that way, I knew. He started the jeep and I sat stiffly as he bounced the car down the narrow, rutted road to the bottom of the mountain, and finally around to where Harbor House waited, toadlike and misshapen. Cary pulled up before the front door and I saw it open and Derek's figure hurry out, a frown touching his face. I stepped from the jeep. Cary stayed behind the wheel.

"Derek, this is Cary Brooks," I introduced. Derek's smile was restrained, his nod perfunctory. I heard Cary's few banal words. I watched the two men eye each other, the moment stiff, almost as if they had met before and held a residue of dislike for each other. Wariness, I thought, that was the word. They exchanged glances with the wariness of distrust. Matland's gray face appeared in the doorway, pulling my thoughts away and I turned to Derek.

"I must see you alone, right away," I said. He saw the urgency in my eyes and turned to the house at once.

"Of course. Come inside," he said.

I started to go with him, turned to speak to Cary and saw that he was putting the jeep into reverse, his head turned away from me. I didn't want to leave without exchanging even a last glance, but he continued backing the car, then putting it into forward and driving off. I went into the house as the motor of the jeep gathered strength.

"I wondered where you were when you didn't show for breakfast," Derek said. "I got in just a little before dawn."

"I was at Cary Brooks's cabin. Something's happened," I said. Derek's sidelong glance was questioning, but I said nothing more till we were in the library and he had closed the door. The words rushed from me in a torrent then, starting with Nora's death, of course, then going back over the events before it, beginning with the letter and the first time I saw it as I handed out the mail. I recounted how angry Una Stenner had been then and on to finding the letter in my room. I quoted it to him almost verbatim, surprised at how completely it had imprinted itself on my memory. I told him of my meeting with Nora, of how frightened she seemed and how she set the place for our meeting. The rest followed naturally, moving to the final moment when my flashlight turned the night into a place of horror.

When I finished, I was drained from the telling. I felt my shoulders move as an involuntary shudder went through me. Derek's first words were of concern and grateful warmth enveloped me as he took hold of my shoulders.

"My poor Stacy, what a terrible experience for you," he said. I found my head against his chest and I was happy to stay there in his arms, strong and reassuring. Finally he moved back but let his hand rest against my cheek and I saw my pain mirrored in his eyes and wanted to embrace him for that.

"You've had a bad time of it, Stacy, and it's pretty much my fault," he said.

"I didn't mean to imply that," I cut in hastily. His smile, rueful, acknowledged a kindness.

"No, of course you didn't, but it's so. You said it yourself. You'd been lied to, and you wanted to find out why. I was party to that," he answered. He turned and drew me down to the couch beside him. I was happy to let my hand stay in his.

"I'll go over things step by step, Stacy. It'll be a start, anyway," he began. "Elise Donner, first. I didn't tell you why Elise Donner left because I thought it might do two things. First, it would have made me sound terribly conceited, perhaps ridiculously so, and secondly, it might have wrongly influenced your decision on coming here and I didn't want that to happen. I wanted you to decide on your own and for your own reasons."

I almost smiled inwardly at how unaware he was of the electricity he possessed. Anyone who came in contact with Derek was overpowered by it making deciding more a matter of responding.

"The letter said it all, Stacy," he went on. "Elise Donner didn't leave here because she was unhappy. The truth is that she had fallen terribly in love with me. That was unfortunate for more than one reason. For one thing, it was entirely one-sided." Derek paused, his eyes flicking to mine for an instant and the echo of a wry smile touched his lips. "She had none of your beauty, your warmth, none of those things that could have made it a two-way affair. But more than that, there was Nora."

"Nora?"

"Yes. Nora has always had a combination of feelings for me, a father-figure image of me and an obsession that we could be secret lovers. She fantasied it all, of course, but she began to make life miserable for Elise. It grew worse, and for the good of my work here, I decided that Elise Donner had to go."

He paused again. "So much for why Elise Donner left. Do you have the letter that came for her?" he asked.

"No, I lost it last night. It fell from my pocket, probably when I went over the edge of the ridge," I said.

"No matter. I just wondered if you'd noted the postmark."

"I didn't have the envelope. Only the letter itself was left for me. It said that no one had heard from her. Do you know where she went when she left?"

"No," Derek shrugged unhappily. "And I'm bothered by that. It was a fairly sticky time when Elise left. She refused my offers to get her to Anchorage and arranged transportation through the Jackson brothers at Bear Landing, she told me." He paused in thought for a moment, then went on. "Now, as to Una. She'd been told that I wanted no knowledge of this to reach you until you'd been here long enough to know us all. I'm afraid she simply overreacted."

Derek's explanations were patient, reasonable, simple—so much so that suddenly I had the feeling that he was explaining things away. "Then why did Nora leave the letter for me? She stole it from Una and left it for me to see," I asked.

"She was there when the letter came, when Una took it from you. I'd speculate that she suddenly saw you as perhaps another rival and she seized the chance to start to get rid of you, sowing little seeds of doubt, subtle thrusts to upset."

Reasonableness again, answers that couldn't be faulted, and yet I was unsatisfied. "But Nora's been killed, horribly killed. Someone did it. She left the letter for me, was to meet me and was killed. There has to be a connection," I said.

"On-the-surface logic," Derek said. "But perhaps only there."

"Surface logic?" I retorted.

"Yes, Stacy," he countered. "I can't tell you it wasn't someone from Harbor House—not yet, anyway. But the surface logic is not absolute. It could have been someone else, someone who came upon her as she waited there for you or perhaps met her as she went to the ridge. We are not the only people in this wild country, as you know."

I stared at Derek. "You can't mean Cary Brooks," I exclaimed incredulously.

"I don't mean *anyone*. I am only saying that there are other possibilities for Nora's death. Up here there are Indians who wear only the thinnest veneer of civilization. There are trappers who roam this land—wild, half-savage men who come and go as they please. And there is the chance that it might have been a wild animal."

I shook my head. I discarded that once and did so again. "And it could have been someone from Harbor House," I said doggedly.

Derek's sigh was long, a grimness in his face. "That possibility must, of course, exist until I can be certain it isn't so," he said.

"You'll call the police?" I said. Derek's eyes fastened on me, deep with gravity, and his hand reached out to take both of mine and enclose them in his.

"I want you to understand, Stacy, and I ask your patience. Of course the authorities will be notified. But I want a few days to make my own investigation. The authorities descending here on Harbor House could wreck what I've taken so long to build. They could make a shambles of attitudes and expectations that I have carefully instilled. They would be a mirror image of all the damaging aspects of society's attitudes toward those they've called disturbed. They will jump to conclusions, come with their built-in prejudices. They will make accusations and apply the harsh methods of police investigation. Some of that must be met, but I must be sure of two things, first. I'm certain it was none of the guests here at Harbor House. But I want to have proof of that in hand before I call in the authorities. I must get that proof in my own way and, equally as important, I must prepare those here for the authorities. I must make sure that the things I've so carefully nurtured here will stand up to the sudden intrusion of the outside world, particularly the police world. After all, I am preparing those here, therapeutically, as well as evolving a new approach to the entire problem. And, last but hardly least, I might even get a lead to other possible killers."

Derek's eyes stayed locked into mine, asking for that understanding he needed. It was not hard to give. His life was here in his work. It was more than Harbor House itself but the concepts he wanted to prove as valid.

"Of course I understand, Derek," I said and his smile was gratitude itself.

"I'll convince you it was no one from Harbor House," he said. I heard his remark and with a persistence of my own, held to those certainties that understanding could not affect.

"Where did Matland and Una come from, Derek?" I asked. "Were they, too, institutionalized?"

"Matland and Una? No, not institutionalized but they did work at a sanitarium. I'd gone to Anchorage—a trip to get some things we needed—and met them there. They had been out of a job for some time, and had come here to try to find something they could do. Frankly, they had had some trouble at the sanitarium where they had worked—a place full of old people, I was told, and their patience was too short. I hired them, and that's the whole of it."

I wonder, I answered in silence. To Derek it was the whole of it, no doubt, but perhaps not to Matland and the woman. Derek's hand against my face brought my thoughts back to him.

"You are more dangerous than anyone here," he said and I frowned at once and saw his smile widen.

"Beauty is always dangerous," he explained. "It is the one thing against which there is no defense. It is the one thing which turns man's discrimination, his sensitivity, his appreciation, against him. His very weapons in life become his downfall, accomplices to beauty itself."

I found a smile. "I'm never one to turn down any advantage," I said, and Derek laughed, a short sound. Then he grew serious at once.

"I think you ought not to try to work today. Stay in your room and rest," he said. "You've had a shattering experience."

"Yes, I'm very tired," I admitted.

"I'll see that the proper things are done for Nora," Derek said. "You just go and get some rest." He leaned forward, his lips brushing my cheek, a quick motion full of understanding and empathy. I didn't draw away, willing to linger close to him. He was so very different from anyone I'd ever known, so much more aware of my every thought and mood. He drew back after a moment, his hand running softly over my hair as though I were a precious, delicate piece of porcelain, hardly to be touched. *I can be touched*, I wanted to say, but held myself silent. He pulled me to my feet and left me at the library door, watching as I went to my room. There, I put the latch on and undressed and lay across the bed, the terribly tired, drained feeling upon me again. Everything Derek had so patiently, logically explained made sense and was clothed in reason, yet something gnawed at me, refusing to let me accept it completely. I closed my eyes, drifting in thought, Derek's explanations in patches, returning to float across my mind. Words, reasons, shreds of phrases, pointing out possibilities I had never considered. Yet the gnawing persisted and I drifted with his words, waiting for it to cease.

Suddenly I was sitting upright, snapped into wakefulness. Nora's face hung before me, not as it had been that last, terrible time, but with her wide, fearful eyes fastened on me in the garden. Nora was still the key to everything, to the gnawing that persisted. Nora believed in love, her every action rooted in it. She had left the letter to help me, not to irritate. The fear I'd seen in the garden was no clever performance, no acting out a role. Was it a fear of Una Stenner and Matland? I couldn't be certain of that any longer. Nora's fears could have been of everyone and anyone. Derek's explanations of Nora's feelings toward him were undoubtedly true, but I wondered if they were complete.

Whether he knew she truly had tried to make life miserable for Elise Donner or had Elise Donner imagined that and convinced him of it. Perhaps others had joined in that. Something about Elise Donner's role here at Harbor House was unexplained; a missing piece and Nora's death had been proof of that. Or had it? The questions whirled, colliding with each other. Derek's reasoned possibilities had to be included. She could have been murdered by someone totally removed from everything at Harbor House.

Damn! I muttered the word under my breath. Nora had left the letter for me. Perhaps she had left other things among her personal possessions? I wouldn't go to Derek now. I valued his wisdom but, in this moment of stress, even he could let his emotions carry him astray. The best thing I could do for Derek was to find anything that might help him, that might provide answers even he did not suspect. His grave, grim countenance as I told him what happened flashed in front of me and I knew that he had been more shaken than he had let on.

I swung from the bed, my decision made. There was more—something else unsatisfied—still ticking away in the back of my head, but for now, this was enough. I dressed and slipped from the room. Lunch was almost over and I went down the hallway, pausing at the stairs, then hurrying on into the other side of the house and Nora's room. The door was closed and I grasped the knob, felt it turn, the door opening. I halted, a coldness enveloping me, not fear but the feeling that I was an invader, a violator of privacy. The dead deserve their secrets, perhaps. Yet perhaps Nora would have wanted me to come here, to discover what she'd been going to tell me. It was rationalization, I knew, but I grasped at it eagerly and hurried into the room, closing the door quietly after me. I surveyed the room, much neater than Marlyn's—almost sparse. I decided to start with the dresser. The drawers

were not very full and I went through them quickly, not knowing what I sought, only that I would know it if I found it. But
the mind demands form and I began to seek a note, or another
letter, or a diary. The thought excited me. Nora could have kept
one. She was the type to confide her thoughts to paper and bring
them back again in moments of solitude. I reached the bottom
drawers of the dresser, found them empty and turned to a small
endtable near the bed. There was a single drawer in it and I pulled
it open. I found photos cut from magazines, loosely scattered in
the drawer, flowers, sunsets, children, lots of children, but nothing else. The closets were next. I'd just started on the first of the
two, going through each dress, when I heard the sound of the
door opening.

I froze, panic gripping me, and I thought about pulling the
closet shut. But the moment had been a moment too long and I
saw Una Stenner in the room, her icy eyes clouded with alarm
for a moment, then fury taking hold. I turned and faced her, my
defiance as much for Nora as for myself.

"What are you doing here?" She slid the question at me in a
low, ominous tone.

"Helping to get Nora's things together," I replied.

"That is my job," the woman barked. "I do the cleaning out
of rooms here."

"Sorry. I was only trying to help," I lied and knew that Una
Stenner didn't believe me. I strolled across the room to the door,
feeling her eyes following me. I avoided glancing back at her and
left, pushing the door wider as I walked into the hall. Once out
of the room my defiance rushed from me as air rushes from a
punctured balloon. But my suspicions had been refortified, that
instant of alarm in the woman's eyes again. It was more than
simply fear of Derek's instructions, more than mere overreacting, as Derek had supposed.

I walked on when, opposite the front door in the hall, Matland appeared, almost blocking the way. I noticed the fresh dirt on his clothes and hands and knew the dreadful meaning of it. He stared at me and his cat's eyes grew smaller, pupils contracting, but not so much that I couldn't see the hate in them.

"She'd still be alive if you hadn't come here, if you'd stayed away from her," he said abruptly. I started to protest and decided better of it. He brushed past me, the hatred glittering in his small eyes, and moved down the hall. I thought again of the sounds of ecstasy I'd listened to that first night here, and of how Matland had gazed at Nora the next morning during breakfast. I'd rejected the very idea then, unable to see Nora's fragile delicacy and Matland's coarseness and brutality. Perhaps I'd no right to reject anything here. Didn't opposites often attract? But perhaps Matland blamed me for taking away not a lover but a goal, a hope. Whatever it was, his eyes had held hatred.

I walked on when I heard the voice calling me and I turned to see Marlyn, her round, short form coming toward me with an aggressive determination.

"You certainly didn't do Nora much good, love," she said. "Ghastly business that."

"I didn't do her any harm," I said defensively, angry at feeling so uncertain myself. Marlyn shrugged.

"Maybe not. Such a nice girl, Nora. She was going to meet you, though," the woman said.

I held back answers and then other words gathered inside me, unplanned, yet suddenly terribly necessary. "I guess your prediction was accurate enough, but misplaced," I remarked. "The right occurrence, but the wong girl."

"Oh, no, love," Marlyn frowned. "I simply missed on Nora completely, didn't get any reception on her at all. That happens, you know. It's got nothing at all to do with you."

She waved a short, plump hand at me and went off. She had held to her prophecy and I had been shamefully ridiculous, fishing for reassurances like that, and I'd been turned away. There was no room for succor at the prophet's inn. I hurried on to my room, slamming the door behind me and flinging myself across the bed, pulling off clothes as I did so. Damn Marlyn and her predictions, I bit out, wanting the silent relief of sleep again and knowing it would be impossible to summon at command. I lay awake, thinking of Nora, Una Stenner and Matland, trying to find possible motives, letting my imagination run free, and finally growing impatient and angry. Wild speculation was no help, perhaps even a hindrance this time. I would put it aside, replace it with patience and facts. I closed my eyes forcing myself to lay still and allowing sleep to creep into my room. But the gnawing stayed, and the sleep was nothing more than a restless, tossing exercise.

The room was dark when I woke, by an insistent, repeating noice disturbing my thoughts. I sat up, defined the sound slowly as someone rapping at the door. Switching on the lamp, I slipped into a robe and opened the door. Derek was there with a small tray—a sandwich and a pot of tea on it.

"You missed dinner, and I thought you ought to have something," he said as he came in and set the tray on the small end-table alongside the bed.

"How thoughtful, Derek," I answered as he drew a chair up for himself and I perched on the edge of the bed. The sight of the food triggered my sudden hunger. Derek's deep eyes examined me intently and I felt the embracing, ebullient strength of him, once more a part of his presence.

"You found out something?" I offered and his smile was warming, perhaps even a little smug and I forgave him for it instantly.

"Enough for me and I hope for you," Derek said. "At the time you were meeting Nora, Rudi, Marlyn and Father Hodges were having a three-handed game of pinochle." He paused, watching my eyes. "I questioned each one separately and their stories fitted perfectly. Aaron was helping Matland unplug a balky bathroom sink fixture at that time."

"And Una?"

"She told me she had gone to bed early. I'll have to take her word for that, but Father Hodges did see her go into her room with her usual nighttime glass of milk," Derek said.

"So everyone is accounted for and accountable," I said with a trace of annoyance, ashamed at hearing it. Except Una Stenner. Her word was not that believable to me. I hunted words myself then, wanting to find the right ones to give form to my question without waspishness.

"So you're really saying it was no one here, that it was an outsider. You're saying that it was sheer coincidence that it happened as she was waiting to meet me."

"Things like that do happen, Stacy," Derek said gently.

"Derek, have you considered the possibility that maybe someone is lying to you, maybe more than one person?" I asked.

"No." He threw the word out instantly, sharply, then softened the impact of it with his smile. "I'm sorry, but there are certain things I'm sure of, Stacy. I know the nature of the relationships I've created here. You've become aware of some of their depths. I'm not being lied to—not about this."

I'd never seen him so absolute. I backed down quickly before his certainty and what I knew was his knowledge in this area. "I came across something else last night," I said slowly. "It came to me as I was thinking about what had happened and I suddenly realized that there is a common denominator among everyone you've brought to Harbor House."

His eyebrows lifted, a gesture of surprise and admission. "You came upon it more quickly than most people would, Stacy. My compliments," he said.

"Because of what happened," I demurred. "I went over what I knew about each person here and suddenly it came to me. An extra susceptibility to the needs of others brought them into conflict with society and eventually here to Harbor House. And perhaps an extra measure of love."

Derek smiled and there were things behind it I couldn't read, a private appreciation. "So romantically put, Stacy," he commented. "And not incorrectly. I refer to it somewhat differently, of course—not as an extra measure, but as a root."

I frowned and he moved to sit beside me, taking my hands in his.

"You see, Stacy, it's the root of sanity. That's right—the root, the basic quality from which everything else grows. Those assembled here possess sanity in its true form. It's that very sanity which created their problems and which results in that extra measure of love and concern you put into words. You are right. They conflicted with and could not adapt to what we term normal behavior. They accepted the behavior of society at large, but not because they were insane but because they could not let go of sanity, of that root. That inability to let go of sanity is their real problem."

He paused and his smile curled around me, wiping away the frown that had set on my face.

"We are expected to let go of sanity. We are expected to compromise with reason and adjust to contradictions. Society demands that of us. It demands that we accept a truth and then deny it in practice. It demands that we adjust to the illogical until that illogicality creates its own logic. For example, we are told that we are my brother's keeper. In a subconscious way, we recognize the sanity of that. We should be concerned with the needs of our brothers; we are in truth each other's keepers. Yet society demands that our own welfare come first. We must keep our interests first. If we do not, society punishes and penalizes us. Are we not then made to go contrary to what all reason and sanity tells us is right?

"In this world, millions of people starve to death and entire cities are made up of beggars. We have the technical knowledge and the material ability to provide food for the world. Yet we look the other way and talk of the marketplace. Is that any form of sanity?"

He paused, but not really for me to reply. I said nothing.

"We are told it is God's commandment that we shall not kill, that it is a direct and unequivocal order. Yet under certain conditions and rules it is perfectly right to make war and to kill. In fact, one can receive medals and an exalted place in society if one is particularly good at it. Isn't that contradictory beyond all reason? We know that life is precious—once lost to us, irretrievable on this earth. Yet we grow germs and viruses so powerful that a single bottle can wipe out the entire population of this planet and for which there are no known antidotes. We make these things and hoard them for use against each other. Is that rationality? Is that not insanity?"

The questions once more were rhetorical. "Yet we do all these things and many more," Derek went on. "And we call ourselves rational, sane. Those unable to adjust to these contradictions, who cannot behave in accordance with them, we term disturbed and irrational. On every level we behave on equally contradictory wavelengths. All you need to do is look about and choose your own examples. And with it all, those who cannot accept such contradictions, who can't do so, who cannot cope with these things or who try to make them less contradictory, we term disturbed, insane. I ask you, Stacy, which is really contradictory, who is really functioning in a world of irrationality—those here and in asylums all over or those of us who sit outside, smug with our own, generally accepted irrationality?"

"You pose the questions so completely that it's almost impossible not to accept the obvious answer," I said.

"You think it's an oversimplification?" he countered.

I shrugged. "Somewhat so," I admitted.

"Oversimplifications contain errors, but that does not affect their basic truths, my dear," he smiled. "My work here is not only to redefine our definitions of disturbed and to achieve a new accommodation, but to show that those we call disturbed are as much value to society as anyone else, just as the wolf and the rabbit, the hawk and the sparrow, are equally important ecologically.

I recalled Derek's words at our very first meeting. *Nature is tolerant. She permits every form of life to live as it sees fit. She renders no judgments.* It made such reasonable sense and I wanted to accept it wholly. Why couldn't I? Why did something in me hang back?

"All my work here is designed to let each person regain the feeling of value society has taken from him or her by its judgments. That includes my outpatient work," Derek said.

"And Nora's murder is outside that. I'm sorry. I guess I'm just not much of a believer in coincidences."

"As I said, they do happen, the unusual conjunction of events," Derek answered, and I knew he was right. "Maybe I just need a little more time," I said. His hands took my shoulders.

"Of course. You'll see I'm right. These are my children, in a way. I know them. But you are a remarkable and lovely girl, Stacy."

Maybe I moved forward first, maybe he did. I didn't know and didn't much care as his lips pressed mine, opening my mouth with a tender strength that was a sudden fire erupting. I felt his hands on me and thrust forward to meet his touch. His fingers moving across the rise of my breasts held a kind of electric wildness I'd never known before and I pulled him to me in answering eagerness. It was he who moved back finally and I saw the struggle for self-containment in his eyes. I wanted to tell him how much I longed for the warm security of someone to hold, to touch and to lie beside, but his words cut off the thought while adding new depth to the message of his lips.

"We'll have to talk about this thing called love, sometime," he said. "It happens so easily with some people."

He rose abruptly then, deep eyes lighted with an inner fire. "Get a good night's rest tonight," he said. I welcomed his lips again, felt the throbbing excitement of him against me again and then he was walking away, closing the door behind him. But the fervency of him stayed, as the reverberation of a thunderclap stays. But then, Derek always lingered on after he left, and I lay back across the bed and knew that half of Marlyn's prophecy would come true. Or had already. It was a flawed happiness. Would the other half also come true?

I sat up, knowing I couldn't just drop off to sleep again. Something to read would help, I knew, a book to fill the mind and lull the senses into drowsiness. I opened the door and went down the hallway toward the library. The sound came to me, drifting from the far end of the opposite hall, familiar, the voice of Father Hodges, the words the singsong cadence of the mass, the mass for the dead. For Nora, this time? I wondered if I should go to the little room at the far end of the corridor and take part. Grimly, I shook away the thought and went into the library, found a novel I'd not read, and started back to my room.

I'd almost reached it when the figure stepped from the dark shadows alongside the wall, noiselessly, drenching me in fear and

I saw Aaron's thin face, drawn and sunken, his eyes looking like empty pits in the half darkness of the corridor.

"I hate you. She's dead now," he flung out. "You didn't want to talk to me, and she's dead now."

"Aaron, there's no connection there," I said soothingly.

"There's always a connection, between everything," he exploded. "Even if you don't see it, it's there. That you don't see it doesn't mean anything. It's there, everything connecting."

"Can you show it to me, Aaron?" I asked.

"No. You're not one of us. That's a connection, too," he threw back. He turned away, sharp, abrupt movements, disappearing down the hall. I went into my room and latched the door, trying not to tremble as I undressed. The meeting had been so unexpected, another sudden, surprising distortion. The book was useless print, now. I read without comprehending. My mind was on Aaron, on what once again seemed to reveal the cracks in what Derek saw as a controlled and reasoned place. Everything skittered across my mind now—words, meanings, the ability to believe, and with it the intrusion of the personal, Derek's lips pressing on mine, wanting and being wanted. He compelled, excited, and held one with his own special strength and I knew that his words, all he'd said had been willed with his own special wisdom. But he had called them all his children and perhaps that was more real then even he realized, I mused, extending the analogy. Parents were often blind in regard to their own children, unable to see what others could see, the myopia of closeness and love. And Derek was human—very much so I had learned tonight, and he could have his own blind spots. If this were so, he needed my help. But I would have to bring him more than just my suspicions.

I snapped off the light and lay in the darkness again. My own suspicions were all I had, really. Could I trust in them? My own suspicions and that gnawing, nagging, ticking something that refused to reveal itself. No, dammit, I answered in anger, I had more than suspicions. I had the memory of Nora's real fear at my questions about the letter and, again, I had that moment of alarm in Una Stenner's face when she'd found me in Nora's room. She was afraid that I'd perhaps found something, it was there in her eyes, the sudden fear. She didn't know if I had or not. There was nothing, at least not that I had come upon, but she didn't know that and I felt a small, creeping sense of pleasure at the thought. Perhaps I could make use of that uncertainty.

I turned on my side and spit out words again in silence. Dammit, it all depended on whether there was indeed something. Derek could be right, I knew. There was always that chance. But I knew one thing without any doubt as I lay in the darkened room. The warmth, the welcome I had found here at Harbor House had been shattered by Nora's death. It wasn't just the hate in Matland's eyes, or poor Aaron's schizoid anger. I felt it in the air, in the very atmosphere, the communication of silent things that somehow make themselves felt with their own brand of ESP. But that would go away, with Derek's help. I was sure of it. I finally slept again but not before the gnawing, nagging and uncertainty poked and pulled at me once more. There was something still unknown to me. Something crucial I could not see yet, but certainly felt with an alarming strength.

CHAPTER FIVE

The house was noisy when I woke, half-shouts, loud talking and an air of people scurrying about. I heard Matland's voice from outside and I dressed, waking as I got into tan jeans and a cream jersey top. The day, as if the duty of daytime, paid homage to the clarity, reason, and logic of Derek's explanations. They ran back across my mind as I dressed with no new insights to add to what was said last night. But I felt a steel-spring tightness inside me and I hurried from the room to investigate the air of commotion outside.

Derek was beside the stairway and he came to me, pressed me to him in a quick, almost furtive kiss, unexpected but not unwanted, a brief reminder of the pleasures of the senses.

"What's all the excitement?" I asked.

"Minor crises, or perhaps not so minor. The goats got out of the barn. They've scattered, and Rudi's organizing a search party."

His words found an echo as the door opened and Rudi burst into the house. "Ah, there you are," he exclaimed. "Good, we'll need you. Damn near everybody else around here has one excuse or another."

"Easy, now, Rudi," Derek said. I heard the door of Marlyn's room open behind me and then another door—Aaron's—just down the hallway.

"Well, it's true," Rudi protested. "Marlyn's not feeling well, she says, and she's not going tramping about. Aaron's in one of his damn withdrawn moods."

Derek's hand was at my arm, steering me to the dining room. Rudi came along. "Stacy has to have some breakfast first, before you involve her in anything," he said firmly. Rudi grunted his agreement. Derek poured coffee and gave me a buttered muffin. I saw Marlyn shuffle in, her face unusually dour, only glancing at me as she poured coffee for herself. Aaron's thin figure appeared in the doorway and rested there against the molding, wrapped in his own solitude.

"Finding those goats is damned important. They supply us with milk when deliveries don't come through, and the best kind, too," Rudi said. "I hope there's no reason you can't help look for them," he added pointedly.

It was not what I wanted to do this day, but I'd alienated enough people here. I'd not include Rudi. "I'll help look," I said.

"Good," he grunted. "Father Hodges is asleep, so that leaves just you and me, and Derek. Una's busy cleaning the kitchen."

"What about Matland?" I asked.

"He went down to Bear Landing to see if a part for the pump has arrived," Derek said. "That was important, too."

"Here's how we'll work it," Rudi said as I finished the coffee. "Derek will circle to the east. I'll look north up into the mountains. You take the pathway west, Stacy. That's on beyond the barn. If they've gone that way, they'll pretty much stay on it, I think."

I nodded. Marlyn finished her coffee, glanced at Rudi who ignored the moment of apology in her eyes, and then shuffled from the room. Aaron stayed where he was, as if pinned to the door frame.

"If you find one, go up to it slowly, then jump it," Rudi was explaining to me. "Get it by the neck. They all wear small collars."

Rudi started for the door and Derek followed, his hand at my elbow. Aaron didn't move and I brushed past him, trying to meet his eyes, but he kept them focused on the floor. Outside, Derek smiled at me and I hid the annoyance I felt. Hopefully, I'd be back in an hour or so and be free to concentrate on the things I was determined to pin down once and for all. I turned and started out, walking quickly, pausing at the line of spruces to glance back. Rudi was out of sight already, and Derek was almost hidden, too. I saw Una Stenner, carrying a pail, leave the house and move toward the line of trees, her figure bent sideways from the weight of the pail. I went on hurrying, and slowed soon enough as the pathway became hardly more than a rock-strewn trail once I passed the small barn.

The land grew rougher, too, the trail lain over with stringy wood fern and tough lichen. On my left, the towering green wall of the mountains rose up, and to the right, smaller, less forbidding trees. I listened for the sound of goats as I trudged on, but I heard nothing. The wilderness closed in around me and made me know my insignificance. I didn't feel threatened, merely unimportant. Only the rudimentary pathway under my feet remained a link with the way I'd come, and I took care not to lose touch with it. I'd gone more than a mile—perhaps almost two—when I debated turning back. Would they have strayed this far, I wondered, and knew well they could have strayed further. I pressed on, angry at this time-consuming foolishness. I wanted to be at Harbor House, talking, listening, seeking some little thing to help me uncover the truth about Nora's death. Out here I would find nothing to aid me in that, and perhaps not even what I was here for, I was beginning to think when suddenly the trees grew wider apart and then I heard the sound, the unmistakable bleat of a goat—one of the young ones.

I rushed forward, pushing through brush and low branches and the bleating sound came again. I continued and then, unexpectedly, the shed came into view, if one could still call it that. It was barely recognizable as a structure that once stood straight with a roof and walls. Now the roof sagged like a swaybacked horse and the walls were no longer walls but a collection of planks hanging at all angles. It was long and narrow and had once been used for storing wood, I guessed. The goat bleated again, the sound coming from inside the shed. I followed it to what once was a door and now was a piece of wood hanging from a single nail. Sunlight streamed through the rotted and cracked boards and I spied the little goat, about halfway into the old structure. I moved toward it, the floorboards uncertain under my feet. I went forward slowly and the goat turned its head toward me, looked at me, and saw me but didn't move. It bleated again and I continued toward it, taking slow steps when the floor creaked loudly and I halted. The goat bleated again but didn't move and then I saw it's left hind leg pulled out straight behind it. It seemed to be caught in something, a crack in the floorboards perhaps. I wasn't close enough to see clearly yet and a length of wood had fallen from the roof and lay across the floor, partially blocking my vision.

I quickened my steps now and was almost at the little goat, peering at its hind leg when I heard the sound—a sharp crack, like the blow of mallet, and the other sound following immediately, the groaning, splintering, cracking roar of wood collapsing, breaking, falling in on itself. I whirled, saw the roof coming at me, the walls turning in on themselves and my scream joined the splintering roar. I whirled again, but there was nowhere to run, the entire old structure was collapsing on me and then I felt the floorboards tilt, rise up and pitch me forward. I was falling, the old shed coming down on me. I would be smashed beneath the weight of it, buried under it. I glimpsed the goat pulling free of something, then leaping, then a board slammed into my shoulder and then another hit across the back of my neck. The world turned orange, purple, and clouds of dirt and dust rose up and I was still falling, falling and the sound of destruction covered everything. Then I knew no more.

Later, life once again was felt in stages, small pieces of me waking, feeling, becoming aware of existence. There was no sound at all now, only the heavy, nose-clogging scent of dust and dirt. I tried moving an arm, found I could do so and then found I could half-turn my body, move my head to each side. I glanced around and saw that I lay inside a hollow of dirt that had been scooped out below the old shed by years of rain and melted snow. This hollow had saved my life. I would have been crushed by the boards of the collapsing shed if the floor hadn't given way, if it hadn't been there for me to fall into. I wondered, not incongruously, how many other creatures it had given shelter and life to over the long years. More than enough, I wagered, and now there was one more.

I looked up to the piles of rotted wood that lay over my head. I could raise myself enough to peer through two crisscrossed boards and see that the shed was totally collapsed, a few boards at the far end still standing. I sat still, letting thoughts drift back to me, reliving the moment of near death and a frown began to furrow itself across my forehead. Bits and pieces swam into place again, mere flashes intermingled with the recollection of falling wood and raining debris. I lifted myself, put a shoulder against one end of the board nearest me and prodded. It moved, surprisingly easily. I pushed harder and it moved again, another board atop it sliding down to push still another aside. I pushed again and more boards slid against each other, enough for me to get my head and shoulders up through the opening. I paused for breath and continued to gather thoughts as I surveyed the area just ahead of me. The goat had been there, only a few feet away, I'd been reaching for it and I saw the length of cord tied to the hind leg. The sharp, cracking sound had come then, breaking into my surprise, the malletlike sound—and then the rest following instantly. I hadn't time to look back at the goat again, but I had seen the cord on its leg. I was certain I had.

I pulled myself up now, through the opening, pushing aside more boards. Finally I was able to crawl out, shaking dirt and dust from myself, the air heavy with the smell of old wood dislodged. I began to push aside the pieces of wood that lay atop each other, a terrible certainty gathering inside me, giving me strength and anger. The goat had been only a few feet from where I now stood balanced precariously on a section of the flooring that hadn't given way. I yanked aside more boards, pulling, pushing, tugging, finally clearing away enough space to see the floor where the little goat had stood. I felt my breath suck in sharply as I saw the nail driven into the floorboard and, hanging from it, the torn piece of cord.

The goat had been tied there, put there so I would find it and go into the shed after it. And the sharp mallet sound had been exactly that—the sharp blow from a mallet at the right spot. It was all the old rotted shed needed to collapse it—a sharp blow at a cornerpiece—and the rest followed. I drew a deep breath, felt a sharp pain in my ribs where one of the boards had obviously hit me. But I wasn't supposed to feel any pain. I was supposed to be under the collapsed shed, killed in a tragic accident. I felt myself trembling as the enormity of it penetrated, the terrible power of comprehension, a kind of totality that overwhelmed. I stood still, took another deep breath, and ignored the pain in my side, and finally I stopped trembling, realization settling itself into a numb shock. Someone had tried to kill me. First Nora and now me. The same person? Of course, I answered myself, and knew that the answer was of itself an assumption. But it was an assumption I would hold to until proven wrong.

I clambered across the boards, over what was to have been my pyre of wood, and started back to the house. I wanted to go back consumed with fury, but all I could summon was fright and the awareness that someone had tried to kill me—a numbing kind of knowledge. I hurried back and realized the incongruousness of hurrying and yet I couldn't slow my steps, a kind of perversity, as though, subconsciously, I wanted to give death another chance. I remembered hearing once that we are all tempted to dance with death, to stare it in the eye and face it down, that terrible, frightening magnetism that pulls us to the edge of a cliff. I told myself I wanted mostly to present someone with living proof of their failure, which was a victory of sorts.

The road, shorter as all returning roads are, wound past the little barn and the line of spruces and then the house was before me, no less misshapen and ugly from the side. I saw Rudi come around the corner and wave at me.

"I found Old Billy and one of the kids," he called out. I nodded, wanting to respond with smooth blandness but suddenly a captive of distrust, the power of my emotions making even simple politeness impossible. Words were dangerous, possible instruments of exposure. It could have been any of them, I knew. Some had heard which way I was going to search and the others had ways of knowing, watching, getting there before me. I would let them all think I believed it had been an accident, except for Derek, of course.

Inside the house, I glanced about fearfully, like an animal afraid of its surroundings. Una Stenner's large form came out of the kitchen, a mop in her hands that looked to me as if it were a spear, a thrusting weapon. I met her quick glance and searched her face, seeking surprise in her cold eyes, but they were as expressionless as pieces of ice. Derek's voice, calling to me, came from behind and I whirled and almost flew into his arms. He saw the tension in my face and his question was instantaneous. "What it it?" he asked. "What happened?"

"Not here," I half-whispered and he steered me into the library, closing the door after us. The library was becoming a place for the recounting of death. The events of my last experiences were still vivid in my memory, and the words tumbled from me as they had when I had told Derek about Nora. When I finished, I was in his arms, my head against his chest. He held me until I finally stepped back and I looked up at him to see his face tight, his jaw set rigidly. He met my glance and let the tightness leave his face at once, bringing his hands up to cup my cheeks.

"You've had a terrible experience, the second one right on the heels of the first. That shakes anyone, Stacy. It's enough to set anyone's imagination going overtime," he said.

I stepped back. "What does that mean?" I asked with a frown.

"It means that no one tried to kill you, Stacy. That old shed has been ready to collapse for years. Your walking into it probably set it off," he answered. His smile was patient, gentle.

"No, I'm not imagining things," I protested. "Just before it fell on me there was that sharp sound, a blow from a mallet or maybe an ax."

"The cracking of wood can sound like that, Stacy—the sharp crack first and then the collapse at once," Derek said. I stared at him, hearing the sensibleness in his words, frustrating in their reasonableness.

"But the goat was tied there, I tell you. I found the nail and the piece of the cord still on it. The whole thing was planned, set up to kill me," I shot back. Derek's face was grave, his eyes deep, serious.

"Darling Stacy, that nail with a piece of string on it could have been in that floor for twenty years," Derek said. "Nerves can play tricks. Did you really—honestly—see the goat tied to it?"

"I *did* see it," I said, hating myself for the lie. I hadn't actually seen the length of string holding the goat's leg, but I dismissed that as unimportant, a mere detail in a larger canvas. I was trembling again, imploring him with my eyes, wanting him to believe me and he pulled me close to him until the trembling stopped. "Nora's death has set off all kinds of tensions," he said quietly. "The things Aaron and Matland said to you—that has to stop."

They're part of the whole picture, I wanted to tell him, part of why I know that shed didn't collapse of itself. But I said nothing, wanting time to find answers for the reasonableness of his words. The sound of tires on gravel made me pull from him, and the short sound of a horn barely touched drifted into the house. I followed Derek to the door and went outside with him to see Cary Brooks just climbing out of the jeep, the small goat in his arms.

"Found him wandering about," he said. "The collar made me think he was probably yours." His words were for Derek, his eyes for me. I brushed past Derek, taking hold of the goat's hind legs. There was nothing on either—no torn length of string, nothing but wiry fur and hard muscle. I looked at Derek, saw the patient tolerance on his face, and grew angry.

"It could have pulled off," I said, knowing how weak it sounded. Derek didn't reply, but Cary's voice cut in.

"Found him near that old shed a couple of miles from here. I came by just a while ago, after it had collapsed."

Alarm can be a cold caution, I found, and it whistled through me.

"How do you know it just collapsed?" I questioned sharply. No one could be trusted now. Except Derek. Cary turned a bland glance at me.

"I'd passed it earlier this morning and it was still standing then," he said. More reasonable answers, more moments of suspicion turned aside so easily. Cary's eyes were searching my face. I saw questions in them and I turned away. Distrust, confusion, uncertainty, they leaped about inside me like so many harlequins with sardonic masks. Did I distrust too much, now? Could I distrust too much? Was I that certain of what had happened? Questions that begged each other and held no answers. I shook them off and watched as Derek took the little goat from Cary. The two men stood for a moment, taking each other's measure, the wariness there again, like fencers who know each other's skills. Derek murmured thanks for the goat to Cary and I saw Cary start to swing himself into the jeep. I felt shame. I owed him my life, probably, and suddenly he was one more enemy—if not enemy, one more unknown quantity. It wasn't right, and the stab of shame I felt joined the other emotions that cavorted inside me.

"Thanks for stopping by," I called to him, trying to make the woefully inadequate phrase mean more. His eyes touched mine for a fleeting instant and then he was driving off, wheeling the jeep in a circle. He knew something was wrong, I was sure. He knew. But how much did he know, and how well? Suspicious thoughts were like an emotional cancer, rushing to spread and grow at the slightest opportunity. I followed Derek into the house, grimly angry at myself, yet holding onto justification for my distrust. I knew what had happened in that shed. I was justified in my distrust of Derek and the others at Harbor House. Justification. The word circled and became unhappily appropriate here where everyone felt they had their own justifications.

Inside the house, Derek called and Una came from the kitchen. He handed her the little goat and turned to me, the warmth of his hand finding mine, enclosing it securely.

"I'd rather you didn't encourage a friendship with him," he said seriously and I knew whom he meant. He caught the question leaping into my eyes at once. "Not till we know more about Nora," he said.

"You can't really mean that," I exclaimed. Derek's eyes held steady.

"I'd feel better about it," he said. "Just until I've had more time to look about. It'd be best, Stacy. I'm not implying anything. I'm playing safe, for you, for me. Or should I say for us?"

My head came against his chest. He was making sense again—too much sense to simply ignore. I'd trust his acuity here, with this.

"All right," I murmured. "But I'm right about what happened at the shed. It wasn't an accident. I didn't trigger the collapse."

"Get some rest, now, Stacy. Think about it some more and tell me later if you're still so sure about that," Derek said. His lips brushed my cheek, then found my mouth. Instant fervor, hunger, then pulling away. "You've become very important to me," he said.

"I like the sound of that," I answered and then, with a flashing, brilliant smile, he went off. I returned to my room.

I curled up in the stuffed chair and suddenly was very weak, drained, consumed with the need to think out every detail again. I wasn't being paranoid, as Derek had so gently implied with his words of reason and logic. I repeated the denial to myself and wondered why I had to do so. My glance drifted out through the window, to the towering green wall, the power of the soaring trees and I had to get up, knowing that I didn't want to think here in this room. I opened the door and started down the hall when

I heard Derek's voice, muffled, angry, coming from the closed door of the library. I couldn't catch his words, only the angry tone, and I remembered he'd said he would put a stop to the things that had been hurled at me. I halted, not wanting to eavesdrop, and caught a shouted phrase ... an *order* ... *won't stand for it* ... *don't forget who* ... and I turned away, retreating back to my room. I left the door open so I'd hear when the muffled sound halted. Derek was lecturing the others, angrily and severely, but I took no satisfaction in it because it was no more than that. He believed no more was necessary while I knew better. Or did I? The uncertainty again. I rubbed hands across my eyes, pulled the skin taut along my cheeks, stretching it as if, by that I could pull uncertainties into form. The sound halted then and I pushed the door open wider and went into the hall. I waited a moment as the others filed from the library and I saw Matland. He'd returned in time to be included in the lecture. When Derek was alone, starting up the stairs to his room, I hurried to him and saw his face was set, tight, as it had been when he'd seen Cary. He let it relax at once as he saw me approaching.

"Sometimes being severe is important," he said to me.

"May I borrow the pickup?" I asked. "I want to get away by myself for a while."

"Of course," he said, and then, "Be careful, Stacy."

"I will. I promise," I answered. His hand rubbed my face gently and then he went on up the stairs. I virtually ran outside to the little pickup and drove off. I couldn't have found the words to tell him what I sought now, what it was I needed, but I'd caught a touch of it that first day when I'd stood at Bear Landing. I drove, following the road, not caring where it went and I wound through narrow, tree-lined passages, between granite rock formations suddenly jutting out. I went on, letting the land surround me, press down on me and then the road rose sharply, widened and I glimpsed azure blue water through the trees. I pulled the pickup to one side, got out, and pushed through the brush to the lake. It was small but so hidden away, so beautifully alone, a slow waterfall feeding fresh water into it at the right. Young spruce edged the shores, like children with their elders standing powerful and tall just behind them. I found a rock, long and flat and sat down on it. A large bird, gray-black patterned evenly with white, a head tinted with deep green-black, swooped down to look at me. I recognized it as a loon. It made another pass and then decided I was harmless and glided down to float on the water nearby. I lay back on the rock and let this land give the strength and clarity I knew it could give. There was order here, uncluttered, simple order and a strength that was both savage and gentle. More important to me, it was a basic, root strength. Nothing here was ever permitted to stray too far from the essence of existence, the beauty of life and the end for survival. Nature rendered no judgments, Derek had said. She also permitted no untruths.

The sun was a soft shawl thrown over me, a gentle warmth on my breasts and I heard the sound of trees moving, a gentle, soothing noise, a conversation of leaves and branches. I cleared my mind of unnecessary thoughts and prepared to go over each detail, step by step, the first question both a beginning and an ending. Had I been wrong about the old shed? I felt my lips purse, grow tight. Had it indeed collapsed from my steps? Had the sharp, malletlike sound I heard actually been the crack of a last, remaining joint? Those were Derek's sensible explanations and they were too sensible to reject. But my own, inner certainty refused dismissal, also.

It could have happened just as he'd said. It could have, but it hadn't. I was certain of that. Perhaps I was uncertain of all the details, but not of the main fact. Reasonableness and perhaps even logic were all on Derek's side, the inner knowing all on mine. Hadn't he told me that we must include the illogical in the logical?

Someone had tried to kill me. It could have been most anyone. I began with Marlyn—first practical aspects, then motivation. She had gone to her room, but no one had actually seen her there. She could easily have slipped out the back way as I breakfasted with Derek. Was Marlyn the one, I mused? I had questioned the accuracy of her prophecy only last night. Had she decided to once again make another of her predictions come true, past practices returning with ease? It wouldn't have taken hate on her part, not even animosity. It would simply have been her obsession with making her predictions come true.

I paused, my lips tightened. It could have been Marlyn. The possibility could not be discounted. But, I recognized grimly, it could have merely been Marlyn's prophecy coming true by itself.

I put aside Marlyn and turned to Aaron next. He was seemingly harmless in his own two worlds. Yet he had thrown real hate at me last night. I remembered how silently he could walk. He could have gone off, silent and quick as a wraith, and been waiting there for me. In his own strange ways, he obviously held me to blame for Nora's death, and I was an outsider, he had said. Enough to murder for? Not to most people but perhaps more than enough for Aaron.

Matland took his place next in my mental notebook. The hate in the man had been all too plain, there even on that first day when he'd picked me up. Had it been hate or fear even then? He was supposedly down at Bear Landing, but he could have been waiting someplace, watching, ready to seize his opportunity. He could even have let the goats loose to prepare the trap.

I pulled Rudi into my thoughts, then. I couldn't define any motive for him; yet he certainly could have set the trap and been there to spring it. He was close with Marlyn, I knew. Had she enlisted his aid in making her prophecy come true? Or did Rudi have some connection with Elise Donner that only Nora knew about? Again, possibilities—all speculative, yet all demanding to be included. I could leave no one out or I risked letting death in.

Una Stenner came next. I thought of how I'd glanced back as she was crossing from the house with the pail in her hand. She could easily have disappeared into the trees, set down the pail and gone off. She knew this land, undoubtedly whatever shortcuts were needed and available. She would have had no difficulty in reaching the old shed before me and waiting there. Her motive was fear, I was certain—fear of me, of what Nora might have told me, fear of something concerning Elise Donner. It had been there from the moment she'd seen the letter to Elise in my hands, Derek's explanation of her overreacting was an unsatisfactory one.

The last of those at Harbor House was Father Hodges. I wanted to exclude his name at once. I didn't do so only because I'd promised myself to examine each one, each possible killer. Of them all, none had ever tried to kill, or even been accused of it, except Father Hodges. He had told me of the accusation himself, dismissing it at the same time. But he was subject to violent anger. Had his dismissal of the accusation been too glib? Had he indeed tried to kill the cardinal? I turned the thought over in my mind. Could Nora have known something about him and Elise Donner that made him enraged when he suspected she might reveal it to-me? It was the most preposterous of my little constructions, and yet I had to include it, for the moment, at least.

I'd come down finally to the very last, Derek's words about someone from outside. What if they had been right? Could someone from outside have killed Nora and someone from Harbor House, blamed me for her death, and sought revenge? Separate yet connected actions? It was a possibility, but I rejected it. It left out Elise Donner and the letter. It was too simple. But it brought me to Cary. I had vowed to leave no one out. Why was Derek so uneasy about Cary? Simple caution on his part? The wariness between the men came back to me. It had definitely been there. Simple, natural dislike—or something more? I was back on a carousel again. Only this time death rode it, too. I had as yet only one belief—the certainty that today had been no accident but an attempt to kill me. Had it been the same person who had killed Nora? Almost certainly, I told myself. It had to tie in. There had to be a connection. What was it Aaron had shouted at me? *There's always a connection. That you don't see it doesn't mean anything. Everything connects.* Perhaps he was more right than he knew.

I closed my eyes and drifted in a half-dream, halfwakened state, all that I'd gone over so carefully floating about in my mind as though if let alone it would assemble itself. And the persistent, gnawing something continued to mock my efforts to pin it down. There had to be a connection, I mused silently. Nora's death, the attempt to kill me—it had to connect. Perhaps Elise Donner connected, too, more importantly than I suspected. But she could give me no help. The letter had made it clear that no one had heard from her since before she'd left. The letter swam before me again, the last lines of it making themselves larger ... *What happened? Let's hear more ... let's hear something.* Elise Donner had left, but hadn't contacted any of her friends. She hadn't written since she'd left. The gnawing, ticking something exploded, showering me with a terrible coldness and I was sitting up, my fingers pressing hard into the rock, as though I could dig into it. The thought chilled blood ice-cold, demanding to be put into words, if only silent words. Maybe Elise Donner had never left here? Maybe she had never left this wild land? Maybe that was what Nora knew, and someone else was aware that she knew it? One killing usually triggers another, I had heard once. I swung from the rock, tiny beads of cold perspiration standing out on my arms. Horrifying as it was, it offered a connection.

It was a shattering, terrible feeling, and I walked slowly back to the pickup truck with it wrapped around me, a numbing cloak that refused to be cast aside. If I were right, if Elise Donner had never left here, then she had been the first victim and I was to have been the third. Things always come in threes, Aunt Catherine used to say. Even that fitted, I snorted silently. I slid behind the wheel, back into a circle, and started down the wandering road that had brought me here. I went over it again and it continued to make a connection, the only thing that did. But it was also clear that I had but one more theory—a better one, perhaps, yet no more than that. Certainly it wasn't enough to bring to Derek. He didn't even believe someone had tried to kill me and he was convinced Nora's death had come from outside. I didn't need more theory, I needed evidence, at least some substance to pull it together in a form he could respond to positively.

If the connection was truly there, if Elise Donner was the first piece, the key to the door, then there had to be a way to prove it. It had to be locked away in Harbor House, or in one of the people living there. I had to find a way to it—not just for Nora any longer, not even for Elise Donner, but for my own life. A shudder ran through me and the road curved, tilted and grew narrower. I slowed, almost to a stop to watch a hawk circling high, his flight slow, wheeling, patient, waiting for the moment to strike. The hawk was not alone in his waiting. Someone else waited for another chance to strike. I had to find the evidence I needed before then. I wouldn't talk to Derek about it till then, I decided, not if I could avoid it. I didn't want to hear his reasoned logic destroying my resolve, punching holes in the theory I had clutched to myself. They were connected somehow, I was certain, Elise Donner, the letter Nora had left for me, her horrible murder and the attempt on my life. Somewhere they all touched each other.

A rock jutting out made me swerve and I paid more attention to my driving. I was rounding a curve when I heard the sound of the other motor coming toward me. I slowed, pulled to the edge of the narrow roadway and almost came to a stop. There was hardly room for one car at a time on the road and then I saw the square form of Cary's jeep round the curve ahead. He drew up alongside me and halted, his grin affable but his eyes sharp, searching my face.

"What are you doing out here?" he asked pleasantly.

"I wanted to get away by myself for a while," I answered.

He made a mock frown. "And you didn't come up to see me? My feelings are hurt," he said.

"I said I wanted to get away *by myself*," I stressed. He reached beneath the seat and then his arm stretched out to me with my flashlight. I took it gratefully, eagerly.

"Came upon it as I was walking along the path," he said. "I assumed it was yours."

"Thanks," I said. I met his eyes as they continued to search, narrowed ever so slightly. His smile was a counterpoint to them in its determined blandness.

"Care to talk about what happened earlier?" he asked mildly.

"How do you know anything happened?" I replied defensively. I felt myself coming alert, that distrust I'd felt on returning to Harbor House flaming up inside me again.

"I have eyes that see. You have a face that says things," Cary replied blandly and my lips tightened. Simple, unarguable answers. I wanted to believe it was nothing more. I would remain guarded, weighing each word, examining each phrase. It was a time for distrust.

"Someone tried to kill me this morning, back at that old shed," I tossed out at him and waited, watching his eyes. Expressions shifted, a form undressing behind a screen again, revealing nothing.

"The same person who killed Nora?" he asked finally.

"I think so," I answered.

"What does Dr. Closter say?" Cary said, the question oblique, asking information more than commenting.

"He doesn't believe me. He thinks I'm being paranoid," I said.

"Are you?" Cold water flung in my face again, blunt, harsh.

"No." I threw the word back at him and Cary smiled, slowly, irritatingly and I knew he had caught the core of my answer, damn him.

"An interesting emotion," he commented blandly.

"What is?" I snapped.

"Defiance. It's a surrogate emotion. We call on it when we want to hide something else," he said.

"Like what?" I stabbed again.

He shrugged. "Fear. Cowardice. Uncertainty," he commented. "I'd guess the last one with you."

"Thanks," I said coldly. "That extra sensitivity of wild animals, artists and the mad again?" I wanted to strike, to uncover anger that could reveal more than itself. But Cary's gray blue eyes remained calm, cool.

"Maybe," he answered. "Speaking of extra measures, did someone try to kill you out of love? Did they try out of that extra susceptibility to the needs and hurts of others?"

Acid mockery, ordinarily angering. It was there in his words, the acid, yet he spoke softly and I had the feeling that he said them as much out of sadness as he did out of sarcasm.

"No, they didn't," I answered, "but I still believe in that extra measure. It's a part of it all, somehow, somewhere. It's there, it exists, and it's important. Derek says that those we call mad really have an extra measure of sanity."

"Tell me more," Cary said, a hint of the cynical in his tone. I recounted the things Derek had said to me, pinpointed the contradictions he had illuminated. Cary's eyes were small lights, his thoughts revolving around what I'd said when I finished.

"We're all mad, then, just in different ways," he tossed out.

"Derek didn't say it that literally," I protested. "He simply raised the question of whether our sane actions were all that sane and theirs all that insane."

"Assuming, of course, that it's all measurable on a Richter scale—mental earthquakes—small ones, medium ones and big ones and none at all," Cary said. He smiled, an enigmatic smile, as though he were laughing at me with a private amusement. Was he, I wondered? Private amusements, the handmaidens of private meanings?

"Do you define it any better?" I asked.

"Not right now," Cary said. Evasions, again, that veiled choosing of words I'd noticed before. A characteristic of his, I asked silently, or something that harbored other meanings? I couldn't help thinking of Derek's warning. It seemed ridiculous, absolutely so, yet I had to admit there was a careful, veiled quality to Cary. But as my dark thoughts slowly turned, I saw Cary's eyes fill with that concern I'd seen in them before.

"You will take care, won't you? You've a way of making people want to look after you, dammit," he said. I wanted to reach out, to put a hand against his face and express gratitude. But I sat unmoving, unable to shake loose of distrust, unable to gauge words any longer.

"Thanks," I managed lamely. I glanced around me and saw that the day had drifted into deep gray, blackness already taking over the interior of the giant forests. "I'd better be starting back," I said. Cary nodded. I turned on the ignition, waved at him and pulled onto the road, feeling his eyes watching me until I rounded a curve. I drove back to the house with haste, recklessness, as if tempting fate here might placate it somewhere else. The darkness had come before I arrived and I parked the pickup to one side and hurried into the foyer. I was glad it was one of the nights when there was no formal dinner. I couldn't have gotten through it. In the kitchen, small trays of sandwiches, tea and cookies were set out along the sideboard. I picked up a tray as Una Stenner entered and I found the boldness to meet her hard eyes. She glanced over me as though I didn't exist. A passing wish, I wondered, as I marched out with the tray. Matland was starting up the stairs with a tray.

"Please tell Dr. Closter I've returned," I said. The tiny cat's-eye pupils blinked at me. What was behind them, I asked myself. My only answer—silence. What was behind everyone here, I found myself thinking, the thought leaping through me growing increasingly important. Not just the highlights Derek had given me but details, the kind of details that might reveal the things I sought. Case histories would have them, I thought, growing excited.

"Where are the files?" I called to Matland as he started on up the stairs. He paused, looked down stiffly at me.

"Dr. Closter keeps all his working files in his room," the man said.

"No, not those, the original case histories of everyone here," I said. "Dr. Closter told me he had them. Where are they kept?"

"In the basement," Matland said and went on. I turned and hurried to my room, excitement running through me on tiny, invisible feet. Perhaps I'd found what I was looking for, a way inside those here, a way to analyze motivations, perhaps uncover some small thing that could lead to other things. Someone here had killed—once, twice, and tried a third time. The seeds of it had to be in a case history. And it was the kind of thing that, could I find it, Derek would listen to, I knew.

I ate hungrily, more than I'd realized, and downed the hot tea gratefully. The room had taken on a sudden chill. It wasn't me, it was the night that had turned cold. This great northland was beginning to send out its own warnings. Once again, they were strong, direct, without the deviousness of those warnings devised by humans. *Winter is coming. A time of danger and hardship lies ahead. Face it*, the land said. Perhaps it was speaking directly to me, I thought, offering not so much a warning as strength. I changed sweaters, putting on a light blue wool cardigan. I carried the tray back to the kitchen, went into the hallway and looked about. The house was quiet, everyone in their rooms. I moved down the corridor, to a closed door on the right. I opened it and found a broom closet. I went on, to another closed door, this one to a linen closet. Grimacing, I kept on to still another door, wider, and behind it I saw what I wanted, the wooden steps leading down to the basement. I left it open, letting the light shine down on the top half of the steps as I went down them, moving deeper into the darkness of the cellar. At the bottom step, in almost total blackness, I paused, peering into the thick nothingness. My eyes made out the dim shape of something hanging down from the ceiling, not far from me. I reached out, moved closer to it, felt the round smoothness of an electric light bulb. My fingers made spiderlike motions around the top of the connection and found the switch, pressing it and the light came on, a dim bulb, unshaded, giving off little light. Still, it was enough.

I let my glance roam across the basement, over old chairs, an upended canoe against the far wall, a few sacks of grain and emptied bags of burlap scattered about the floor and then, against the far wall, a single file cabinet standing beside an old, rolltop desk.

I picked my way across the floor to it, wondering if I could read in this dim light, deciding I'd take them all up to my room. I pulled at the top drawer. It didn't move. I pulled again. It refused. I tried the middle drawer and saw that it stayed shut, too. *Damn*, I muttered silently. The file cabinet was locked. I examined the lock, rusty, and certainly not too strong. Yet I hated to pull it open. Perhaps there was a key. I glanced down at the old desk alongside it, the green blotter atop it crumbled away into dustlike bits of paper. I opened the top drawer and it came easily. There was no key in it, but there was an old album. I lifted it out and opened it. I saw old newspaper clippings, odds and ends of articles, yellowed newsprint photos.

I picked up the first newspaper clipping, saw Derek's name on the caption. It was a report of a dinner given for him in Vienna, an award for a paper he wrote and I glanced up at the newspaper dateline. It was the *London Times* and I felt the frown pressing down over my eyes, my mind making automatic calculations. The date of the article made Derek almost seventy years old.

I felt drenched in ice, a jumble of thoughts I dared not sort out pulling at me, a stabbing moment, mostly of incomprehension but not without a terrible unnamed, undefined fear. I stared at the article, transfixed by it, when I heard the creek of the stairs behind me and I whirled. Derek was there, almost at the bottom step, his handsome face a dark mask of anger, his jaw tight, his eyes deep, blazing pits of black fire.

"What are you doing, Stacy?" he asked, frigid tones, ominous.

"I wanted to go through the original case histories," I said. His angry, tight face did not detract from his handsomeness, I thought almost incongruously. He was before me now, reaching out, taking the newspaper clipping from my hands. He looked down at it and then his eyes lifted to mine and he knew the questions that whirled inside me. He knew it and that knowledge was in the steady, piercing depths of his eyes and then his face, the severe anger of it, suddenly dissolved in a smile made of patience without instant forgiveness.

"My father," he said. "He was very ahead of his time. He started me on my own concepts."

"Your father," I echoed and felt so terribly small, so absolutely unworthy and totally ashamed of that fleeting, stabbing moment of panic.

"I'm sorry, Derek," I said, my voice very small, pulling my eyes from those deep, burning orbs.

"About what?" he asked mildly and I kicked myself inside. He let me avoid the need to reply by going on. "Why did you come down here to go through the case histories? I told you about each person here," he said.

"I know, but I wanted to go through the originals myself, through each detail. Perhaps there is something in them, Derek, something I could see, looking with a fresh eye."

"Something to help find Nora's killer?" he asked, his tone chiding now. My lips pressed together until they were but a tight line.

"Yes," I admitted. "I'm sorry, Derek, I still think it's all tied in with someone here."

"And with what you still claim was an attempt on your life today?" he said.

"Yes," I said, nodding again, feeling very small and contrite.

His hand reached out and took mine and he put the scrapbook back in the desk drawer. His arm went around my waist and he started to take me back to the stairs.

"You would have wasted your time, Stacy," he said. "You'd find nothing in those case histories. I know, believe me. There's nothing to find."

He started up the stairs with me, turning out the lone, dim light bulb just in time to hide the stubbornness that touched my face. I couldn't accept that, not even from Derek, not anymore. There was a blind spot in him. He was believing what he wanted to believe. The anger in his face just now had been proof of that. He wouldn't change until I faced him with things he couldn't turn away from. I didn't reply to his remarks and he went to my room with me. Inside, I faced him and saw anguish touch his eyes as his hands took me by the waist.

"No matter how it happened, Nora's death has upset me terribly, Stacy. It'll bring the outside world in on us before I'm completely ready for it. I only hope Harbor House is ready enough," he said. "I wrote the authorities today. I expect they'll be here by next week."

"By next week?" I exclaimed.

"Everything takes time here, Stacy, especially mail," Derek said.

Death doesn't take time, I wanted to say. *It comes swiftly, in the night, in clever traps.* I wouldn't wait till next week. I couldn't. Death wouldn't permit it.

"You're very important to me now, Stacy," Derek said. "More important than you know."

"That's nice to hear," I said. His eyes were deep flame, almost hypnotic in their intensity. His face came to me, his lips finding mine, pressing hard on my mouth and a rushing over me, a tremendous wanting. It had been like that with Philip sometimes, when nothing had gone right, a plunging into the senses, a shutting out of everything else but pleasure. It was always a temporary thing, but it sufficed, draining and filling at once. I thrust forward, meeting Derek's touch, the cardigan opening, feeling his hands against my skin, fingers running lightly over my breasts, tiny flames of excitement. I wanted him, my hands answering his, and then, abruptly, he pulled away. Once again, I saw him fight himself into control, his face finally touched with a wry smile.

'It's not that I don't want you, but then you know that, don't you?" he said. "It's that you're special. I want it to be the right moment, the right place, the right everything. I want it to be perfect, the way it must be, as perfect as you are."

I almost told him I'd be willing to compromise, but I said nothing and wrestled with my own need for refuge. His was a refreshing stance in today's world, a recognition of importances and subtleties. But that would be Derek, that extra sensitivity that was him. His lips kissed mine again, quickly, and then he was at the door.

"Get some sleep," he said. "We'll talk more tomorrow." He closed the door and I put the belt on and shivered, the coldness of the room rushing to embrace me once I was alone in it. I undressed quickly and pulled the bedcovers tight around my neck. Turning out the lamp, I stared at the darkness and knew that sleep was impossible. The dusty, old file cabinet formed before me in the darkness, standing in mid-air, mocking, taunting, telling me it held secrets to help me. And then I saw Derek on the stairs, the fury in his face, almost a fury of fear. Almost? I toyed with the thought. I had believed there were things here he could not see. He was blinded by his own feelings for the "guests"—Derek's own word—at Harbor House. The same blind spot parents have for their children. But perhaps there was no blind spot. Perhaps there was something he knew all too well, something he feared my knowing. The thought grew, mushrooming in my uncertainty.

Poor Derek, I felt myself saying with a rush of warmth. His eyes had held love in them just a little while ago, when he had held me in his arms. Was he trying to serve two masters? Was he trying to protect what he had so painstakingly built here, the meaning and very existence of his life's work, and protect me, too?

Was he trying to do what he felt he had to do, for his work and for me? Was he trapped in something? Other men before him had faced the anguish of being torn between conflicting demands. He was possessed by no immunity to that very human dilemma. I had to find out, not just for myself, but for Nora, and for Derek, too. I became certain that the answers, or at least part of them, lay in that old file cabinet, in case histories and detailed backgrounds. It was my own sixth sense at work, now, and Derek's face on finding me there. Or was it simply that I had no other direction in which to go. Whatever it was, need and fear had filtered too deeply into my thoughts to be ignored and I rose and dug into my things for a gray sweater and a pair of dark gray slacks. I donned them and hunted through my suitcase, finding a strong nail file and some bobby pins. Only pitiful tools, but they would have to do. I'd worked in enough offices to know that file cabinets had locks that succumbed to such things. The flashlight Cary had returned to me came next. I stuck it into the waistband of my slacks and then sat down in the stuffed chair, letting the house go to sleep.

Finally I rose and crept into the hall. I wouldn't risk meeting someone, or being heard opening the cellar door. Instead, I moved to the rear door, using both hands to open it noiselessly. Outside, the night air grabbed at me with cold hands and I stood still for a moment. The temperature had dropped sharply. I looked at the trees rising upwards, an endless procession, and I imagined I could see the yellow light of Cary's cabin somewhere up in the wild, dense mountainside. I had the urge to take the path and go up there. I didn't understand why the sudden urge tugged at me, only that it did, too strong to deny. The attraction to danger? Or the urge for sanctuary? I didn't want to analyze it. I moved alongside the house, staying close to the sides. A swath of yellow cut into the night from the second-floor windows—Derek's rooms—and I passed under it hurriedly. I moved on, around to the other side of the house, when I found what I was looking for—an access door to the basement lying almost flat against the ground.

A rusted handle hung from it. I leaned over and pulled. The door moved and I pulled again, short, inching tugs, risking no unexpected noise. Finally it was pulled open far enough for me to step inside it and I used my flashlight now, lighting a small flight of wooden steps. I closed the door after me, stood in total blackness for a second and switched the flashlight on again. I used the beam to spear my path across the cellar, lighting up the old chairs, three large sacks of grain near the far wall, and the old file cabinet. The light moved across it, from top to bottom and back again. It waited implacably, like an ancient carved god inside a cave, waiting for its secrets to be uncovered. I went to it and, holding the flashlight in my left hand, I probed along the upper edge of the top drawer with the nail file. I pushed the nail file in deeper, probing with it, finally finding the catch of the lock. Pausing to wipe my hands dry, I pressed hard with the nail file, working the slender edge of it along the top of the latch. I was about to give up with the nail file when I felt the tip of it catch. I moved it slowly along the top edge of the latch, twisting and pressing it at the same time. Feeling its tip pushing against the latch, I pressed it down harder and then heard the soft click as the lock snapped open. I pulled the nail file back and returned it to my pocket. The drawer opened reluctantly on dry and rusted tracks. Obviously, no one had been into these original case histories for a good while. The thick beige folders came into view and I gave the drawer another tug until it hung three-quarters open, enough for me to get at the folders comfortably.

I took out the first two and set them on top of the old desk alongside the cabinet. Then I let the flashlight find one of the old upended chairs, righted it, and set it down at the desk. I propped the flashlight on the desk, making a small lamp out of it, and opened the first of the folders. It was Aaron's—the name AARON LIEB neatly typed across the first page. Physical examination records came first, photostats of court orders, commitment papers, admission reports, the technical and clerical accompaniment to the human condition. I went through those pages quickly, impatiently, and then the section I wanted lay open before me, neatly typed pages recounting the attempt to understand a life.

I began to read each word carefully, analyzing each page and paragraph. It was a very thorough case history, including statements from his parents. When I had finised it I had a detailed knowledge of Aaron's history. But I had nothing more, the picture essentially just as Derek had told me. There had been nothing in the pages to hold itself out to me; no insights, no ingredients to help my search for a killer. There was a final page following the end of the case history. On it, written in hand, were brief comments signed by Derek Closter. "Acceptable," I read, my lips moving silently. "Schizoid prepotent reflexes, undoubtedly, yet he will fit into the connotive behavior pattern. Derek Closter."

I closed the thick file and set it aside. The next one was Nora's and I read it with the pangs of violating privacy. I pushed aside the feeling and began to read. Like Aaron's, her case history was thorough and complete. It was like his in still another way. When I'd finished, I knew nothing more than Derek had told me. On the final page there were a few lines again scrawled and signed by Derek: "Very acceptable. I'll be able to use this girl as a keystone in my work."

The files closed, pushed aside, I stood up and took the next two from the drawer. Rudi's was the top one and once more I pored over each word of the detailed history and once more there was nothing that held me, nothing to make me stop and wonder. I finished it and Derek's few lines of acceptance closed the file again. I pushed it aside. I sat back, rubbing my eyes, aware that they hurt—the flashlight too intense a circle of light. I waited a few moments, pressing hands to my forehead and then started in on the next folder. It was Marlyn's and it seemed the thickest so far, her background the most active. I felt the damp cold of the cellar begin to seep through me as I read, tiredness adding to the chill. When I completed her folder, a grimness had joined the seeping cold. The case history had revealed nothing I sought and I glanced at the few lines of acceptance at the close. Derek had indeed chosen each one with that singular character in their makeup. I had been right in calling it that extra susceptibility to the needs of others. I pushed away the two folders, stood up and took the last one from the file, that of Father Hodges.

I began reading again and saw that the folder included a number of statements from fellow priests and teachers at the seminary. It was the most interesting of them all. There were numerous references to his intensity as a young man. I tried to find a pattern in that, but soon gave it up as hopeless. There was nothing there to grip, nothing to help me, only that as a seminarian he had a pronounced empathy for those in need. Altogether, his folder was no more revealing than any of the others had been, and I finished by reading Derek's comments at the close.

"Am anxious to include this subject in group. Please make all necessary arrangements with the appropriate diocesan authorities," he had written.

I closed the folder and felt more than tiredness, more then the seeping cold. A despair gripped me as I stared at the thick folders in front of me, objects of hope that had so quickly become objects of disappointment. I half-smiled grimly. They were, in their own way, echoes of the lives they chronicled, lives that had been objects of hope and had become objects of despair, at least to those who loved them, bright fires into ashes, love into pain. Had I been wrong in thinking I could find answers in the case histories? Was it wrong to explain the present in the past? I shook my head slowly. Didn't all psychiatry seek today in yesterday? Aren't we formed by our yesterdays as a tree is formed by the earth, the sun, the wind, and the rain? There was simply no place else to seek.

And yet, I wondered if perhaps it was not *where* we sought but *what* we sought. Were we like explorers with lead weights attached to their shoes? Were we tied down by our own limitations, our inbred need to discover reasons we could understand, motivations we could grasp? Were we doomed to failure so long as we continued to seek the recognizable? I grimaced, knowing I was in unchartered waters, yet suddenly as dissatisfied as Derek with approaches to understanding. I'd found nothing to give me answers and yet something was here—it had to be—the knowing hard inside me. Dammit, why had Derek been so furious when he found me down here, I muttered to myself. Because it revealed my disbelief of his explanations? Not enough, I answered, not enough. Angrily, I gathered up the thick folders and began putting them back into the cabinet. I reached one hand into the rear of the drawer and felt the surface of another folder.

A little stab of something shot through me and I yanked at the drawer, pulling it out the rest of the way. Another folder was wedged into the rear of the drawer—as thick as the others, perhaps thicker. I stared at it. A sixth folder, but at Harbor House there were but five guests. The stabbing excitement grew, poking harder at me. A sixth folder, I murmured, and I started to

reach into the drawer for it, felt my hand hesitate, muscles replying to the mind, sudden spears of guilt. Derek had not wanted
me to see what was here. Perhaps it was best that way. But I had
already decided that he was perhaps as much in need of help as
I, perhaps a prisoner of his own blindness, a captive of his own
hopes. I reached for the folder, tugged at it as it stayed wedged.
I stretched, my leg pushing out backwards and I heard it strike
the chair. Twisting, I tried to catch hold of the chair rung, but
missed. The chair went over on its side, sounding like the crash
of thunder.

The silence that followed the crash of the chair was tomblike, that unique, apprehensive stillness, and I thought grimly,
not at all inappropriate. Then I heard the sounds overhead, along
the far side of the ceiling where it bordered the hallway, footsteps echoing clearly in the stillness. I learned that terror was
a thing of magic. It made my throat go dry as a desert and my
face wet with tiny drops that sprouted from my skin. The footsteps had almost reached the cellar door that led down to the
basement and I wrenched myself out of frozen panic. I yanked at
the thick folder, tearing it out of the place where it was wedged,
and then shoved the drawer closed. I heard the click of the lock
as it snapped back into place when the drawer shut. The sound
of the cellar door being opened reached me, the knob being
turned. I swept the light low to the floor, found the three sacks
of grain, and switched the light off. I darted forward, almost fell
against the three sacks and sank down behind them, trying to
fold myself into invisibility. The loud, pounding sound I heard
was coming from inside me, I realized. Footsteps were starting down the stairs and now I could see a dim outline from the
weak light of the opened door. The figure paused, then moved
down another few steps. I lowered my head behind the sacks and
waited, my breath a shallow trickle of air. I heard the figure pause

again and then the dim light bulb came on and I was grateful, now, for its dimness. A narrow, vertical space between two of the sacks revealed Matland standing on the bottom step. His cat's eyes traveled slowly around the basement and his neckless figure leaned forward, his head turned, listening for sounds.

My fingers suddenly hurt. I realized I was holding the flashlight so tightly they were cramped around it. Matland continued to wait and then, with a sinking feeling, I saw him move from the step and go down onto the basement floor. He walked slowly, peering first to one side and then the other while I drew on all the prayers I'd learned during those four years at Saint Theresa's Academy. I watched as he moved to where a group of the old chairs lay carelessly against each other. He halted and pushed out one foot, yanking one of the chairs away. One of the others fell on its side, the sound not as loud as the one I'd overturned but close enough in tonality. Apparently satisfied, the man turned and started back to the stairs. I watched his squat figure reach up one arm and switch off the light bulb and then, a dark bulky shape, move on up the stairs. I waited till I heard the cellar door close before I let breath rush out in quivering relief.

I looked down, not seeing but feeling the thick folder in my hand. I couldn't risk staying here to read it. He could return, the man possessed a stubborn suspicious nature. More important, he might go to Derek who would certainly return to see for himself. I had to be out of here. I rose, turned on the flashlight, holding it just in front of me, taking small steps in the little circle of light on the floor until I reached the access door that led back outside. I put my shoulder against it, lifted it a fraction, then a fraction more and held it for a moment as I snapped off the flashlight. I pushed against it again, enough for me to squeeze outside and held it until I'd silently let it close down again. The cold of the night seized me almost gleefully. The temperature had plummeted. I glimpsed the moon, high over the mountain, theatrical in its roundness and clarity, as though a part of some stage set. The file folder clutched to my breasts, I edged my way around the house, the light from Derek's window out now as I hurried beneath it and then to the rear door. I grasped the doorknob firmly and turned. Nothing happened. The door stuck. I turned again, pulled harder and the door continued to hold. *Damn*, I muttered softly. I put the folder down on the grass, reluctant to let go of it for even an instant, and used both hands on the knob. I pulled again and the door stayed shut and icy realization descended upon me. The door wasn't stuck at all. It had been locked. *Matland.* I swore the name silently. In his night rounds, he had latched the door.

I picked up the folder, holding it against me again, trying to keep down the moment of panic that tried to seize me. My eyes went upwards, to the black bulk of the mountain where Cary's cabin lay hidden. But I heard myself refusing, forming the silent words with my lips. No, not there. Not with the folder, certainly; not even by myself at this moment. It wasn't time for trusting, yet, not even with the concern I'd seen in his eyes as he left me earlier. Strangely, the only thing I could place trust in was distrust—one more distortion here at Harbor House, one more mirror that reflected the shadows, not the image. I stared into the black depths of the wall of trees a few yards away. Perhaps I could stay the night out in their safety, I thought. A wind drove cold needles through me almost as if in answer. But I hugged the folder against me. I had to go through it, to see what it was, this strange sixth folder. If I were deep enough in the forest, I could cover myself with leaves for warmth. I'd heard of that being done. Then, in the morning, I'd wait till the door was opened and find a moment to hurry back inside. But would there be a moment in the light of morning? I started toward the trees, shaking away the thought. There would be an opportunity in the morning, I told myself, with a confidence that was more desperate than reasoned. Inside the trees, I let my feet find their own path, afraid to use the flashlight this close to the house.

A wind swept through me again, carrying ice in its touch, harder, colder, this time and I halted, shivering as I stood. I shuffled a few steps further and knew I would spend no night in these woods without freezing to death. I had found no leaves under my steps, no sound of leaves, no touch of them, nothing I could make into a blanket. These forests were mostly pine, spruce, and hemlock, dropping a soft carpet on their forest floor but no blanket that could cover. Once more the wind grabbed at me, and once more I shivered. I turned and started back to the house. I had asked the land for strength, for purpose, only so few hours ago and it had given of itself and now it was being kind, delivering its warning directly. Only if I ignored it would it retaliate. Find another way, it said to me, for in the forest this path leads to death. A wry sound almost escaped my lips. Perhaps, now, every path I took led to death. I gripped the folder, holding it hard against me, clinging to what? A thousand speculations? An answer to what I sought to know? Or simply another reasonable explanation, meaningless, without consequence entirely. No, I answered. It held answers of some kind. Derek had not wanted me in these files. His anger had shown that. Was it because of this sixth file, this case history for someone not here?

I was back before the house, now, turning aside speculations, thinking of how I could find a way back inside. I let my eyes slowly go along the first-floor line of windows. The latticed ones were shut tight, I knew. I'd noticed that from inside. The others to the right of them led to rooms, Marlyn's, Rudi's, perhaps Matland and Una Stenner. I couldn't risk trying to open one. I moved sideways, following the line of the house, my eyes moving to the second floor. I despaired of finding a way in, and feeling the cold deep inside me now, when I halted along one of the projecting bulges in the house, beneath a Dutch Colonial dormer. The window was open from the bottom, the window dark, moonlight faintly glinting on the glass over the black strip where it was open. There was nothing along the wall of the house I could pull up on, not even if I had both hands free, certainly not with a folder in one. I stared up at it and it seemed to become an opened mouth laughing down at me with a black, toothless grin. My eyes moved from it along the edge of the dormer, tracing the edge of the roofline. A copper rain gutter edged the roof and I followed it to the corner of the house where it connected to the copper drainpipe that came down to the ground.

I moved toward it. Small bands of metal anchored the drainpipe to the side of the house, nailed into the wood. I followed it up to the roofline and the excitement gathered inside me. *Maybe,* a small voice whispered to me, *maybe.* A sudden gust of wind speared me with coldness and whispered something else. *You have no choice*, it said, *none but this. You cannot stay here, and there is no other way in. There's Cary's cabin*, I answered voicelessly, and knew that was no choice, either. I looked down at the file folder in my arms. I couldn't climb with it. I'd have all I could do to make it with both hands free. I held the folder away from me, my lips thinning to a tight line. Whatever secrets it held it would hold onto them a little longer. It was one more decision without choice. Poring through the folder would have to wait till tomorrow.

I turned and almost ran, crouched over, to the soft, turned dirt of the garden. I went to the edge, where Nora had spaded, and working feverishly, using my hands, digging and clawing at the earth, I buried the folder. Covering it then, I fashioned a row of dirt to match the other spaded rows and rose, perspiring though the cold air chilled me to the bone. Running, now, I returned to the corner of the house. Wasting no time, afraid something else might happen to make the night a complete disaster, I put my foot on the first of the metal brackets. It held and I pulled myself up on the drain. There was room only for the barest toehold on each bracket and I felt the pull on my calves, muscles crying out after the first four brackets, screaming after the next four. I was halfway up, breathing heavily, and I halted, feeling the sharp edge of the metal pressing up into the bottom of my toes. My shoulders were beginning to join the protest of muscle and flesh and I continued to climb. Each one grew slower, more painful and the edge of the roof seemed too far away, too high. I halted again, barely able to cling to the copper drainpipe now, my leg muscles trembling. From someplace, I found a reserve of strength, a wellspring of desperation, and I lifted myself upwards, my toes groping for still one more metal bracket and finally my hands felt the thicker edge of the roofline. I got a leg up onto it and found enough push left for a final, grasping effort. I lay against the slanted roof, my chest taking in deep, heaving breaths. I lay still until the trembling of strained muscles subsided enough to call on them again.

I turned my body carefully around until my back pressed against the slant of the roof. Using the drain gutter as support for my feet, I began to inch toward the dormer window, muscles protesting again. Night moisture made the roof slippery and I caught a half-scream as my foot went out from under me. The scream, stifled, became a shuddering gasp as I pulled myself back against the roof again. I moved on, more slowly, sliding myself along until the dormer rose up in front of me. Sinking onto my knees, pressing flat against the sides of the house, I reached around and got one hand onto the sill of the open window. I pulled, let myself come around in a half-arc and grasped the sill with the other hand. Clinging to it, I pushed my head into the open window, then shoulders and then, arching upwards, I used my back to press the window wider. Finally I crawled through it, arms outstretched, going headfirst down onto the floor to lay still, listening, the loud pounding inside me again. But there was only silence and I rose. I snapped on the flashlight for a fraction of a second, enough to see that I was at one end of the second-floor corridor. I started down it, moving on the balls of my feet, using my hands along the wall to guide me.

I finally caught the glow of a very dim light ahead and as I drew nearer I made out the stairway leading down, the light emenating from the few lights left on along the downstairs hall. I quickened steps as I passed the closed doors of Derek's room and then I was going down the stairway, moving fast now, into the hall below and then into my room. I felt the dryness of my throat again as I opened the door to my room and slipped inside it, latching it after me. My legs were trembling again, not from muscle fatigue now but from the weakness of relief. I dropped clothes to the floor as I sank onto the bed and pulled the cover over me. The room was cold, the night cold, I was cold. I couldn't separate the shivering any longer, relief, muscle reaction, simple cold and fear.

But I had gotten back to my room unseen and now even the shivering couldn't stave off the sleep of physical and emotional exhaustion. Tomorrow I would return to the garden. I would find a way to retrieve the sixth folder. Six folders for five people. Tomorrow would tell me why.

CHAPTER SIX

woke to bright sunlight and muscles that still protested, particularly those in my legs. It was still cold and I drew as hot a bath as I could and soaked in it, letting the heat and the wetness penetrate aches that seemed to shift about with deliberate maliciousness. When I'd finished I felt only slightly less wrung out, but any improvement was gratefully accepted. I dressed and went downstairs where breakfast was over but I found coffee and a lone biscuit.

Matland was clearing away dishes. Marlyn still sipped her coffee. She cast a bright-eyed glance at me.

"Morning, love," she sang out. "My, didn't it get cold last night? You did notice, didn't you?"

I glanced at her with sharpness, the paranoia of the guilt-ridden rushing to the surface, every innocent remark suspect.

"Yes, it woke me. I had to put on another blanket," I lied blandly. Marlyn's round face revealed nothing.

"It's going to be a hard winter," she said.

"Prophecy or just weather forecasting?" I asked. Marlyn shrugged.

"Same thing. I'm always right," she said. Her face turned fully to me, her eyes growing smaller, staring at me with a directness that was somehow veiled. It was almost as though she were evaluating me with a personal, special measuring tape. She turned finally and walked from the room, passing Derek as he entered. He came to me at once, cupping my face in the warmth of his hands.

"Had trouble sleeping last night because of you," he said sternly. I grimaced inwardly, words suspect again, the guilt instantaneous.

"Because of me?" I managed.

"Yes. I kept thinking about everything being perfect, that right place and right time. It could be closer than I'd realized," Derek said. His hands dropped to my shoulders, softly kneading fingers and from his eyes, a deep, dark lightning that would have surprised me had I not come to know it as part of him. He stepped back then and a gravity, almost a strained sternness came into his face. He smiled, but the smile failed to erase it.

"You really don't want to work with anyone here, not till this is settled," he said. Once again I felt that acuteness, that sensitivity that was so warming. I nodded, thinking of the real reason I wanted to be on my own and to myself. He didn't deserve being lied to, but maybe he'd thank me in time, I reasoned.

"You do whatever you want to do, Stacy," Derek said. "We'll talk more tonight."

He turned and walked from the room. I heard his voice calling Matland in the hallway. I finished my coffee and went back to my room. I'd already formed a loose set of plans, and now I pulled them together. I rummaged through my things for the big tote bag I always carried for casual moments. I found it and pulled it out. It was deep and roomy. I stuffed my note pad, a few paperbacks, and a sweater into it. There was still ample room to spare inside. Slinging it over my shoulder, I went out to the kitchen. Una Stenner was there and the woman turned her big-boned body as I spoke to her from the doorway.

"I want to tend to the garden," I said with a boldness that surprised me. "Where are the garden tools?"

"In the closet to the right," the woman said. Her eyes stabbed me with cold dislike and I turned away. Inside the closet I saw the gardening tools. I took the spade and the shears, putting them into the tote bag, also. I started for the door and saw Father Hodges in the library, writing a letter. He waved to me as I passed and I nodded back. I strolled outside, forcing myself to be unhurried and casual. I wandered to the garden, my eyes immediately finding the spot where I'd buried the folder. I sank to the ground some three or four yards up from it and began to spade the earth, uprooting small, weedlike growths, smoothing the soil after each overturned mound. Fighting down impatience that pulled at me with invisible hands, I finally reached the spot. I turned, moving so that my back blocked out any direct view from the house. I began to spade, furiously now, and felt the spade strike the smooth surface of the folder. I cleared away soil, spading with one hand. With the other, I pulled the folder out of where I'd buried it and pushed it into the tote bag I had lain close beside me. I draped the sweater over everything in it and then smoothed down the earth again.

I continued to spade and weed for fifteen or twenty more agonizing minutes. Finally I halted, picked up the tools and my tote bag and returned to the house. I put the gardening implements back in the closet and headed for my room. Aaron passed me, half-halted, his eyes going down to the totebag and the sweater on top and then he went on. I wanted to race back with my prize, excited triumph seizing me, but I forced myself to saunter casually. Only when I closed the door to my room did I explode in eagerness. I pushed the latch shut and dumped the contents of the tote bag onto the bed. I climbed onto the bed, sitting cross-legged, using the headboard as a back rest and took the thick folder on my lap. I opened it, annoyed at the way my hands fumbled, almost trembled. The first page, as on all the others, bore a name neatly typed. I stared down at it:

NORRIS KINCAID

Unformed thoughts speared me and I refused to heed them. I wouldn't entertain any thoughts, no more moments of wild panic as I'd had when I read that old newspaper clipping on Derek's father. I would hold back and read all there was to read, first, about this name *Norris Kincaid*. I rifled through the pages of the folder, passing over the judge's statements, rulings, the detail of commitment orders and all the legal detritus. I settled down with the first page of the actual case history and began to read, an anticipation of secrets to be revealed dancing in the lines in front of me.

"Subject, Norris Kincaid, aged thirty-four years," I began. "Subject is male, white, born in Pennsylvania. Norris Kincaid is above average height, an attractive, well-built, mesomorphic-structured individual. The outstanding element in the subject's case history is a background of astonishing brilliance and almost total sociological conformity. Prior to admittance to the State Hospital for the Mentally Ill, subject was given tests on the Binet-Simon Scale. He tested beyond the high point on the curve of the scoring scale. After confinement, subject was again given tests. CAVD tests showed absolutely no interference or impairment with intellectual functioning.

"Norris Kincaid is the product of an apparently normal or average environment and of comfortable economic circumstances. His father died two years ago and till then, owned a small chain of laundromats. Subject's mother is a woman of ordinary intelligence, entirely average in every respect. There is no immediate hereditary association with the extreme brilliance the subject showed at the very earliest age. His extraordinary grasp of things as a preschool child encouraged the parents to take him to a psychologically oriented testing center where he was, in time, enrolled in a school for gifted children.

"The complete conformity of subject background was borne out during the entire investigation of this case. The importance of this lies in its very unimportance. The case of Norris Kincaid indicates that there can be severe emotional disturbances without any important verifiable environmental elements. The items that were brought out during the investigation were far from conclusive, and their subtleties must be left to further evaluation.

"The subject, as a school-age child, excelled at anything he tried. He exhibited marked artistic talent, a mind for mathematics, a liking for the sciences. But most importantly, he exhibited a lightning comprehension of complex thought problems that astounded his teachers. In this connection, the subject was definitely held in awe by both parents and teachers though investigation indicates no preschool or early school emotional problems."

The case history began to detail the childhood of Norris Kincaid, his family's move to Philadelphia so he could attend a particular school, his daily home routine. Exacting research had been done and through it all, like the *leit-motif* of a Wagnerian opera, ran the theme of Norris Kincaid's astounding brilliance. I continued to read on, a life chronicled and capsuled in neatly typed lines, as all the others had been and yet, as I read, I found myself wondering if there was anything here but facts that revealed only themselves, that actually masked truth.

"High school and college records show continued brilliance," the case history went on. "Peer-group popularity seemed secure enough. Investigation revealed that Norris Kincaid was considered to have an unusual empathy for others. More significantly, investigation also revealed the subject, even in early high school, held a degree of selfesteem that was unusual, perhaps almost autocratic. At various times he was heard to say that he believed he had special gifts to bring to the world. At a family holiday dinner, he announced that he deserved to be admired because of what he had to offer the world. This unusual ego development has a marked associative relationship with a single incident that occurred when subject was thirteen.

"He had developed a tremendous affection for a girl classmate. Apparently the girl rejected him peremptorily and coldly. Subject continued to approach the girl who continued to reject him. One afternoon he waited for her outside the school and beat her until others intervened. All records pertaining to this incident were carefully examined. Subject showed no sorrow. Instead, he stated that he had wanted to do good things for the girl and she had turned him away. School records show that subject placed all the blame for the incident on the girl's attitude toward him. Under questioning, he did not dispute her right to reject, but her right to reject *him* and what he could offer her. For that, she needed punishment. She had to be taught that her attitude was wrong. The ego development association was disregarded by those present then, but to the trained psychiatric investigator, there is a definite relationship.

"The incident was finally forgotten and relegated to passing adolescent behavior. It was the only such incident during early formative years.

"Norris Kincaid graduated from the university with highest honors. He had excelled in every subject and teachers interviewed attested to his brilliance. Only one, Professor Herbert Breander, biology, voiced any reservations about the subject. Professor Breander told the caseworker that Norris Kincaid was so brilliant there was something frightening about it. It was as though, said Professor Breander, Norris Kincaid was laughing at the world behind his brilliance. Quotations from the remarks made by the professor are helpful here.

" 'Norris Kincaid seemed to be indulging in a very private joke. It seemed to me that his brilliance was both very real and also a facade, a front for something else. Frankly, the youth always left me with a rather eerie feeling—a personal reaction, of course, but one I couldn't shake.'

"In-depth investigation revealed that Professor Breander was one of the few people who received any such acute reactions to Norris Kincaid and he, of course, had nothing but his own emotional or psychic responses to go on. The remainder of the subject's formal academic training revealed no further evaluative instances. Interviews with classmates reveal only that he had shown a definite interest in social causes and worked, for a summer, with underprivileged families.

"When he graduated, Norris Kincaid received numerous offers from leading universities and businesses, many of them in the heart of the academic and business communities. It is interesting that he turned down each of these offers. The reasons he gave to most of the personnel people who sought him was the same one. A check of this revealed that he told each one, with minor variations, that their operation was too contained for him. He sought something and someplace that had more need for his talents.

"He apparently found such a place when he accepted the offer of a small college in northern Pennsylvania near a complex of modest suburban communities. He took up residence at the college and began teaching English literature from Chaucer to the contemporary writers. Subject kept fairly much to himself, staying out of the social life of the academic community. Fellow professors assumed this was due to normal shyness as a new member of the community. Subsequent investigation revealed that he had frequently gone to pools and clubs in surrounding communities and had become very close to a number of young women.

"He had been teaching there for almost a year when a number of rapes occurred in the surrounding towns. The assaults— six of them—spanned a period of about a year. In addition, there were two rapes in which the victims were killed—both strangled. The police had no leads besides the two unifying elements common to each assault. The attacker always wore a stocking mask which disguised both face and voice and each victim was told generally the same thing: 'You don't want me to do this. Fight me, deny me. You must, but I know what's good for you. I know what you need. I'm looking after your needs. I'm going to give you pleasure you cannot have anywhere else.'

"The assaults continued until the attacker made a mistake. He dropped a college I.D. card at the scene of one assault. It carried his name: Norris Kincaid. When police faced him with it, he admitted the assaults only. He denied the stranglings. No strong evidence could be found to link him with the two murders, though the presumptive evidence was obvious. The prosecution decided to convict on the basis of the six assaults and the two killings remain unsolved. Norris Kincaid was convicted. A court-appointed psychiatrist found him criminally insane. During the trial, the subject handled much of his own defense and, according to observers, presented brilliant philosophical arguments while admitting guilt.

"The trial judge asked Norris Kincaid for a final statement before pronouncing sentence. The subject's remarks, as recorded in the trial transcript, are as follows.

Kincaid:	Do you speak Chinese, Your Honor?
Judge Ford:	I do not and I fail to see what bearing that has on this matter.
Kincaid:	It is simply that anything I say will be Chinese to you.
Judge Ford:	Why?
Kincaid:	You will not be able to understand it because I speak a language you cannot know and I live in a world you cannot enter.

"Norris Kincaid was sentenced, judged criminally insane and committed."

So the case history of Norris Kincaid came to a close. But I found myself staring again at his last remarks to the judge. There was a familiar ring to them, an echo of other words. Suddenly I was hearing Father Hodges on that afternoon when he had told me about himself. *You cannot see through my eyes, feel with my emotions, and think with my mind.* I had scoffed at that, then, and thought I'd proved my point only to receive that gratuitous smile afterward. I'd thought, then, he had meant the difficulty of one person's understanding another's feelings, but now I wondered if he had not meant something far different. His words and those of Norris Kincaid were but variations of a single attitude, I realized with growing grimness, almost a feeling of alarm. Were we really those explorers with lead weights tied to their shoes, doomed to flounder about, moored by our own inabilities? Did the disturbed, the really mentally sick, live in a world we could not enter?

Weren't Derek's concepts almost a recognition, an admission of that, I asked myself. Wasn't his accommodation not so much a way of reaching that other world as a plea for the inclusion of it, the rational including the irrational? I had no answer, of course, but the folder on my lap had fortified one thing again. Even Norris Kincaid, the most aberrant in his behavior of them all, saw himself as doing good. Distorted and twisted as his actions may have been, it was clear that *he* believed he was helping the women he had attacked. They were unfortunate creatures in need of what he had to offer them—variations on a theme, again.

I turned to the last page of the folder to see Derek's comments, reading them with a grim satisfaction.

"I have decided to include this individual among those I have chosen for Harbor House," the words answered me. "The homicidal evidence was strictly presumptive and never proven. Although he is potentially dangerous, this subject's extreme brilliance and underlying motivation make him a tremendously interesting addition for my work here."

I closed the folder. Derek had been consistent in his choice of guests; each of them carrying, in his own way, that extra measure of empathy with the needs of others. But now I stared down at the closed folder and felt my fingers trembling. What I had read was terribly important of itself. What it meant to me was even more vital. But exactly what did it mean? Assumptions leaped about like leaves in a sudden wind. Conclusions presented themselves like so many puppets jumping up and down. They flew at me, raced at me, clawing, pummeling the mind, demanding to be sorted out. The few I could quickly sort out were antiphonal, answering but a part of the whole, begging the rest.

The folder on my lap seemed to vibrate with an evil of its own and I pushed it from me as one pushes away something suddenly distasteful. But it continued to glower up at me, a sixth folder. Derek had assembled six guests here, and now there were but five. Norris Kincaid was missing. He existed once, here, proof of that lay in front of me. He had been a brilliant mind and a convicted rapist—perhaps murderer—but Derek had seen more than that in him and brought him here to take his place with the others as part of that experiment in communication and understanding, that new accommodation for tomorrow. What had happened to Norris Kincaid? Had he been sent back? No, I answered quickly. His case history would most likely have gone with him then. That was the usual procedure.

Then—if he had not been sent back—where was Norris Kincaid? Alive, someplace? This thought slowed my racing mind. Was he here someplace, not in the house itself but somewhere near? Was Derek very much aware of that? Norris Kincaid had a base, motivational relationship with the others here, perhaps, but he was very different in other ways. Had he been Derek's mistake? Had the things Derek disregarded in accepting him proved to be of terrible importance? I was going in circles, I realized angrily. I had to stop, to make order out of chaotic thoughts, to bring form into being. I would construct possibilities, build hypotheses and see what I really had to go on and, fittingly enough, I would start with Derek.

It was clear now why he didn't want me poking into the files. He didn't want me to find that sixth folder. Because he feared what I would ask? Was Norris Kincaid outside of Harbor House, yet near enough? *Outside.* The word hung before me. Outside— outpatient? I rethought Derek's concepts of outpatient work as he'd explained them to me ... *a period in which the subject tests his ability to develop solitary self-reliance.... If you can adjust to yourself, to the inner-directed tensions of your own being, then you can adjust to any outside tensions.*

Derek's words, his beliefs, and I'd been unable to accept them, then, I recalled. Was Norris Kincaid alone somewhere in this rugged land, an outpatient testing Derek's theories? Had he failed that period of self-adjustment? Had those inner-directed tensions overwhelmed him? Was that what Derek knew? The questions raced after each other, now, and I thought of Elise Donner. Where did she fit, I mused. But my construction was building itself, now, adding pieces with a momentum of its own. Had Norris Kincaid killed Elise? The frightening possibility gathered its own logic. Is that what Nora knew? Is that what she had wanted to warn me about? Was Norris Kincaid, a homicidal killer, somewhere in the deep mountain forests, watching, staying out of reach, waiting. Had he been watching me? Had he seen his chance at the old shed? And what of Derek? Did he suspect? Was he trying to buy time to find Norris Kincaid? It was a dangerous purchase, then, a grim rigadoon with a homicidal maniac. But it was all so very possible. Derek would want to find him on his own, to put an end to everything without bringing the authorities in. He would, perhaps, feel bound to correct his one failure.

I stepped back, figuratively, putting aside that first construction as a child puts aside something it has built to build another. I sat back and began again, shifting pieces, the same pieces but fitting them together in different ways. What if Norris Kincaid had not been an outpatient at all? What if he had simply run off one day, fleeing into the wild land, Derek's failure? What if he had stayed beyond capture, living off the land in his own ways while Derek waited, hoping he would return? The construction moved on under its own direction, now. Elise Donner had left, for the reasons Derek had explained, and he had said she'd insisted on going on her own. Then letters came from friends, complaining they had not heard from her. Derek would have feared the worst, then. With his knowledge of Norris Kincaid's background, he would have suspected that Elise had been seen leaving, followed, attacked and slain, somewhere in this wild, silent land so capable of swallowing up everything.

Derek had waited then, I went on building, and finally decided that Norris Kincaid had finally fled entirely or had perhaps succumbed to the wilderness. He hired me, and Nora, for her own reasons, wanted to warn me of what had happened to Elise. She was going to tell me at the spot she had chosen for our meeting. But neither she nor Derek knew that Norris Kincaid had returned, or never really left, and he saw her and acted. Derek would have realized what happened then. I recalled the sternness of his face as I told him of Nora's death. It would also explain his certainty that none of the guests here at Harbor House had been responsible. And the attempt to kill me? Norris Kincaid again, of course.

I put that construction beside the first one and began still another, this time starting from another point entirely, the fear I had seen in Nora's eyes. It had been real, vivid. She had feared someone here at Harbor House, not Norris Kincaid. The certainty in that was sobering and made its own pathways in the mind, taking me far from the other theories I had built. Two things—two facts—leaped up as one. Norris Kincaid had been a part of Harbor House once, but Nora's fear had been of the present—of someone here now. I decided to play at reconstruction for a few moments. Norris Kincaid was Derek's outpatient, living not too far away in the solitude of this wild land. But Elise Donner had indeed been killed—not by Norris Kincaid, but by someone else here at Harbor House. When the letters to Elise came, Derek had grown suspicious— even fearful—but he had nothing to go on. But Nora knew the identity of the real killer. Perhaps he confided in her. When I came, she first tried to warn me that things were not all what they seemed here at Derek's Eden. Then the killer struck when she went to meet me. And then tried to kill me. Nora's death had turned Derek's fears into certainties. But he looked in the wrong place, now. He suspected Norris Kincaid of recedivism when the real killer was here at Harbor House.

I set this premise with the others I'd built and went to my last thought. Derek simply didn't believe it was anyone he worked with here. He insisted on believing it was an outsider, a passing trapper. But he didn't want me to know about Norris Kincaid, and especially the man's history, afraid that I would come to only one conclusion. He was a prisoner of his own involvement. To face the fact that the killer was here—part of Harbor House and his work—was to face more than he could. No one likes to face failure and, if he faced the truth, that someone here was a killer, it would mean that his concepts held deep flaws.

I unfolded myself abruptly, standing up angry, and unsatisfied. I had built a series of theories and in reality they were no more than that, speculation on top of speculation, a child's game. Only death was a player in this game. Everything I'd put together was possible, yet in each one there were gaps, pieces that refused to fit properly. Una Stenner was one such piece. The woman had feared my seeing the letter and Derek's explanation of her overreacting to his orders was even less satisfactory now. Matland's hostility—where did that fit? It had been present from the very first moment of my arrival, before there had been any letter to Elise Donner. It had another basis of its own. That I was the outsider? I shook away the reason. It was too simple. He feared my presence here. Because he and Una Stenner knew of Elise's death? Because they were involved? What about Cary and Derek, facing each other with wariness too real to have been a product of my imagination. Where did that fit? Did it mean anything other than natural dislike? Derek had told me to stay away from Cary till this was all settled. Did he really include Cary as a suspect?

Did he know more about Cary than he let me know? What did he know about Norris Kincaid and never reveal?

Finding the file on Norris Kincaid had set me off into building constructions involving the missing man and Elise Donner. But they had no room in them for these other things, those pieces that wouldn't fit neatly, and with all that I'd fashioned, only a few pieces could stand unchallenged. Something had happened to Elise Donner. That was becoming more and more clear. Nora had known and had been killed for her knowing. There had been a sixth guest at Harbor House, Norris Kincaid. Whether he still existed or not, he had been a part of this place once. I felt my hands curl tightly as I thought of my third possibility. If I were right, if Norris Kincaid lived as an outpatient not too far away in actual innocence, then the real killer lived here at Harbor House now.

I rose, the grimness settling upon me again. I put the file folder at the very bottom of my suitcase and covered it with sweaters and slacks. I'd find a way to return it when this was all over. Thoughts turned to Derek again. Would it be simplest and best if I just told him what I'd learned, that I knew about Norris Kincaid? That was what I wanted to do, rush into his arms and tell him what I'd learned and that I understood his inner conflict. But I recalled the cold fury in his face when he'd found me in the basement and I realized I could say nothing yet. All I'd be telling him is that I had disobeyed him, that I had no faith in him, and he didn't need more hurt now. I had nothing to make him listen to me, nothing but theories I'd constructed upon learning of Norris Kincaid. But Derek already knew all there was to know about Norris Kincaid, and he still hadn't believed someone had tried to kill me. Stubbornness, blindness, whichever it was, it wouldn't be pierced simply by revealing that I'd learned of Norris Kincaid.

No, I assured myself. I stared at my suitcase, envisioning the folder hidden under the clothes in it. The file had helped me fill in pictures—enough for myself, but not enough for Derek. Not yet, not without something more that would make him see what he refused to see or could not see. I had to probe further, to question more, to find a new jumping-off point. I thought of where to start and whom to start with. I suddenly realized that boldness is not a base character trait but a flame that flares, fed by the coals of desperation. I'd talked to the others but never really to Una Stenner. The thought grew quickly. It might well rattle her— perhaps trip her into saying something revealing. It was worth the try, if only to see the woman's surprise. I turned quickly and went into the hall, hurrying down toward a stream of afternoon sun cutting across a hall window. I was almost at Marlyn's room, about to step through the yellow barrier of sunlight when I heard Derek's voice, then Marlyn's and I halted, rooted to the spot. Derek's tone was low, confidential, almost conspiratorial, and it flung shock at me. Not just because it was an unexpected moment, but because of what his tone said. It seemed to me to be a step across an invisible line. Derek's relationship with the others here was unique, the result of careful work on his part and I'd realized that my first day here. Yet with it all, I'd always felt there was a line—the subtlest of distinctions perhaps—yet there, known to all and intrinsically observed by all. Calling them into the library and lecturing them angrily had been an example of that line. "Sometimes being severe is important," he had said to me then. Was being confidential important, too, I asked myself. I wanted to accept the answer and couldn't. The two things were not the same.

"Have you come to it yet?" I heard Marlyn's voice ask.

"Yes, I'm about ready," Derek said, a soft reluctance in his voice.

"I think you're running out of time," I heard Marlyn answer.

"I'll decide that," Derek said in quiet firmness. "Things went too fast, not the way I wanted."

"Nora's fault, that," I heard Marlyn comment.

"Mostly," Derek answered flatly. "I'll have to move soon. Very soon."

I heard Derek turn, his footsteps coming toward the door and his words a last aside to Marlyn. I shrank back, then turned and fled, passing my room, down the hall to the rear door, opening it and slipping outside. I hadn't been certain, and once outside I halted to draw a deep breath of cold air. The brief exchange burned inside me. "I'm about ready," Derek had said. Ready for what?

I heard Marlyn's answer again. "You're running out of time."

Running out of time for what, I asked myself. Time to move against Norris Kincaid? Or someone else? Did Derek know the killer? The question clawed, flung itself at me with a silent scream. Had he known the killer all along and been holding back? Had he hoped to work small miracles? Had he been playing a terrible, dangerous game? Or had he simply hoped against hope about one of his "children"?

If so, then why the shared confidence with Marlyn? It was Nora's fault, the woman had said, and Derek had half-agreed. Nora's fault that she'd gotten herself killed? That she had precipitated something Derek had wanted left alone? Or that they *all* wanted left alone? Suddenly, the shared confidence made its own kind of sense. Was there a terrible secret Derek shared with the others and all wanted it kept that way?

I began to walk, almost as though in a daze, into the trees and the shadows there made the cold bite more. I didn't care. I was almost numbed from the realization that what I'd heard put an entirely different picture on Derek's involvement. Did he intend to keep his secret, *their* secret, whatever it was, however terrible it was? Was he getting ready to move to do what he should have done long ago, apprehend the killer? I felt my lips form a tight line. The next question tore itself from me with its own anguish. Was Derek trying to shield me from everything until he brought in the killer himself, or was he trying to cover up all that had happened with one more secret? The latter was all too possible, given Derek's intensely personal stake in all he had built here at Harbor House. To take care of one's own failure, to clean one's own house, would remove the need for the authorities. Explanations could always be found, stories concocted later.

I halted, leaned against a thick white pine, felt the roughness of its bark press into my back. It was a strangely reassuring touch—solid, real, a little painful, but a pain one could grasp, know, recognize. I had been fighting with shadows too long. The distortions of Harbor House were indeed distortions and they had engulfed Derek, too, I realized, the creation absorbing the creator. Or is it always so? The exchange with Marlyn, the quiet confidences back and forth, had added still another construction to my others, the most terrible of all because it made Derek into a prisoner instead of a knight in armor.

A wind curled around me and I looked up at the sky. It had turned gray with long, delicate pink streaks at the edges and I let my eyes move down to the forest stretching before me. I glimpsed a hare leaping through brush to his burrow. The wind wrapped itself around me again and I shivered, glanced up at the sky once more and saw it change as I watched, growing bleaker, the pink edges turning purple and suddenly it was a Sibelius symphony, all of it—sky and land and endless mountains, bleakly beautiful, austere, uncompromising. It was a part of—yet apart from—all that mere men could wreak. Suddenly I knew what I would have to do, the only thing left for me. I would run to it. I would ask refuge of it as I'd asked strength of it. I would flee Harbor House, flee Derek, flee my own fears.

It would be best that way, for everyone, and perhaps especially for Derek. My coming here had obviously not worked out as he had planned; his quiet words to Marlyn had said as much. But more important, I couldn't stay here any longer. It was suddenly crystal clear with a clarity that frightened and sent shudders through me. I was afraid, not only for my own life, for what was now the unknown, but for whatever I might unwittingly trigger here. My presence here had caused Nora's death. I hadn't faced the ugly truth of that till now. She had wanted to help me and had been killed for it. Had I not come here, she might well be alive now. The secret of Harbor House, whatever it was, would have stayed secret. And now I was the one who could endanger that secret—the outsider—to someone who wanted that secret kept inviolate. Derek had brought me here, knowing of the secret of Harbor House, but hoping it was buried and done with. But my coming here had made it come alive again.

I realized one thing more. I had made my own harbor here at Harbor House, and its name was Derek. With his sensitivity, his acuteness, intense brilliance, he had become my refuge first, something much more later, and now I felt something that edged betrayal. I didn't know what Derek believed or didn't believe anymore. I didn't know how deep his blindness went, or how far he would go to protect his work here. I only knew I couldn't toy with speculations any longer, building theories while the killer moved closer to his next try at finishing me. Or her next try, I added grimly. Derek had suddenly turned into a kind of stranger, yet one I wanted to run to and cling to protectively. The heart is indeed an incongruous piece of machinery, I thought.

A small gray animal leaped from the brush nearby and I almost screamed. I closed my eyes and drew a deep breath. My fear was more thoroughly into me than I'd realized. I pushed myself from the tree and, under the lowering sky of the day's end, I returned to the house. I made plans as I walked, grateful for the mind-filling character of prosaic thought. I'd wait till the night was deep enough, then take the pickup truck and flee with it.

Bear's Landing would be no hiding place, but there would be someplace else farther south. I'd find a map and study it. I had almost reached the house when I turned and gazed up at the mountain in the flickering last daylight. Would Cary Brooks's cabin be a place to hide? I paused, wondering, then turned away. No, I could trust no one now, neither the most unlikely nor the most likely. I was alone, but there was a certain grim safety in that. I almost laughed at the thought. Once, only such a very short time ago, I would have said that safety is being held, protected, yes, loved. And now it was being alone—one more distortion here at Harbor House.

I opened the door and went inside to see Derek turn in surprise from Father Hodges, the two men standing in the foyer, Father with a packet of letters in his hands.

"Well, hello. I thought you were in your room, resting." Derek said, his smile quick, a soft tenderness in it, making me feel instantly unworthy.

"Hello, Stacy, my dear," Father Hodges added. I nodded back.

"I was in my room; then I decided on a walk," I lied. Derek's eyes went over the light sweater I wore.

"It's gotten too cold to be out long in just that," he said, concern in his deep eyes. Father Hodges interrupted, giving me time to think of a reply.

"I'll see you later, Derek," he said. "We can talk about the philosophy of impatience, then." Derek smiled his agreement and then his eyes returned to me.

"I wasn't going to stay outside long," I said. "I met Cary Brooks and he took me for a ride in the jeep. It was warmer there."

"I see," Derek said and I caught the instant of displeasure that touched his face. I hesitated; then, boldness being an infectious thing, plunged on.

"Do you really suspect Cary Brooks of being a killer?" I tossed out. Derek said nothing for a moment, his eyes holding mine. Then his hands reached out to cup my face.

"I'm not going to say any more on that now, Stacy. But I will, soon. Till then, please stay away from him," he said, and his eyes became soft, tender depths of unstated meanings. It had been clear again, the warning without a direct accusation. Why, I wondered. Because he really didn't know? Or because he did? Derek's hands dropped from my face and his smile exploded, dazzling, pulling me to him with its warmth. I felt his mood change, that vibrant, compelling intenseness taking hold of him again.

"Soon you'll understand a lot more, Stacy," he said with an almost airy cheerfulness. "Till then, just trust me."

Trust. I swallowed the word. Trust when I was filled with distrust. There was no room, not even for him. Yet as I stood before him I knew I wanted his arms around me, his lips on mine, his warmth and protectiveness. Distrust and need, an uneasy coexistence and then, as if in answer to my silent thoughts, his lips pressed mine, his hands finding my breasts. I clung, for a moment, and this time I was the one who drew away, afraid of my own weaknesses.

"I'm sorry, Derek. It's just that I'm on edge." I groped out the words and saw his smile broaden.

"I understand. And it's better that way," he said. Better? I wanted to ask, but I knew what he meant. At least I thought

I did. That perfect moment and right place he had spoken of the last time we kissed. He turned, blew me a quick kiss, and was off down the hall. I wanted to race after him, to tell him I had heard his talking to Marlyn and that I believed in him, that whatever he had decided was right. But my legs tightened, held back, and I stayed where I was. As the creation can absorb the creator, so can distrust absorb the fearful and I gathered all my turbulent emotions around me and harnessed them again into the one avenue that offered any real clarity—flight—a flight from so much more than simply physical fear.

I pressed my arms to my breasts and glanced around me and saw the walls of Harbor House seem to lean down toward me as if to challenge my resolve and cry out that there was no escape from anything for me. Suddenly I had some recognition how those in a sanitarium cell felt—the walls not merely walls but curving in on one, oppressing not simply the body but the spirit and the mind, adding to whatever else throbbed in disturbed minds, the terrible supplement of resentment. Derek was right. There had to be a better way.

I wrenched myself from the spot and went to my room where, in the dimness, I stood at the window and watched night throw its noose over the day and stuff it into its black sack. Fear stole upon happiness in much the same manner, I thought, silently slipping a noose over it and taking command. I turned from the window and lay down on the bed, waiting till the dinner hour was over, forcing myself not to think, to keep my mind in a state of blankness. Questions kept trying to slip into my consciousness, stray thoughts, probing little spears of the psyche and I busied myself fighting each one away until finally the hours drifted on. I rose, then, and went down to the library, scanning the shelves with quiet desperation. I finally found what I sought not on the shelves but tucked away in a magazine rack. I opened the atlas, glanced quickly at it, and then made off to my room with it. I glimpsed Una Stenner as she stepped from the kitchen, her eyes sharp as they swept over my receding figure.

Once in my room, I opened the atlas and, using Bear Landing as an orientation point, I traced a line, avoiding the heart of the Talkeetna Mountains, circling eastward to a place called Tyone, then moving south to Nelchina and then west again to hook up with the Glenn Highway that finally ended in Anchorage. I could do it, given a little luck and a minimum of wrong turns, I told myself. Many of the roads would be hardly passable, I knew, but I'd stay with them to safety. But distances here would be bound by conditions and travel time. I would have to be prepared for the unexpected, detours, delays, road problems. I put the atlas on the bed and turned out the light, then slipped into the dark hall. I crept along the wall and saw that the kitchen was dark, just enough light entering it from the hallway to let me see my way about. I opened closet and cupboard doors silently and poked about. I wasn't trying to outfit myself for the entire trip. At one or another place I'd be able to pick up more supplies. I wanted only enough for an emergency. I found a box of chocolate bars and took it, then a container of biscuits. A tin of prepared luncheon meat was next, equipped with its own opener. I took some tea bags and envelopes of instant coffee and a Thermos jug I found. My arms loaded with stolen booty, feeling determinedly immoral, I hurried back to my room.

I put everything on the bed and got out the tote bag. I put everything in it, added as much clothing as it could carry and the atlas. I would take only the bag. I wouldn't risk being met carrying out my suitcase. Finally, everything readied, there was only one thing left to do. I took a sheet of stationery from my suitcase and wrote the note:

Dear Derek,

Please forgive me. I am running. I've learned too much not to fear and not enough to trust. I think it's best this way. Call it my way of including the irrational in the rational.

Maybe, sometime later, we'll both know more and understand more. I'll be in touch.

Love…. Stacy.

I creased the single sheet of paper and placed it atop my suitcase. Going to the closet, I put on a heavy sweater, slung the tote bag over my shoulder and stole from the room. I went out the rear door, moving carefully. It was not all that late yet, but I was driven now by the desperate desire to flee—a tugging, churning impatience that fed on itself, telling me that I was in danger. I'd known that all along, of course, since that collapsed old shed. Now everything had come together to turn knowledge into fear.

The night air speared me with its cold dampness, and I glanced up quickly to find the sky hidden by clouds, the distinct feel of snow in the air. Another of Marlyn's predictions coming true of itself? I shifted the bag on my shoulder and hurried on. I wouldn't wait to test her abilities any further. Hugging the side of the house, the lights on in Derek's room, I made my way past the front door and turned the corridor to where the pickup truck was always parked at the left side of the house. I halted, feeling my stomach muscles contract, pulling in as though a fist had rammed itself in them. The pickup was gone! I stared at the dark emptiness as if, by concentrating, I could make materialize the short, squat shape I wanted to see there. But only the darkness stared back at me.

My stomach drew itself in again, short, tight motions of the abdominal muscles. The little truck had been there earlier. I had seen it. Perhaps it had been put into the little barn. I let hope leap up in thought. Perhaps because of the threat of early snow it had been put there. I began to run around the end of the line of trees hiding the little barn, trying to keep the leaden weight that had formed in my stomach from growing. The barn waited, a small bulk in the dark night and I yanked at the doors. The truck could just fit inside it. The one door came open and I peered into the blackness beyond it, letting dark shapes form themselves. I heard the sound of small hooves coming toward me and I closed the door. The barn was empty, the truck not inside it. I felt denied, suddenly stripped naked.

I stayed for a moment against the barn, leaning on it, and as curdled milk turns sour, I felt a sourness inside me turning into a sick nausea, as despair wrapped itself around me. Some people carry despair as part of their emotional baggage. They are quick to call on it, familiar with the feeling. I was never one of them. I was unfamiliar with the feeling, the constricting, total hopelessness it brought and I felt physically sick. I pushed from the barn and started back to the house. As I rounded the line of trees I looked again for the little pickup, as though it would magically appear, as though I had somehow missed seeing it the first time. The yawning emptiness laughed back at me and I halted before the house. It seemed to look down at me in silent triumph. I disdained going to the rear door, a sudden moment of bitterness pushing at me, and I went in through the front. I was in the foyer when I heard a door opening, from upstairs, Derek's room. I took the few strides to the darkened library, pushed the tote bag behind the door and returned to the hall as Derek came down the stairs. His eyebrows lifted as he saw me.

"Felt like a little night air before turning in," I lied. "I stayed close to the house."

Derek's eyes were bright dark lights, looking at me appreciatively. "That's good," he commented. I decided on boldness again, bitter disappointment prodding a certain recklessness.

"I noticed the pickup is gone," I remarked.

"Yes, I gave Matland and Una a few days off. They have the time coming. They'll probably drive down to Saint Anne's," Derek answered.

"That's nice," I managed while fear flared inside me. Fear and confusion. They were becoming my two most used emotions. Matland and Una had been sent away. That had to mean that they were not involved. It shattered theories, eliminated suspects with a single sweep. I felt a sense of incongruous disappointment. Whatever Derek was preparing to do, it was to be private and, as he himself had said, Matland and Una were outsiders, hired help. But wasn't I an outsider, too?

Derek's voice pulled me from racing thoughts that only plunged deeper into confusion. "Beauty such as yours deserves only the best things, appreciation, loving," he said, and his eyes danced with tiny pinpoints of light. He seemed his old self, more vital than I'd seen him since Nora's death. Because decisions had crystallized in his mind, I wondered.

"Then I'd better protect it with a little beauty sleep," I answered, surprised I could toss off light answers. I'd return for the things I had left behind the library door. They were unimportant now, anyway—tools for which there was no use.

"Sleep tight, Stacy," Derek said, his hand brushing my cheek. "I just came down to lock up for the night and check things. Matland's job, usually."

I nodded, remembering all too well. I wanted only to get back to my room, now, and I hurried away, not looking back. Once inside the room, I found myself at the window once again, staring out at the dark night and feeling the damp coldness seeping in. Did I dare flee on foot, I asked myself. Did I dare try to make it to Bear Landing and hope to find some way to go on from there? Or would I be walking to certain death?

My eyes scanned the blackness outside. There was a killer out there, watching, waiting, certain to see me leave on foot. Or there was one here, within these walls, waiting just as carefully, watching just as closely. I could be followed too easily on foot, caught too easily. My eyes rose, ran along the tops of the trees, following their own unseen pathway to the unseen little cabin in the mountains. But that was no refuge either. That was but one more question mark. The feeling of despair closed in again with a renewed vengeance, as though I'd had no right to discard it so quickly and it would punish me for it. I was beginning to know this feeling of despair for what it really was, the knowledge that one has no place to turn, no one to look to, nowhere to go. It is a thief, this despair, robbing one of all hope. There is only an empty void, a nothingness that corrodes itself into a kind of living death.

I turned from the window, back into the room and wondered if it hadn't been a kind of symbolism. Perhaps I ought to turn back to Derek, I reflected. Perhaps I could summon up trust and go to him with everything I'd learned. I reached for the doorknob, my hand closing around it, but refusing to turn. I was afraid—of everything and everyone, I realized   too afraid. I could perhaps conquer distrust, but not fear, and together they held me in a relentless grip. My hand was still closed around the door-knob when I heard the sound of an engine, then tires skidding to a halt. I turned, ran to the window, opening it to peer out to the front of the house. Had Matland and Una returned for some reason? I saw headlights, twin yellow eyes opening paths in the dark and I heard voices and then I recognized the outline of Cary's jeep. Frowning, I closed the window and hurried to the door, yanking it open and going into the hallway. I rushed down the corridor, but I was too late. Derek was just closing the front door and I heard the engine outside, being gunned, the jeep roaring away fast.

Derek turned to me as I neared. In one hand he held a large, flat package, the front of it wrapped in brown paper, the back open, revealing the rear of a stretcher and canvas. His eyes held curiosity and the hint of disapproval as he held the canvas out to me.

"Your friend Brooks," Derek said. "He said it was for you."

I took the canvas and held it tentatively in one hand. "I don't understand," I said honestly.

"It's a painting, obviously," Derek said coolly. "Hadn't he said anything to you about it?"

I shook my head and saw his eyes narrow slightly as he watched me.

"Perhaps you'd best have a look at it, then?" Derek commented.

I nodded and began to pull at the brown paper covering the face of the canvas. Derek came around to stand beside me as I got one corner opened, then pulled at the rest. The paper fell away and I stared down at the canvas, hearing the soft, sibilant sound of my breath being sucked in. I stood riveted before the canvas, looking down at myself. The portrait was excellent, almost life-sized—from the waist up, and completely nude. I continued to stare at myself, my breasts as excellently done as my face, as much mine as the eyes and hair and nose. He'd done me with hair flowing loosely, behind round white shoulders slightly arched forwards. I found myself thinking that Cary Brooks was not only an excellent artist but the possessor of a very good memory. But the thought disappeared in an instant and I turned, wide-eyed, to Derek.

He was still staring down at the canvas, his eyes burning into it, his face a thing of stone. Then he turned to me and I saw the muscles along his jaw ripple and in his deep, dark eyes I saw a consummate rage.

"So this is what you were doing in his cabin," Derek said, his words coated with ice, pushed at me through lips pulled back in tightness.

"No," I exclaimed. "No, I never posed for him at all. I don't understand why he sent this."

Derek snorted in disbelief and his smile was thin, more a grimace. "It seems I had you quite wrong," he said. "You're quite an exhibitionist, aren't you?"

There was hurt, terrible hurt behind the rage that seemed to explode from him with a frightening electricity, I was sure. But all I could see was the towering fury.

"No, please, Derek, you've got to believe me," I tried. "I never posed for him."

His hand shot out, fingers digging into my shoulder, hurting, pressing deep, then whirling me around to face the canvas.

"Look at it, dammit. That is you, isn't it?" he shouted. "I can't vouch for all of it, not having had the pleasure, but tell me that's not you."

His rage sent terror through me. He was almost beyond control of himself. "Please, Derek, you're making the wrong conclusions," I said placatingly.

His hand dropped from my shoulder and he turned to me, a still, deadly fury on him now, as terrifying as the other.

"Don't lie anymore to me," he snapped. "Just don't. Take that to your room with you. Get it out of my sight!"

I opened my mouth to say something else placating but closed it. His eyes were terrible, dark pits of coldness. He had cared much, much more deeply than I had thought. I took the canvas and hurried away. This was no time for further protestations. They would have to wait till he was calmer, capable of listening to me. Besides, I had no explanation for the canvas, of why Cary had sent it. Had he thought I alone would see it? Did he think it would please me? Was an offbeat sense of humor behind it, an elaborate bit of wry sarcasm? Whatever his reasons, they were secondary to Derek's rage. I set the painting against the wall of my room, stared at it again for a long moment, then went back outside. I would try Derek again, now. Perhaps he had calmed down enough.

I went to the stairs, saw the light coming from his rooms above and started to climb the steps. I was halfway up when I heard his voice, talking to someone and then I recognized Father Hodges's quiet tones. I kept climbing until, almost on the top step, I could see into the first of Derek's two rooms, the door open and Derek's back to me. He was standing before an opened closet door and then I saw part of Father Hodges as he moved into view, his left side, his arms folded.

"Is this necessary?" I heard Father Hodges say. "You'll bring it all down. You're risking everything."

"No, I'm protecting everything," Derek answered. "I know what I'm doing."

I saw Derek turn and my hands tightened on the bannister, digging into the hard wood until they hurt. The long, polished object in Derek's arms was beautifully evil, but then guns always frightened me. They seemed possessed of waiting malevolence. I watched as Derek put the gun down against the desk and my lips formed the silent words *no, no, no!* Derek reached into a desk drawer to take out a small, square box as he spoke to Father Hodges and I pressed myself against the bannister.

"I'm not having any more," he said. "He's got to be stopped now. I won't tolerate him any longer around here."

The first shock at seeing the rifle had given way to a new sense of disbelief but as I saw Derek begin inserting cartridges in the gun a grim horror gripped me. I began to back down the stairs. Everything here was past my understanding, including Derek's astonishing rage. Was I to blame for that in a very real way, too. I had done nothing to stop him from falling in love with me. On the contrary, I had welcomed it, wanted it to happen. But now anything I said would fall on deaf ears, on the rage of a lover crazed with jealousy. Or the rage of a man whose emotions had stepped beyond the bounds of normality. Had this world he had created here rubbed off on him, I questioned. Had daily, intimate, insulated contact with the others here brought its own distortions to Derek, his concepts and beliefs sliding into an indiscriminate concordance of thoughts and attitudes. In his intense efforts to see as they saw, think as they thought, had he entered understanding too deeply? The Heisenberg Principle of which he was so fond carried to the extreme lengths?

I couldn't know—not now, at least. All I knew was that he was gripped by a fury that no words from me could stem now, that would subside only of itself in time. But before it did, it could bring tragedy. I had reached the bottom of the stairs now and I halted, my thoughts on Cary Brooks again. Once more I had to wonder if Derek's rage at Cary had other things behind it. But I pushed the thought aside now. I had to push away confusion and distrust now. I owed my life to Cary Brooks, whoever he was and whatever he was. It was a debt I could repay now.

I raced out the front door, across the lawn to the rear of the house and plunged into the trees. I swore at myself for not having stopped to take the flashlight, but I didn't dare go back now. Derek could well have come downstairs, could be only moments behind me. I found the little path in the blackness and stumbled forward on it, using my hands and feet once again to do what eyes could not do. Branches kept springing at me, slapping into my face and I kept my head down and pushed forward. I was perspiring in moments, but the cold damp filtered through clothes to make my body a chilled, clammy thing. A vivid, horrible vision of what I had found the last time I climbed this path in the night flashed before me and I closed my eyes as though that would make it go away. I hurried my pace and fell, feeling my slacks tear at the knee. Pulling myself up, I went on, as fast as I could, falling too often, finding that speed actually slowed me down. My chest was beginning to strain. I felt myself taking in deeper draughts of the cold air. The path widened under my feet. I was at the ridge, the spot that would stay with me as long as I lived. On the dark trees I saw the image of Nora's hanging, bloodied form and I ran on, as I once ran past graveyards at home when I was a child.

The blackness continued and the path seemed endless. I was moving too slowly now but my lungs wouldn't permit anything else. A moon would have filtered some light down into the forest, but I had been denied even that aid. The path rose sharply and I fell again, lay there for a moment, and then yanked myself up again. I wondered if Derek had started up yet, and if so, how close he was behind me. I pushed forward, using the low branches now to pull myself along, and then, ahead of me, a pinpoint of light. It was like an injection of adrenalin to a heart patient. I began running again. The light grew into a square, scattering to the trees, giving form and shape to the night. I saw the cabin, solid, the light streaming from the door which stood open wide. I expected to see Cary appear at the door. Certainly I was making enough noise as I pushed through the brush. But the doorway remained empty, the cabin still, a tiny oasis of light against the towering mountain forests that rose up all around it. I hurried the final few yards to fall into the doorway, resting there, hearing the harsh, strained sound of my breath.

"Cary," I called and waited for an answer. There was none. I stepped through the doorway, the cabin assuming a familiarity at once for me. "Cary?" I tried again. Once more there was no answer. I peered into the little adjoining alcove, wondering if perhaps he were fast asleep there, but the cot was empty. I turned back into the main room, frowning. He wasn't here. Yet the door had been left wide open, the lights full on, as though he'd been expecting someone. Frustration pulled at me. I couldn't wait here for his return. I couldn't be here when Derek arrived. Dared I leave a note? I glanced around the cabin at the sketch pads and canvases and decided against a note. If Derek found it, it would only add renewed fury to his rage. And he could be here soon, I reminded myself and I found myself wondering if he would kill me if he found me here. How absolute, how beyond all reason was his rage? I dared not risk finding out. I started for the door when my glance fell on the square little table nearby. A small pile of clothes lay atop it and I halted, frowning. I saw a skirt, a bra, girl's clothing. I moved closer, saw a blouse. It was stained, irregular blotches of a dull, rusted red and the front of it was torn. I picked it up and saw the bra partially under it carried the same dull-red stains. My eyes went to the blouse again, to the collar where a name tag had been sewn on. I read it and a terrible, sick feeling welled up through me, filling every part of me until I was quivering with it. The name tag stared back at me: ELISE DONNER.

The tag swam in front of me, grew dim, then ballooned to fill my mind with its meaning. My fingers dropped the blouse and it fell atop the other clothes. The dull-red stains took on their own meaning, now. I was looking at Elise Donner's blood-stained clothes.

"Oh, my God!"

I heard my own voice—barely audible, as though it were a stranger's. Derek's caution had been right all along. Or had it been more than caution? Was Cary Norris Kincaid? Derek may well have had him use a new name for a new beginning. It all fitted, now. The portrait had been a device to bring me up here. My thoughts reached back, picking up little things, making quick associations. *You've a way of making people want to look after you*, Cary had said to me. *I'm looking after your needs*, Norris Kincaid had said to each of the girls he had attacked. Derek had disregarded his homicidal possibilities and been tragically wrong. It was plain, now, why Cary Brooks had known so well about that extra measure of sensitivity given to wild animals, artists, and the mad, as he had phrased it.

A sudden explosion of terror erupted in me and I wrenched myself away from the little table, the pitiful little pile of clothes. I ran out the door, racing into the night and heard the voice calling.

"Stacy."

I half-turned, saw Cary coming down from behind the cabin, in his belt a revolver, his face set, unsmiling. The horror was stark in my eyes, I knew, and I paused but an instant, then turned and plunged into the trees.

"Come back here," I heard him call, his voice hard, urgent. I ran, harder, pushing aside the branches that seemed to clutch at me, sudden allies of his trying to hold me back.

"Damn you, come back here," I heard him call out again. I ran, heedless of anything but escape now, fear plunging through the forest with me and then I heard the sound of him coming after me. I changed directions, ran on, then shifted again and the sound of him still followed and suddenly I knew that if I kept running he would catch me. All he had to do was follow the sound of my body crashing through the trees and underbrush. I turned sharply, plunged into thicker, heavier brush and trees where the branches grew low and full. I stopped then and sank to the ground, curling myself into a little ball, hidden by the thickness of branch and brush. Somehow I kept the hard sound of my breathing down and listened to him as he made his way through the trees. I heard him halt, then go on again, and I lay curled up, like a frightened animal. My hands moved along the ground, touched something cold, hard, closing around it, a rock, big enough to kill, small enough for me to throw. I moved it, inched it closer to me, taking it in my hand. Stillness closed around me now and I knew that feeling I'd tasted so briefly on that day when the plane had winged away from Bear Landing. There was no place to turn, now. I was utterly and totally alone and I knew that the end product of despair was a thing called panic, the end product of panic a thing called survival—first, foremost, at all costs.

CHAPTER SEVEN

And so I wait now.

To be killed.

Or to kill someone. The unthinkable no longer unthinkable, all things turned upside down, utterly changed. To kill someone. An act beyond all morality, beyond all normality, an insane act, no less so than for the madman who stalks the forest to kill me. An exchange of insanities. Perhaps that's what it all comes down to—simply that and nothing more—an exchange of insanities; ours for theirs, theirs for ours.

I wait here and I am as naked, stripped of all pretenses. I will kill if I must. I will commit the insane act, the irrational act. The moral and the rational are such weak exercises when faced with survival. I know that now as I wait.

I felt a wetness on my face, a drop first, then more but I dared not move. I glanced down and saw the ground starting to turn white as if by magic. It was snowing, not hard, the soft fall of an early snow. Light, hardly a pinpoint at first, still startling, broke the total darkness and I stiffened. Cary had a flashlight and he was using it, sweeping the ground with it. He moved toward me, slowly, and I heard him pushing through the trees. Where was Derek? He should have reached me by now if he had left soon after I did. If. The lone word mocked. Perhaps he had contained his fury. It was what I had hoped for, only now I wanted the opposite. Death carried its own grim humor.

The light was growing larger as the figure moved closer. I saw the narrow beam slowly moving across the ground, a probing eye and now I could see the form behind it. The light had sound again, his form pushing aside low branches. I dared not run. He was too close, now. My hand closed around the rock and I felt muscles as they grew taut. He was very close, the flashlight lighting trees, the brush just in front of me. It swept past me and he moved with it, to the left. I held onto hope. The light moved away from me and I heard him halt, stand still and listen as he sent the light probing in a semicircle. He turned, started away and I felt breath rushing from me and my muscles start to relax. I breathed a sigh of relief and with unexpected suddenness, an afterthought on his part, he spun around and the light swept over me, stopped and darted back. I was bathed in its whiteness and he crashed through the trees toward me.

"There you are, dammit," I heard him snap. The light was full in my face and I picked up the rock and threw blindly, knowing I had missed even as it left my hand. I heard him move quickly to the side and then the light lowered and I blinked up at his form standing over me.

"Get up, Stacy," he said sternly, standing over me as though he stood behind a curtain of gentle, white lace that waved in front of him. I started to uncurl myself, saw the small shower of snowflakes that fell from my shoulders. I was starting to push myself up when the night exploded, the blast deafening. I saw Cary Brooks whirl and then the side of his face erupt in red. I knew I was screaming yet I was unaware of any physical effort at doing so and I watched him pitch forward to lie on his face in the thin layer of new snow. The flashlight had fallen to the ground to throw a penumbra of light over the still figure.

I tore my eyes away as Derek came toward me through the trees, the rifle carried in one hand and I stood on weak, wavering legs, afraid I was going to collapse. He came to me, looked down at me, unsmiling.

"I saw his light and I followed it, moving each time he did so he wouldn't hear me, getting a little closer each time," Derek said. "I knew he was hunting for something. I didn't know it was you until just now."

I drew a deep breath and nodded grimly and the snow felt good against my face, clean, strangely comforting.

"What were you doing here, Stacy?" Derek said evenly.

"I came here to warn him," I admitted. "I saw you with the gun. I didn't know what to think except that you were crazed with anger. But he saved my life once. I decided to repay that. You see, I didn't really know then, I wasn't really sure of anything."

"You didn't know what, Stacy?"

"That he was the killer, not until I saw Elise Donner's clothes inside the cabin."

I saw Derek's face fill with surprise and he stared at me for a long moment. Finally, he pursed his lips thoughtfully.

"He had her clothes?" he echoed.

"Piled on the table, all blood-stained and streaked," I said. The surprise still lingered in Derek's face.

"How interesting, indeed," he said, thinking aloud, really, I saw. He turned to me then, and I held back saying all the things that crowded the tip of my tongue.

"I never posed for him, Derek," I decided to reiterate. "Believe me, I never did."

Derek's smile was sudden warmth, embracing, the smile I had come to know so well. "Come on, let's get you back to the house," he said. I knew he believed me now.

I followed, the path too narrow for us to walk side by side. He'd retrieved the light to help find the way. Questions sorted themselves out in my mind. I was grateful for the silence as

Derek strode on purposefully. When we reached the bottom of the path, the dark bulk of Harbor House rose up and he crossed to it in a few strides, using the rear door, holding it open for me. I could see he was still reflecting, his eyes slightly narrowed, thoughts pressing hard on him. He took my arm and guided me into the library. The long, soft couch was terribly inviting, but I paused to glance at Derek again as he put the gun in the corner.

"Why were you so surprised at what I said to you back there," I asked. He turned to frown at me.

"Surprised about what?" he answered.

"About Elise Donner's clothes in his cabin," I said. Derek came toward me, a small smile touching his lips, rueful, almost shy.

"I had underestimated him badly," he said.

"Didn't you think he had killed Elise Donner?" I asked. "Wasn't that why you wanted me to stay away from him?"

Derek looked at me with a patient amusement in his eyes that suddenly irritated. "You must have known he was the one who'd killed Nora," I said. "After all, you did know who he was. You did know his case history."

"Exactly what did I know, Stacy?" Derek said. The tolerant amusement stayed in his eyes and I felt myself growing angry. I didn't like being played cat-and-mouse with ever, certainly not now.

"You knew he was Norris Kincaid," I snapped. I waited, watching Derek and I saw the patient amusement drain from his face, his eyes, first, emptying of it, then the small smile sliding away from his face and now he stared at me with an unnerving stillness.

"Where did you learn about Norris Kincaid, Stacy?" he said, finally, his words spaced out slowly. I answered impatiently.

"In that sixth file folder," I said. "I'm sorry, but I had to find out for myself."

"My you have been a busy little person," Derek said stiffly. "It seems I underestimated you, too."

His icy anger seemed misplaced now, after the fact, unnecessary. Unless—and I held the sudden thought, felt my stomach draw in as though I'd been struck a blow. Words rose in my throat, stayed there. I had to push them out.

"He was Norris Kincaid, wasn't he?" I offered.

Derek's face was stone as he dropped the single word from his lips.

"No."

I felt cold suddenly, terribly, unexplainably cold. Everything that had fitted together suddenly seemed to be exploding apart. I heard myself repeating Derek's answer in my mind. No. No, he was not Norris Kincaid.

"Then who was he?" I heard myself ask. Derek's little shrug broke his stiffness.

"A friend of Elise Donner's, I suspect," he said.

The coldness was hurting now, all inside me, all through me, pressing up into my every vein. There was no sense to anything again. "Where is Norris Kincaid?" I managed. "Is he alive? Is he somewhere near?"

Derek continued to stare at me, his eyes deep, dark pits. Then, with startling suddenness, he began to laugh. He threw his head back and laughed, but I heard no humor in it. I could feel only the coldness constricting me, making breath come harshly, painfully. Then he stopped as abruptly as he'd begun, and his eyes fastened on me again. I saw his slow smile reach out to me.

"Oh, yes, Stacy, he's near, very near. I'm Norris Kincaid," he said softly.

The coldness took over and I was drenched in its consuming pain. I stared at Derek, but I saw only a procession of images racing in front of me, leaping, coming apart, drawing together, moments, words, sounds, all different now, all new, all wearing new faces. I caught hold of a few as they rushed past, as one catches hold of a dandelion pod blowing by. The first—the very first, suddenly clarionclear—was Nora on that first morning when we had talked of Derek. *He's one of us*, she'd said. I could almost laugh. She'd been telling me the truth, then, but I was too rational to see it. The price of rationality, I snorted silently. I stopped chasing images to focus on Derek.

"That newspaper clipping—that wasn't your father," I said, wanting to hear thoughts spoken aloud as if, in some magical way, that might change them. "That was really Dr. Closter."

His smile was patient amusement again as he slowly nodded in agreement. Words caught again at the next question but I had to ask it, to hear the answer voiced.

"Where is Dr. Closter?" I said.

"He's dead. I killed him. He was first, of course," the calm, soft voice answered.

"And after him?"

"Elise, naturally. I hired her and she became very special, just as you are, Stacy."

"And Nora?"

His eyes hardened for an instant. "I couldn't help that. She had insisted on going her own way with you. She was trying to leave us, I suspect."

"She was slipping into normal, rational behavior?" I flung at him, bitterness bursting from me. He shrugged again.

"If you like. Poor Nora was never really at home in either world. She didn't really belong in either, completely. But she would have ruined everything if she'd gotten to you," he said.

Something still refused to fit. "That time at the shed, you tried to kill me then?" I questioned.

"Oh, no," Derek said quickly, his face taking on shock. "That was one of the others here, resentment at Nora's death, blaming you. I'm not really certain who. Aaron, I imagine."

I looked around the room and Derek caught my glance and the thought behind it. He smiled pleasantly. "The gun isn't loaded, my dear," he said.

"Why?" I flung at him. "Why all of this? Dr. Closter was trying to help you, all of you. I assume you have quoted his concepts to me in your role."

"Indeed. I know everything about his work. He told all his concepts to me. I read everything he had written. It was necessary for me, of course."

"In order to become him," I said.

"Precisely."

"Didn't you believe in anything he was trying to do?"

Derek's laugh was short this time, harsh, not really a laugh at all.

"He was an old fool, less of one than some of the others, perhaps more of one in some ways," he said. "What was he trying to achieve? What was his grand design? Accommodation? To include us in your world, some ability to feel, to sense, to experience things we cannot. The truth is that your world is a dull, dim place. You experience none of the things we do. You reach none of the heights we do, none of the acuteness of the senses, none of those very special pleasures we do, even when you try to do so with drugs. Your minds are leaden, anchored to the ground. Our minds can soar to places you cannot imagine. I laugh at you. We all laugh at you."

"A world we cannot enter, a language we cannot know?" I paraphrased and his smile was instant and full of charm.

"Exactly," he said, and the smile vanished abruptly to be replaced by a cold, angry frown. The words he spoke were echoes—the same, yet so different now—the reason in them steeped in new depths, rising out of unreason.

"You judge us," he went on. "You pass judgment, and you call us mad, and by that you make beggars of us. But we are not beggars—not of the spirit, not of the soul, not even of the mind. But you will help us to rejoin your world, to sup at your table. What arrogance!"

"No judgments. The tolerance of nature. Every form of life is allowed to exist as it sees fit to exist," I echoed. So much fitted now, completely, perfectly, terrifyingly. I had found reason in those words once. Was it any less there because I knew that Derek was a madman? I stared at him, at Norris Kincaid, and the file folder came alive in his words. His brilliance was more than brilliance, his egomania more than just that. It had become twisted into madness, the extra measure of love in it more twisted than with the others. He had used the word arrogance, and suddenly I realized that love can be arrogance, their kind of love not love at all, but the certainty that they held the secret of helping others. And yet, that root had to be there, I told myself, that extra empathy had to be a basic, root concern. I felt terribly tired suddenly, a swimmer in waters she could no longer cope with, no longer navigate. Only one thing was clear. I had feared the madman who would kill me and now I faced him. The panic had long gone, replaced by a numbing acceptance.

"Matland and Una Stenner, do they know who you really are? Why were they so hostile to me?" I asked.

He shook his head. "They worked for a home for the aged. They were fired after beating two of the patients in a fit of anger when they'd soiled their beds," he answered. "They knew they had a good thing here. They wanted no outsiders coming in and maybe changing it. They were happy to look the other way at anything that went on here."

I was aware of movement behind me and I half-turned. Marlyn was slipping into the room, moving to stand at my right. Rudi came next, then Aaron, slinking in, hugging the wall and then Father Hodges. They formed a semi-circle around me and I looked from one to the other, unable to keep the plea out of my eyes. Perhaps one of them would help. That extra measure of love, or concern for others, would it extend to me? Was it strong enough in this moment of truth? Hope faded quickly as I met each pair of eyes and saw a wall between them and myself. I lingered on Father Hodges.

"I understand your remark at dinner now," I said to him. "This was what you meant by Derek's setting up his own Goddess of Reason, this little world of its own here, this masquerade."

His eyes nodded to me and I turned to Derek. Hope was a thing of many lives, dying and coming alive again at the slightest opportunity. Perhaps, if I could hold the light of rationality high enough, one of them might see with different eyes.

"Hasn't there been enough of it now? Isn't it time to stop? You can't go on like this," I said.

"But we can." It was Derek's voice interrupting, Norris Kincaid's own arrogance. "A state Inspector stopped by one day. He accepted everything without question. I am Dr. Closter, and there is no one to know differently. I will burn those old clippings. I should have done it before now. Things will go along perfectly."

He spoke with that embracing, vibrant enthusiasm I had come to know so well. It carried him high, stimulated him, the exciting pleasure of fooling the world. The ego of Norris Kincaid was past reaching. He was past reaching—were they all? The normality, the rationality I had once seen seemed to have dissipated into another posture, the root one, that other language, a cameraderie of its own.

"It won't go on," I said, turning to the figure standing so casually, so pleasantly in front of me. "You have to keep bringing girls like me here. Someone came looking for Elise Donner. Others will come."

Derek's smile chided. "This land can hold more secrets than can be uncovered. It will go on," he said, and I felt the sick feeling that he could just be horribly right. I turned to Rudi.

"Stop it now, before it gets worse," I said to him. He met my plea with a shrug, a defensive hostility coloring his florid face.

"I'm not going back to those places. No more cells for me. They had some nerve in the first place. I like it here fine. I'll stick it out with Derek. What's there to lose?" he said.

I caught the appellation. He was Derek, Dr. Closter to them, one of them yet their leader, standing apart. Rudi would have no help. He had put it so rationally. What did he have to lose here?

"I was right once again," I heard Marlyn sing out cheerfully. Hardly a prophecy, I thought, and I passed over her to Aaron, his thin frame against the wall, his ascetic, linear countenance reflecting a kind of petulant hostility.

"You didn't want to talk to me," he said accusingly. "I remember things. I don't forget, and everything connects. I told you it did."

I returned to Father Hodges. The priest stood watching me with his sad-stern, contained face, his hands folded in front of him. "You can't be a party to this, Father," I said. "Not to what has gone on here and will go on. You know you have to stop it. You are a priest of God."

His eyes stayed with me for a moment and then his lips tightened with regret. "Yes, I am a priest. I must do what has been given me to do. Please excuse me, Stacy," he said. He turned and began to stride to the door.

"Father!" I called after him. He didn't look back as he left the room and I heard his footsteps hurrying down the corridor. Was he going to help me, I wondered, seizing on hope again. Had he left only to return and help me? I glanced at Derek. He wore the patient amusement again, no concern at Father Hodges's abrupt exit touching him.

"It's time, now," Derek said quietly. I saw Marlyn start from the room, Rudi following, then Aaron sliding against the wall as he left and I was alone with the man who faced me.

"And now, Derek?" I asked and I almost smiled. He was Derek to me, too. Norris Kincaid was still someone in a file folder. I saw deep eyes watching me with something that looked like tenderness, the look of love.

"I love you. But you know that," he said. I felt rage grow. I'd had enough of distortions, rationality that was not rational at all.

"No!" I flung the word at him. "No, you don't love me. What you call love isn't love at all. It's twisted, warped. It's mad."

"Call it whatever you wish. I know it's love," he said.

"And what are you going to do with that love, now?" I asked. His erraticism was clear, now. Perhaps it could take unexpected turns. Hope leaping again, the perennial emotion.

"Each man kills the thing he loves," he said. I recognized the quotation at once. Wilde. "The Ballad of Reading Gaol." He went on, almost dreamily.

> Some do it with a bitter look,
>   Some with a flattering word,
> The coward does it with a kiss,
>   The brave man with a sword.

I met his almost-sad eyes, moods that shifted with quicksilver speed. "How will you do it, Derek?" I asked. His answering smile was so warm, so charming, so normal.

"As I am both a brave man and a coward, I will do it both ways. First, a sword of the flesh, then a sword of steel," he said. He moved toward me and I backed away. I knew it was a useless attempt, yet I had to try. Survival recognizes no closed doors. I lunged, trying to get around him and reach the door. Quick as a cat, he moved to his left, his hand shooting out to catch my wrist, spinning me around. I clawed at him with my other hand and he ducked away and I was free, backing away from him. His lips drew back in a tight smile and I saw the excitement in his face. I glanced about desperately, found the heavy glass ash tray on the desk, more than an adequate weapon. But it was halfway across the room and Derek blocking my way to it. He started toward me again and I backed away. I heard the sound then, faint yet clear, from down the hall.

"In Nomine Patris, et Filii, et Spiritus Sancti."

I felt the grim smile touch my face. The Mass for the dead. That was fitting, indeed, and Father Hodges was being a priest of God. It was the most terrible distortion of them all here at Harbor House, and so perhaps the most fitting. The chant continued on in the background as Derek came for me again. I clawed at him and he pulled back.

"Good," he smiled. "Very good." The excitement fairly glowed in him now. He started toward me again, made a small motion to his left and I lunged in the opposite direction. But he had only feinted and was ready for me, hands fastening around my waist. I brought my leg up and came down hard on his ankle and he cursed in pain and I twisted away once more. The ash tray seemed miles away but Derek was smiling again as he came toward me.

"Of course you don't want me to do this. But I know what you need. Fight, deny me, you must, but I'm doing what's good for you. I'm looking after your needs. I'm giving you pleasure," he said. The words flew out of the file folder, echoed now in terrible reality. His hand shot out, caught my blouse and I felt it tear down. I halfscreamed and twisted away. "That's right, Stacy," he said. "Only by fighting me will you know what pleasure I'm going to give you."

I backed away, but the words clung to me, suddenly finding new meaning, revelations of their own and out of the past, textbooks and teachers leaped into the mind, classic examples studied and analyzed, bits and pieces of nearly forgotten learning. His words were not just words, but a mirror to the twisted mind, a door opened to the reality of unreality. The mirror revealed flaws amid flaws, or was it simply hope against hope? Whichever it was, it was all I had left and I seized upon it.

Derek came at me again, reaching out for my blouse. This time I didn't pull back. I tore open the rest of it and moved toward him.

"Yes, all right, I understand," I said. I saw him halt, the frown instant in his eyes. "Please, I want what you have for me," I said and I reached for him. He slapped my hand away and I saw his face contort in dark anger.

"No, stop that," he said. I reached up quickly and unsnapped my bra, starting to wriggle out of it.

"I know you're trying to help me, Derek. I want you to do it," I said, moving at him again. He backed away and now disgust had come into his face.

"What are you doing, damn you?" he barked at me. I reached out for him, rushed at him and he almost fell as he stumbled backwards.

"Please, please," I breathed. "Oh, yes, please."

"No!" He shouted the word at me. We were almost at the desk. His hand came around and I felt the slap spin my head, sharp pain, stabbing. "Stop it, you little slut," he roared.

I made myself laugh and flung myself at him, arms out-stretched. He sidestepped, avoiding my grasp, and I felt his hands flinging me around, against the desk, bending me backward over it and he was slapping my face, back and forth, vicious slaps and I refused to acknowledge the pain of it.

"Stop it, stop it, damn you, stop it," he was shouting, each slap an accompaniment to his words. His body pressed against my thighs. I forced myself to cry out, pushing ecstasy into my voice as I thrust my hips upwards.

"Oh, yes, Derek, oh, yes, please," I said. I felt his body move away, his hands loosen on me and my arms were half over my head. My hand groped, felt the cold smoothness of the ash tray. I gripped it, all the frantic desperateness taking split seconds that seemed days. I brought it around with all my strength, smashing it against the side of his face, seeing the instant spurt of red. He staggered back. I brought it down again, hitting his temple this time and he dropped to the floor, his body making little convulsive movements as he tried to cling to consciousness. I threw the ash tray down at him, saw it hit against the top of his head and then I was running, leaping over him, racing into the hallway. I was beyond reasoning, now, panic my only companion. I raced down the corridor, heard noises behind me, doors opening, the faint, clear sound from the end of the hall ... *whom thou has redeemed* ... and I ran, murmuring, *dear God, whom thou hast given renewed hope, please help me again, don't forsake me.* Last words for me, too, I wondered, and I ran on.

I raced outside into whiteness, the ground a pure blanket like the soft white coverall of a newborn baby's crib on which every impure fingerprint shows. My every footprint would show here, and I heard myself cursing as I ran. I halted just inside the line of the trees and glanced behind me. My path was traced there with absolute clarity, written in the new snow. "Damn," I sobbed aloud. "Damn you!" I cried the curse upward at the sky showering whiteness, the massive mountains and the giant trees. The obdurate land was showing its utter disdain for the affairs of men, taking no sides, revealing its own relentless judgment. Survival—the reality behind all others once again.

As I watched, I saw the figure move from the house, Rudi's square shape. Another figure followed, moving catlike, hunched over. That would be Aaron, of course. I saw Marlyn's form follow and then the figures were bunched together, looking at the footprints. I saw another form appear in the doorway, pausing in the light there, a handkerchief held to the side of his head. He moved out with the others, still holding the side of his face. I felt an incongruous relief at seeing him. I hadn't killed him, and rationality made me glad for that. As I watched, Rudi and Derek started out along the path of footprints while Marlyn and Aaron fanned out on both sides.

I turned and ran, the very act seemingly a fruitless gesture. I would have gotten away except for the snow. It would be a little harder for them in the forest but only a little, not enough for me to elude them. But I ran. One does what is left to do, hopelessly or not. Each time I glanced back, I saw the path I left. I might as well be carrying a candle for them to see, I thought angrily. It was still in the snow-covered forest and I could hear them moving toward me, spread out. I halted, a trapped hare wondering which way to flee and I thought the stillness was appropriately tomblike. I started forward again, choosing a direction at random, when the figure moved out from behind a tree, directly in my path. I could see the side of his face made rough with dried blood, a dash of color against the white that covered his hair and clung to his brows. I saw him and closed my eyes, opening them quickly to see if I was hallucinating. But the figure remained in front of me and I saw him lift one hand to his lips in a gesture of silence.

I hurried forward and now, close before him I could see the terrible streaks of red that had dried to stain his shirt, showing through the snow on his shoulder. Cary Brooks spoke in a whisper.

"His shot only grazed me, enough to make me black out for a while. I just came around," he said. "I was heading down to the house. I was afraid I'd be too late."

"No, I got away," I said. "Cary, I'm sorry. I just assumed...." I let the sentence trail off. His voice whispered again.

"There's no time now to go over everything. I'd made plans to get away if I was discovered or trapped," he said. "I think we can still do it. But they must keep thinking they're only following you. Walk in my footsteps, understand?"

I nodded and he turned and started off, taking strides not too long so I could follow in them. I placed each foot in the footprints he pressed into the snow. I could hear the others closer behind, catching up, but Cary maintained his steady stride. He turned sharply and I followed in the footsteps and in a few moments I heard Aaron's voice behind. "This way—she turned here," I heard him call, his voice near, too near. Cary continued on and then, as we rose atop a small, snow-crusted mound, he halted, turned and beckoned to me. Walking in his tracks, I came too-to-toe with him and as he bent to put his lips against my ear, I felt the handle of the revolver at his waist. He spoke softly into my ear.

"We're close, but not close enough. A little further on is a lake. I've a canoe and supplies there. We need another five minutes, but they're almost up to us. I've got to buy us time—with this," Cary said and I felt his hand move up to touch the gun.

"You think they'll stop if you shoot at them? I feel as though I'm being chased by a wolf-pack," I whispered.

"No, but Closter—or whoever he is—knows I'll kill him if I have to," Cary said.

"His real name is Norris Kincaid," I said.

"He can't stop, but he'll back off a little till he tries to figure a way to get us. That's all we need—those five minutes," Cary said.

"What do you want me to do?" I asked.

"Stay here now. Face them," he said. "We've got to have surprise on our side this time. Surprise and time, they're equivalent. I'll be near. Just let them think they've caught you."

I nodded and he turned. I thought his lips brushed my cheek, but it could have been just an accident. He disappeared in seconds behind the white curtain and I turned back, trembling. I was cold, but it was not the cold that shook my body. It seemed I had hardly more than a minute to wait. I heard them before I saw them, sounds moving behind the falling snow and then dark forms taking shape, distinction, to my right, first, moving closer. Aaron materialized first, then Derek, directly in front of me. Two more forms took shape behind him. I could see Marlyn's round shape beside Rudi. Father Hodges was the only one missing. I took no satisfaction. He was here, in his own way. Derek stepped closer and I felt the rage of him. Cary is near, I told myself, Cary is near.

"Bitch!" Derek hissed at me.

"Here?" It was Marlyn's voice, almost an eagerness in it.

"No, that would be too easy for her. I want her back at the house. I want it the way I first planned," Derek spit out. His hand shot out, the slap stinging, knocking me backward. I half-screamed and fell. *Cary is near*, I kept repeating inside. Derek was reaching for me when two shots split the night. I heard the sound of them thudding into a tree nearby.

"Goddamn," I heard Rudi cry out. Derek made a hissing, snakelike sound when the third shot rang out and he dived to one side, rolling across the ground. I started to rise. Aaron seemed to have vanished and then I glimpsed him huddled beside a tree.

"Stacy, run! This way," I heard Cary call and I ran toward the sound of his voice. I heard still another shot explode past me and then Cary was beside me, running with me. Behind, I heard muffled oaths, sounds of caution.

"I couldn't see clearly enough to wing him, dammit," Cary said as we ran. "The damn snow made everything fuzzy. I was afraid I'd hit you if I shot too close."

Cary was pulling me along now, his long legs driving for us both. I followed him to the crest of the mound. The lake appeared before me, a long expanse of darkness behind the white lace. Cary had let go of my hand and was plunging into a clump of young trees. I ran to help him as he began to pull the canoe out from its cover. I took the other end and pushed, sliding it almost to the water's edge and then, with Cary, rolling it on its keel.

"In the trees—two rucksacks," he said, as he started pushing the canoe into the water. I pushed into the clump of young spruce, found the two bags and dragged them out. I'd just flung them into the canoe, half into the water, now, when the figures appeared, spread out, moving fast toward us. Cary whirled, raised the revolver as Derek's shape came toward him. Derek leaped to one side, a diving motion and Cary fired. I heard the metallic click of the hammer as it misfired. I saw Cary squeeze the trigger again and the gun remained silent.

"Damn!" I heard him exclaim and then Derek was rushing at him from one side and the lithe, quick form of Aaron from the other. From the side of the canoe I saw Marlyn circle up behind Derek and then Cary bring the gun down as Derek tackled him.

I heard Derek's muffled oath as the blow struck him and he slid down to Cary's feet.

"Cary!" I screamed the alarm as Aaron came in from the other side, leaping forward. Cary whirled, struck out with one arm in a backhanded motion and Aaron fell half-atop the prow of the canoe. Cary's hands were on him, gripping his shoulders and flinging him away. I gasped as suddenly Cary went down and I saw Derek's arms wrapped around his leg, pulling him to the ground. The two men grappled, rolling in the snow and with astonishment, I saw Marlyn move in, saw her arm upraised. In her hand I glimpsed the dull shine of a kitchen knife. She circled the two men as they grappled, her back to me, looking for an opportunity to strike at Cary. I looked around frantically, reached out to seize the nearest of the two paddles inside the canoe. A thin piece of rope tied it against the side and it broke as I yanked the paddle up. I swung the paddle, using both hands, stepping in as I did. I heard it smash into Marlyn, the impact sending a shudder up through my arms. The woman pitched forward into the snow, tried to pull herself to her feet, and collapsed to lie still. I turned to Cary and Derek just in time to see Derek fling Cary from him with a tremendous burst of strength. Cary's form staggered back, dropped to one knee almost beside me. I pressed the paddle into his hands as Derek leaped forward. Cary brought the paddle up in a short, half-arc blow, time only for it to smash into Derek's chest, edge-first. Derek staggered backward, dropped to both knees and I heard his heaving, pain-filled efforts to regain his breath.

Cary shoved the canoe into the water. "Get in!" he yelled at me. I got one leg over, trailing the other in the water as he pulled me into the craft and hopped in after me. Rudi and Aaron were running to Derek, helping him to his feet. I saw Aaron go to the shore, yelling after us and then the snow curtained him off. Cary was paddling and I took the other paddle and joined him. "Straight out into the lake," he said to me, calling over his shoulder from the prow. I bent to the task, trying hard to match his powerful, easy pull and finally we were well away from shore. "Turn right," Cary said, and he eased the canoe down the length of the lake. He shifted positions, moving to the center and I knelt beside him, paddling on the right.

"Slow down, now," he said softly. "There's no way they can get to us now. The lake narrows and becomes a river that runs into the Chickaloon and finally to Palmer. We can get help there."

"I'm afraid to believe anything anymore," I said. "You had a plan of some kind, didn't you, and I wrecked everything."

His body close against mine as we paddled side by side was warming, in so many ways. The snow continued to drift down, to disappear as it touched the lake waters.

"You couldn't help it, and I was improvising at the last of it," Cary said. "I was a good friend of Elise Donner's family," he went on. "Elise had gone off on her own up here, but she always wrote. When she stopped suddenly, I knew something was wrong. Her parents are both ill. When one of her friends showed me her last letter, I became more and more certain something had happened to her. I decided to come up here and look for myself. I did a lot of snooping about. I couldn't get much of anything on Harbor House and Derek Closter except that the hospital was there and there were reasons for its existence. I checked out the Jackson brothers at Bear Landing. They knew of no arrangements Elise had made with anyone for transportation out of here. Little things kept building up my suspicions, and one day I had a piece of luck, if you can call it that. A raccoon dug up some of Elise's clothing and left it scattered about. I found it and dug up the rest."

"And you started looking for Elise," I said softly.

"I found her, where they had buried her, not far from where they'd buried her clothing. She'd been killed—it was too damn easy to see that. But by whom? I'd nothing to connect anyone at Harbor House—nothing except a certainty that something was very wrong there. I kept waiting and watching with no results."

"Then one day I popped up at Bear Landing," I cut in.

"Yes, and I was certain you'd been brought here to replace Elise in more ways than you imagined," Cary said. "But I'd still only my own feelings—nothing I could even convince anyone on, much less act upon. I still hadn't a damn piece of substantive evidence."

"I know the feeling," I said.

"When Nora was killed, I knew a homicidal maniac was down there someplace, and every day I grew more afraid for you," Cary went on. "And I'd already seen that Dr. Closter ran the place with a firm grip on all that went on. I became more and more certain that nothing happened without his knowledge of it. Then, I got to thinking, perhaps nothing happened without his making it happen. I'd looked up Closter's reputation in advanced psychological thought before I came here. He was a well-known European doctor. The Dr. Closter I'd met here wasn't European. I got more suspicious. He was getting more edgy, too, I noticed the last time I met him. If he was a phony he was a damn brilliant one and a damn careful one, I knew, but I also knew that he had to be playing some private game of his own, operating on some mad set of private motivations. I decided I had to do something that would make him break—something that might push him into some action that'd reveal him for what he was."

"The portrait," I said, sudden realization pulling at me with delayed insistence.

"That's right. If he was the killer, I was sure it would trigger him into action. I put Elise's clothes out on the table in the cabin and left the door open. If he was the murderer, that would be the last touch. I took up a spot just above the cabin. I expected him to come gunning for me."

"And instead I showed up, saw the clothes and assumed you were the killer," I added grimly.

"I realized what you'd think when you went into the cabin. I came down just as you stormed out and started running. You know the rest—one piece of bad luck piled onto the other," he said.

I nodded and looked up at him. His face was strained and I saw the small grimace of pain he made with each stroke of the paddle. The redness caked on the side of his face was evidence that he was pushing himself on the edge of exhaustion.

"Cary, can we stop someplace?" I asked. "I think we'd better."

He glanced at me, drew a strained breath and nodded.

"Swing to the right, the shore's not far," he said. I pulled hard on my paddle and the canoe swung obediently and suddenly I noticed the curtain no longer hid the shoreline.

"It's stopped snowing, Cary," I said and saw Cary's head nod, the simple motion an effort now.

"Sleeping bag's in the canoe," he muttered. The shore came up, trees hugging it, yet enough room to beach the canoe. I paddled hard and felt the prow rise up on the hard soil. Cary stepped out with me and pulled the canoe up further. I opened the sleeping bag back near the trees. Cary was on one knee near the canoe. I helped him into the sleeping bag and then found a cloth among the pack. I soaked it in cold lake water and, as he lay half-awake, I washed the dried, caked dirt and blood from his face. His hand reached up to hold my wrist when I'd finished.

"I'm afraid I didn't figure out all the possibilities very well," he said. "Sorry about that. Not a very bravura performance at all."

"Bravura enough," I answered. "If it hadn't been for the portrait, everything would have gone off exactly as Derek planned." Damn, I swore silently. Why did I keep calling him Derek? He was Norris Kincaid, a homicidal maniac. I shivered as a sharp wind speared deepening cold into me.

"It's big enough for two," Cary half-whispered. I smiled down at him and crawled into the sleeping bag beside him. His arm moved, lifted, and I fitted myself against him. I lay awake beside him, letting the warmth of our bodies encircle us to heat the sleeping bag. Thoughts slowly arranged themselves in my mind. So many things to sort out, to recognize for what they really were. When I felt Cary's arm tighten about me later, I knew he was not sleeping either.

"What happens to them now?" I wondered aloud.

"Before we send the authorities descending on Harbor House?" Cary said. "They might scatter. I doubt it, though. This is no land to hide in unless one is experienced and equipped. They'll probably stay, quarreling among themselves, aware that the charade is ended."

"The Goddess of Reason," I murmured.

"What?" Cary asked.

"Something Father Hodges spoke about one night, another attempt at replacing things that failed."

I turned my head into Cary's shoulder, pressed tight against him. Questions had been answered and questions had been left. Irrationality had proven itself to run true to its own course. Yet things had been seen, things said, and things learned that would not disappear. Dr. Derek Closter, Norris Kincaid, they overlapped and their words melted together, the truths about insanity by the sane, the truths about sanity by the insane and suddenly I thought of a line from Dryden, *And thin partitions do their bounds divide.*

I closed my eyes and reached a hand up to touch Cary's face. I felt his lips press against my fingers and I finally slept with the touch of his lips staying on my hand.

CHAPTER EIGHT

Cold, bright sun woke me and I opened my eyes, rubbed sleep from them and saw Cary beside me, watching me, a gentle smile touching his lips.

"You look just as lovely asleep," he said. I turned his face with my hand, looked at the seared, red flesh. It was raw, but clean.

"We've got to have that treated by a doctor, first thing," I said.

"There'll be one in Palmer," he said and I wriggled out of the sleeping bag and he followed. "I've coffee and oatmeal and a pan in the pack," he said. "I'll start breakfast."

I went down to the lake and washed in the crackling blue water. The day was almost cloudless, a pure, clean morning. I'd always felt that mornings like this one washed away the clinging things, giving pains and problems a new look. I was silently commenting on the fact that it didn't always work that way when I returned to Cary. He had a small fire going and handed me a tin cup of hot coffee, his eyes studying me as I sat down.

"Want to try sorting it out verbally?" he asked casually. I held his quiet glance for a moment.

"I'm not sure I can yet. So many feelings are crowding me, strange bedfellows, some of them."

"Like being glad and being sorry," Cary remarked.

"Yes," I admitted. "I'm glad it's over—glad to be alive, glad to be here with you. But I saw so much and heard so much that made sense, Cary, so much that was wise and sound. Then it all blew up in my face. I feel cheated, or maybe betrayed is a better word."

"A madman can say things that aren't mad at all," Cary said.

"I know, and yet I can't find separations, now. I keep thinking of him as Derek Closter, the doctor, the man trying to bridge a gap. I think I do because I want to believe in the things he said. I want to believe he wasn't just a madman saying mad things. Yet that's what he was. Where did Dr. Closter's thoughts stop and his begin? Whose sense was I listening to?"

"Both, I'd say, Stacy," Cary answered.

"That extra sensitivity to everything around them, that extra measure of empathy, that extra measure of love—it's there, Cary, I'm sure of it. It's one of the root causes."

"He told you their root was sanity, the real sanity they can't let go of the way the rest of us can. Stripping away the self-justification in that you find a truth but that truth is a minus quality, not a plus one. They lack the ability to bend. They are rigid, inflexible, unable to bend to the irrationalities of existence. They lack balance, and without balance you eventually have only distortion. Everything that concerns us, internally or externally, is a matter of balance. Love requires balance. Love without balance is something frightening and self-consuming. Sadness without balance becomes suicide. Art is nothing without the discipline of balance."

"Why are they without this balance, then?"

"I have the feeling that most of us, as part of our makeup, have a built-in balance factor, call it an emotional pendulum, if you will. But I think it's there and a vital part of our emotional and mental defenses. When it's missing, or not functioning for some reason, you have an individual without balances. You have distortion—a person who sees everything and feels everything through a different set of eyes and emotions."

"His different language," I murmured, hearing bitterness in my voice. "You ally yourself with him. You imply there's no meeting place."

Cary's lips tightened. "I don't say that. I don't know. But I do think we've walked too many wrong paths. I agree, also, that we must redefine our thoughts and treatment of mental illness. It seems to me we keep treating the slightly disturbed and the truly mad as part of a whole. They occupy different ends of the spectrum, different extremes of that Richter scale of emotional earthquakes. I think we have to reexamine that. I don't think they are parts of the same whole, any more than that all the problems of the body stem from childhood."

"Where do we look if not into yesterday?"

"Somewhere not tied down by our rational concepts of ids and egos, our explanations of a language we cannot speak. Johnny may not be the way he is because of something that happened to his psyche in childhood. What happened to his psyche in childhood may have been due to what he is. We look for the missing factor, that emotional pendulum or faulty ectoplasm or excesses of the soul, if you like, but a root imbalance that goes beyond what we understand now."

Balances and imbalances, I reflected silently. Sane acts and the acts of insanity; they slide so easily into each other. They take only the right push at the right time. I understood that in a way Cary couldn't. I knew and I would know forever. It would be a terrible bond I would carry forever with Norris Kincaid, with Father Hodges, and with all the others.

I rose abruptly, and Cary got up and put out the fire as I rolled up the sleeping bag. "After we reach Palmer, what then?" I asked.

"Telling the authorities about Harbor House, signing sworn statements, all the technical details," Cary said. "We'll be in Palmer by late afternoon, I'd guess—certainly by nightfall."

I went to him, rested my head against his chest. "I don't want to be alone tonight, Cary," I said. "I want to be close to someone."

"Anyone?" he asked gently and I looked up quickly.

"No, not anyone. You—is that bold enough?" I said.

"It'll do," he said and his smile was full of understanding.

"After Palmer, what happens to you, Cary? Where do you go?" I asked as we put the gear back into the canoe.

"Wherever you go, Stacy," he answered simply and I turned to him. His smile was quiet, secure.

"That's nice. I'd like that," I said. "I want to go to a soft, lazy land where no one thinks much about anything because they're too busy doing and enjoying."

"Wonderful," Cary said. "I know just the place. A friend has a house on a small Caribbean island. It's a place made for indulging the senses." He took my arms suddenly, pulling me to him. "I should warn you that I'm not planning on an interlude," he said.

"Good. I've had too many interludes," I said. His kiss was short, a touch of tomorrow in it, promises of things to come. We pushed the canoe into the water and I took my place beside him, paddling with easy, matching strokes. We glided down the lake as it narrowed and became a slow river. I didn't look back. I didn't need to. The past would never be that far away, I knew, and the real would always include the unreal.